SOME BRIGHT NOWHERE

ALSO BY ANN PACKER

The Children's Crusade

Swim Back to Me

Songs Without Words

The Dive from Clausen's Pier

Mendocino and Other Stories

SOME BRIGHT NOWHERE

A NOVEL

ANN PACKER

HARPER

An Imprint of HarperCollins*Publishers*

Without limiting the exclusive rights of any author, contributor or the publisher of this publication, any unauthorized use of this publication to train generative artificial intelligence (AI) technologies is expressly prohibited. HarperCollins also exercise their rights under Article 4(3) of the Digital Single Market Directive 2019/790 and expressly reserve this publication from the text and data mining exception.

This is a work of fiction. Names, characters, places, and incidents are products of the author's imagination or are used fictitiously and are not to be construed as real. Any resemblance to actual events, locales, organizations, or persons, living or dead, is entirely coincidental.

SOME BRIGHT NOWHERE. Copyright © 2025 by Ann Packer. All rights reserved. Printed in the United States of America. No part of this book may be used or reproduced in any manner whatsoever without written permission except in the case of brief quotations embodied in critical articles and reviews. For information, address HarperCollins Publishers, 195 Broadway, New York, NY 10007. In Europe, HarperCollins Publishers, Macken House, 39/40 Mayor Street Upper, Dublin 1, D01 C9W8, Ireland.

HarperCollins books may be purchased for educational, business, or sales promotional use. For information, please email the Special Markets Department at SPsales@harpercollins.com.

hc.com

Excerpt from "Night's Thousand Shadows" by Christian Wiman from *Hard Night*. Copyright © 2005 by Christian Wiman. Reprinted with the permission of The Permissions Company, LLC on behalf of Copper Canyon Press, coppercanyonpress.org

FIRST EDITION

Designed by Bonni Leon-Berman

Library of Congress Cataloging-in-Publication Data has been applied for.

ISBN 978-0-06-342149-3

25 26 27 28 29 LBC 5 4 3 2 1

To Rafael

SOME BRIGHT NOWHERE

1

AND THEN IT WAS OVER, the final visit to Claire's oncologist. Eliot rose and shook the doctor's hand. Claire inched forward on her chair, grimacing a little as she mustered the strength to stand. Always petite, she had become tiny, her weight down to a distressing ninety pounds. Her hair was about an inch long and clung to her scalp in tight curls.

Dr. Steiner waited until she was steady, then took her hands in his. He said, "It's been a privilege treating you, Claire."

Eliot watched as Claire pursed her lips: preamble to a small witticism. She said, "It's been a privilege being treated by you, Dr. Mark Steiner."

Steiner squeezed Claire's hands and then took a step backward and held out his arm. He wanted them to leave ahead of him, a first.

The corridor was busy and Claire stayed near the wall, pausing every now and then to catch her breath. She needed the bathroom, and Eliot stationed himself opposite a photograph of a mountaintop at dawn that he'd walked past a thousand times and somehow never noticed.

In the car she gave him a long look. "Are you OK?"

Eliot wasn't really a milestones person, but she was—the anniversary of their first kiss, the packing of the final school lunch, the first Christmas without her mother—and sometimes she yearned to have him make a big deal over things. Today of all days he wanted to get it right. But making the cessation of treatment official with Steiner was far less emotional to Eliot than any number of other moments during the long and agonizing journey to this bleak juncture. There was a night in January when she was a few days out from her next treatment, deep in an Ambien-induced sleep because even after so many years she still got anxious before chemo, and Eliot sat in front of a basketball game and leaked tears, his whole face flowing though he didn't cry, didn't sob. They had still been under such pressure then.

"I am," he said. "What about you?"

She gave him a thoughtful look. "You know what I was just thinking? If he finally buys that cabin I won't get to hear about it."

She meant Steiner. He'd been renting in Maine for years, two weeks every August, and had told Eliot and Claire many times that he was thinking of making an offer on the place. His rental was twenty miles from the house where Eliot and Claire always stayed, close to the lobster rolls they liked best, the small, pebbled beach. Spending time in Maine was Eliot and Claire's favorite summer pastime and had been since shortly after they were married, when they joined friends for a long weekend south of Portland. After that they rented their own place each summer, at first for just a week but increasing to two once they had kids and three once their work schedules allowed for longer vacations. Packing up to leave at the end of the previous summer, they both knew it might be Claire's last visit to Maine, but the chemo was still working and they didn't talk about the possibility that she might not return. She was a milestones person, yes, but also someone with a remarkable capacity not to get ahead of herself.

"I guess not," Eliot said.

Claire shrugged lightly. "Among so many other things."

He gave her an understanding smile, a smile he hoped conveyed an opening to say more if she wanted. She tapped the dashboard, ready to go.

At home he helped her into bed and took her empty water bottle to the kitchen so he could refill it with filtered water. When he got back she was burrowed under the covers, her frame as small as a child's. "I really am wiped out today," she murmured, her voice in a register of mild unhappiness.

He kissed the side of her head. "I can tell. I'm sorry. Get some sleep, OK?"

He closed the door on his way out. There was laundry for him to start, the dishwasher to unload. He longed to be truly busy but couldn't bear to begin any of the more involved tasks that might occupy a few hours. In three to six months he'd have all the time in the world to organize the garage or take up woodworking or go to Vietnam by himself.

Late in the afternoon there was a soft knock at the front door. It was Holly, with an armload of Tupperwares.

"She's asleep," Eliot whispered.

"I'll be quiet."

In the kitchen Holly put the food in the fridge, explaining what was in each container as she went. "How was it?"

Eliot shrugged.

"Anticlimactic?"

"He was sweet. In the waiting room beforehand we saw that girl."

"Shit. Did she talk to her?"

The girl had appeared in the infusion suite some months earlier, occupying the chair next to Claire's. Ewing sarcoma, twelve years old. Claire had fallen in love with her a little, the two of them chatting about the girl's preference for small dogs over big ones and her attempts the previous summer to learn how to do flips off the diving board. It was one of Claire's talents, forming swift, sweet friendships. A couple weeks later she invited the girl to the house and taught her how to make meringues.

"Just waved," Eliot said.

"How was she?"

Eliot knew Holly meant Claire, but he had answered this question too many times over the past eight-plus years. His heart had withdrawn, and he felt wooden when he was forced to answer anyway. He pretended to think Holly was asking about the girl. "She was pretty far away, beyond the aquarium. Hard to tell."

Holly gave him a searching look. Now she'd ask how he was.

"How are you, Eliot?"

"It was just a formality, going in."

"I know."

She reached into her purse and pulled out lip balm, apparently in no hurry to leave. The understanding was that the two of them were a team, president and vice president of Claire's support system. They traded information, observations. But Eliot wanted to be alone. He wanted to do his back exercises, maybe have a beer.

In the distance the bedroom door opened. Eliot heard Claire's walker bump the door frame, the familiar sound of her cough. When she saw Holly, she broke into a smile. "You're here."

They fell into each other's arms. Tall, robust Holly with her thick auburn hair, her muscular body. Claire was engulfed. Holly's shoulders shook, and Claire made soft shushing sounds, then wept a little herself. She tilted her head in the direction of the bedroom, and they headed off together, likely to be out of sight for hours.

To Eliot's surprise, Holly reappeared just ten or fifteen minutes later.

"Leaving?"

"She wants ramen. Is that OK, if I pick some up for her?"

Eliot doubted Claire would eat it once it arrived, but it was certainly OK. "Of course."

"Do *you* want some? She specifically said we should 'all have ramen'—it was like a vision. Remember in the old days when we had those Friday night dinners and the littlest kids wouldn't eat the pizza?"

Eliot remembered children kneeling on the ladder-backed dining chairs he and Claire had inherited from his grandmother. The chairs had high centers of gravity and sometimes tipped over if their occupants were too rambunctious. Eliot pictured the noisy, crowded dining room, three, sometimes four families squeezed together. Claire in her prime, seeing everything, knowing everything. Late on those evenings, as Eliot loaded the dishwasher, Claire told him everyone's business, information gleaned as much through observation as report. Dave Moulton had some kind of secret—gambling maybe, or drugs; or who knew, maybe an affair. The Baxter boy was having trouble in school, and the Baxter marriage was in trouble again. Eliot loved hearing Claire talk about people, her combination of warmth and dispassion. Holly called her "Oh Wise One" for how evenly she viewed the small, ordinary problems of family life. In those years especially, Holly could be quite judgmental.

"Right," Eliot said to Holly now. "They ate ramen instead. I might have a few packages here."

"No, she wants it fresh, from the place. I'll get you one, you can decide later."

Once she was gone he went into the bedroom. Claire was propped up against the headboard and talking on the phone. In the six months since he moved to the guest room, afraid of disturbing her sleep, what had felt equally owned had become entirely hers. Clothing, books, magazines, her water bottles, pills, photographs recently pulled from albums to keep at hand. Moisturizer, a heating pad, a small notebook and pen. It was her den. Eventually he moved his bathroom stuff to the guest bath, ceding the entire space.

"Michelle," she mouthed, pointing at the phone, and he retreated.

Abby visited on the weekend, leaving the grandchildren home with Isaac. The kids couldn't do the round-trip from Virginia in two days, it would be hell for everyone. Nor could Abby wait; she too was very much a milestones person and needed to see Claire right away. At one point Eliot entered the TV room and found Abby with her head on Claire's lap, Claire stroking her hair. It could have been twenty years earlier, Abby a heartbroken middle schooler. It was almost too much for him, thinking about the passage of time. He couldn't go into it, the past, all those feelings; he couldn't or he might never come back.

"Dad," Abby said that evening, once Claire was asleep. "You need to reach out. You need support too."

"I've been taking care of your mother for a long time. I'll be OK."

"Emotional support."

"I knew what you meant."

Abby was on the window seat and got up, antsy, crossing the room to lean against a wall and moments later crossing it again to pick up an abandoned mug. Her hair was short these days, severe to Eliot's eye, though it made sense given her busy life. She said, "I should've tried harder to get you guys to move." Her voice had the tight, desperate quality that frustration had triggered in her during childhood. Frustration born of ambition, Claire always used to say, reminding Eliot that Abby was a lot like him. If you substituted a group of headstrong little girls for a group of business executives, Abby was no less determined than Eliot to impose her will.

"You honestly think that would've helped?" Eliot said. "Trying harder?"

Claire's first metastases, found in her lungs three years earlier, had caused a great reckoning in the family. Within a year Eliot retired, and Abby launched a campaign to relocate her parents. Eliot was agnostic on the subject, saw pros and cons, but there was no missing how much Claire wanted to make the move, to be close to Abby and the grandchildren. Nor was there any missing how adamant she was that they couldn't, wouldn't do it. Abby was a pediatrician, spending hours every day taking care of other people's children before spending hours taking care of her own. Claire was terrified of being a burden.

"Dad, come on," Abby said now. "All I'm saying is I wish you were closer."

"And all I'm saying is don't blame yourself that we're not."

"You're suggesting I'm not all-powerful?" she said, fighting a smile. "I have children, I think I know that by now."

"Fair enough," Eliot said. Then: "I'm glad you're here, sweetheart."

In the morning they Zoomed with Josh. It was still the dead of winter in Chicago, and he wore a beanie and two sweaters, his house old and very drafty. He said, "Mom, do you feel like getting a massage? Can I gift you a massage?"

Claire glanced at Eliot; Josh barely made ends meet. She said, "You're sweet. You having that thought is all the gift I need."

An hour later it was time for Abby to go. She clung tightly to Claire and said, "I can come back anytime. Literally anytime, this is exactly why I'm in such a big practice. Wait, do you have a fever?" She reached into her bag and pulled out a forehead thermometer.

"Always prepared," Claire said—amiably enough, but it made Eliot remember earlier moments when Abby's professional identity bumped up against her identity as a daughter. Soon after Claire's diagnosis, medical-student Abby insisted that Claire meet with her mentor, an academic oncologist she'd gotten to know during a summer research project. Claire and Eliot made a special trip to Boston . . . only to have this doctor give them the exact same recommendation they'd received at home. Since then, Abby had kept any doubts to herself.

"Ninety-eight point three," she said, reading the thermometer. "So more like ninety-nine point three, but that's still fine. OK, I feel better leaving."

Once she was gone the evening lay ahead of them. Eliot delivered pills, prepared small snacks because Claire felt nauseated and though hungry could eat only a little at a time. Awake very late, she sat with him in front of the TV while an oldish comedy played. She liked to guess the year a movie had been made using only what clues were provided by hairstyles and clothing. "Those shoulder pads!" she said. "Where's my phone, I have to see if Holly remembers this movie. I had a blue linen dress kind of like that, with shoulder pads like wings. Will you get me my phone so I can call her?"

"It's almost midnight."

"She'll be up. Or she'll call me back in the morning."

Eliot found the phone and handed it to her. "What if she has your number set to wake her?"

"She'll go right back to sleep. She wants me to call. She keeps saying so."

"Of course."

Holly was Claire's oldest friend, her dearest, going back to second grade. At the beginning, when Eliot and Claire had been dating for a month or so and it was time to be introduced to family and friends, Eliot slightly dreaded meeting Holly. Claire had reported various cutting things Holly had said about other guys, and Eliot knew she wouldn't soft-pedal any doubts. After the first encounter, Claire reported that Holly found Eliot "quietly witty," such an unrousing endorsement that Eliot for the next week or so made a point of being as noisily witty as he could. At last Claire asked what was up with him, and he confessed that Holly's comment had caused him to try to be more dynamic. "Well, don't," Claire said. "You're being weird." She reported the whole thing to Holly and came back saying she'd had it wrong, Holly hadn't found him "quietly witty," she'd found him "quiet and witty," which was so much worse. But the entire back and forth delighted Claire and served as a small stepping stone on her path to feeling Eliot was the man for her. He was smart and competent, he knew how to move through the world. Those were the qualities she prized.

"When we were young," Claire said now, setting the phone down absently, "I was in such awe. I always felt so dumb and ordinary in comparison."

"To me?" Eliot said, puzzled.

She laughed lightly. "To Holly, honey. She was such a sparkler, she had so much verve. I mean, in retrospect it was probably agita over all the stuff at home expressing itself, but to me she was magically funny and energetic. I was really a little dullard."

"No, you weren't," Eliot said, but he was lagging behind, wounded by her amusement at his mistaken assumption.

"If I said I was," Claire said, "that means I felt I was."

Now Eliot was flustered. "OK. Sorry."

"You're so literal."

"And yet so unliterary. It's amazing we lasted." He looked at her and waited, wanting just an agreement, an acknowledgment of his value, something. In the old days she sometimes called him "my businessman," a label that an observer might assume she employed to emphasize how different she and Eliot were, when the point was that she loved his practical, efficient side.

She motioned at the TV. "I think I'm done with this."

2

EVENTUALLY SHE WOULD NEED a hospital bed, but for now she didn't want one so much as waiting in the garage. The hospice woman told Eliot this was not unusual. During the initial visit the hospice woman used the phrase "not unusual" several times, giving Eliot the impression that speaking in this manner was a careful choice, a way to avoid words like "typical," "average," "normal." Claire had chosen this particular organization because it was the one used a couple years earlier by her friend Susan Simmons, a woman she'd met in a breast cancer support group, back at the beginning. Their illnesses had mirrored each other to a sometimes comforting and sometimes sickening degree—comforting when Susan arrived at a milestone Claire had reached first because Claire could give her the lay of the land, be helpful; and sickening when the opposite was true and Susan's bad news heralded a development Claire had yet to experience but would now dread.

Then Susan's cancer spread to her liver, and her end came swiftly. Claire spent hours at Susan's bedside, coming home sad but also somehow giddy, the visits creating a mood Eliot didn't recognize.

"Susan got her hospital bed two weeks before she died," Claire said once the woman was gone. "If you have enough people taking care of you, they can do the things the bed does."

"Go up and down?"

"They can help you do the things the bed's different motorized whatevers help you do. Like sit upright to eat."

"You mean stack pillows behind you."

"Or just hold you."

Eliot imagined that, holding her up to take a bite of something. Or more likely a sip. They had weathered the years of her illness with great ebbs and flows in their intimacy. Her original diagnosis leveled him, he could say that now—leveled him and exposed how essentially ill-equipped he was. One night, sick beyond bearing with poison, she fell apart, cried that he didn't love her. She was on the bedroom floor, thinning hair preemptively shaved, dizzy and having what he would later learn were rare but not unheard of hallucinations. "Wires of light," she'd said earlier in the evening, trying to explain. "Needles of blue." From the floor she said, "How can you love me and stand by while I'm going through hell?" And he said (stupidly, so stupidly): "What choice do I have? Would you rather I not stand by?"

Later there had been periods of great closeness. Physical closeness, reaching for the other in bed, at the kitchen table, in the car. But emotional too. Probably the closest communion of their marriage.

"We'll get it when you want it," he said now, of the hospital bed. "Maybe that day won't come."

"And I'll die in my bed," she said. "Our bed." She smiled. "Should you move back in with me?"

He shook his head. "I'd hate to cost you any precious sleep."

Her gait was getting worse, and a wheelchair was delivered. Eliot brought it to the living room and had her hold on to the arm of the couch while he maneuvered the chair behind her. Her hips were so narrow that the seat behaved more like a sling, dropping her several inches below the frame.

She said, "Let's just go around the house."

He pushed. The trick going up on a rug was to move quickly. A slight bounce as you came back down.

"This is the kitchen," he said. "The dining room. Down this hall is the TV room."

"You're showing me around?"

"It's a very good value," he said. "Good schools."

"We're thinking of homeschooling."

Eliot stifled a laugh. "Interesting. How old are little Dick and Jane?"

"They're ageless, like all good suburban children. We get to see Dick run forever, always wearing the same little khaki shorts."

"Does Jane run too?"

"Jane wears a pinafore and plays with dolls."

"I'm so sorry, ma'am," Eliot said. "That must be very hard for you."

Claire laughed with pleasure. She raised her hand above her head, and he grasped it and kissed it. He loved kissing her hand, had always loved the cords of her tendons, how pretty her nail beds were, the pinky scar caused by a jagged piece of metal on her first bicycle. When they were first together he found the daintiness of her fingers exquisitely sexy.

"Eliot," she said.

"What is it, love?"

She twisted around so she could look up at him. "I'm so lucky. I mean, I'm so unlucky—but I'm also so lucky that I have you. I'm so lucky it was you on that Metro North train. And that I wasn't the type who got offended when men offered to help."

They had met on the New Haven line: she heading home from a morning in the city, he to meet a client in Bridgeport. Seated side by side, they chatted a little at the beginning, friendly, then settled into their separate reading. That should have been it. But midtrip she rose to fetch a bag she'd stowed on the overhead rack, and without thinking he stood and retrieved it for her. He still remembered how her shirt had pulled out of her pants as she reached up, how it was the sight of her belly button, glimpsed without her awareness, that got him to his feet. She joked later that he was too gallant to enjoy such a sighting without offering something in return, but in the moment he just felt embarrassed.

He circled the wheelchair and crouched in front of her. "You know what I'm going to say."

"You're the lucky one."

His eyes stung as he nodded.

"I'm so sorry about this."

"Baby, don't."

"I am. I'm abandoning you." She gave him a plaintive look. "How are we going to do this?"

She meant get from this moment to her last one, whatever it turned out to be. Get there practically, get there emotionally. She was asking how they were going to bear it.

"We're going to make sure you're as comfortable as possible," Eliot said, aware he was answering only the narrowest version of the question. "I mean I am—you're just going to take it easy."

"I know," she said, "I know. You've taken such good care of me, El. But—"

"No 'but,'" he said. "Nothing is more important."

She sighed and leaned back. The reassurances they'd traded back and forth over the years of her illness, in moments between hard times, moments that could last minutes or months: there were just so many of them, and so few ways to differentiate one from another. They'd had conversations about how repeating these proclamations—how grateful she was, how sorry; how devoted he was, how grateful—robbed them of meaning.

"Shall we go outside?" she said. "What'll we do to get me from the front hall down to the porch and then down the front steps?"

Eliot didn't know. Someone had mentioned building a ramp, but that seemed—what? Unnecessary? Its purpose too short-lived?

"Never mind," she said. "Don't worry about it now. Michelle is calling soon and I think I'll take it in the bedroom."

Once she was occupied, Eliot stepped outside. The house was in a newer part of town, a tract built in the 1950s. Yale people and other professionals. Quite Yale-heavy, in fact: a law professor around the corner, an economist two blocks over. A couple of English Department people lived directly across the street: a literal couple, an Americanist married to a Chaucerian. "What an unlikely marriage" went the joke, when of course Claire had almost been an Americanist married to a management consultant. Halfway through her dissertation, when Abby was just seven months old, she got unintentionally pregnant with Josh and said she was quitting, she wanted to focus on the kids. Everyone thought she'd go back once Josh started kindergarten, but instead she took a nonacademic job, working in the Yale development office. So long, "Pale Horse, Pale Writer: Katherine Anne Porter and the Literature of Illness." Ironic now to have become so ill herself.

A ramp on the front of the house seemed impossible, but Eliot went around back, stood at the edge of the woods, and looked at the deck. Maybe along one of the short sides, making a 180 halfway down the slope and extending forward to the concrete pad leading to the driveway. He texted Josh, who said definitely, do it, surprise her. But did Eliot want to surprise her rather than discuss it with her, plan it with her? They'd always worked on projects like this together.

In the kitchen he loosened the skin of a chicken and slipped garlic and tarragon into the pockets. This was a method he'd first tried for dinner club, a monthly meeting of six men who gathered to share food and discuss recipes and techniques. The club had grown out of a men's cooking class Claire had urged Eliot to take after her initial treatments were finished. She was back on her feet and in the kitchen (following so much lasagne from caring friends that Eliot still couldn't bear the stuff), so in some ways it was the exact moment when Eliot didn't need to learn to cook. Her point was that he should do it for fun, this class she'd heard about from a colleague. She said it would be something just for Eliot, that he deserved it after all the hours he'd spent helping her through the effects of chemo, radiation, and surgery. Eliot had always felt awkward in the kitchen, his contributions few and far between and either fussed over like a child's fingerpainting or consumed without comment. The class focused on the foundations of cooking, on how and why various methods worked, and to his great surprise he loved it. By the end he was rethinking all those dinners Claire had made for him and the kids and recognizing that cooking could be incredibly satisfying. That he'd missed out.

He'd put the chicken in the oven and moved on to slicing radishes for a salad when he heard Claire approaching. She appeared in the doorway looking red-eyed but upbeat, reminding him of how she was after those visits to Susan Simmons's deathbed, full of a deeply satisfied contentment that Eliot could never square with the impending loss of her friend.

She said, "Michelle wants to come up."

"For a weekend?"

"Maybe longer. She took a buyout, you know. She's done. I told her to talk to you before she settled, but—"

"I'm sure she did just fine on her own."

Michelle was Claire's college roommate. Smart and lively, but not someone Eliot had ever really clicked with. She'd never married, never lived with anyone. Her Chinese-born parents viewed her as a disappointment, hilarious given her stellar career in hospital admin. Her most recent position was chief strategy officer of a healthcare network with locations across seven states. Eliot imagined she'd walked away with a nice package—without any help from him.

"What do you think?" Claire said. "About her coming? It would be soon. Maybe even next weekend."

"She'd stay with Holly, I assume."

Claire nodded. Her expression changed to the dreamy look that sometimes accompanied reminiscence. "Susan Simmons said the funniest thing about her once. You know how Michelle is really into hiking? And she does those trips?"

Now Eliot was confused: Susan, the local cancer friend; Michelle, the Atlanta-based college roommate. "Susan knew Michelle?"

"Well, she never met her, but I talked about her a lot. Or did she meet her? Was Michelle at my sixtieth? Susan was because I remember she had this abscess and was in such pain but came anyway." Claire nodded as she reconsidered bits of information in her memory bank. "Right, and I sat her next to Abby because I knew Abby would be fine talking and drawing her out or not talking, whichever. But I can't picture Michelle there. Why wouldn't she have . . . no, wait, she had a work thing come up last minute. That's right. So no, they never met."

Eliot waited a moment, but Claire didn't go on. He said, "Susan said the funniest thing?"

"Oh, right. She said Michelle with her hiking was using one kind of ascent to . . . damn, no, it was that she was ascending . . . oh, shit!" Claire stopped, hugely frustrated.

"She was ascending?"

"I can't remember! Oh, my God, I knew it a minute ago, I remembered the whole thing."

"It's OK."

"It's not! It was right there. I hate this." Tears flooded her eyes.

She was at the kitchen table, and Eliot took the chair next to hers and pulled her close. "Don't worry. Happens to me all the time."

She stiffened. "You don't have lesions in your brain. God, I don't want to do this."

He looked into her eyes. "Do which?"

"Any of it! Eliot, my God!"

His face burned and he bowed his head, aware that the gesture was a manipulation and thus doubly ashamed.

"Eliot!" she gasped. "I'm sorry, I'm so sorry." She put her hand on his shoulder, pushing a little to get him to straighten up. He waited a stingy beat and raised his head.

Her eyes were red, her mouth carved in a tight frown. She said, "I'm so sorry. That was awful."

"Don't worry, I get it." He needed to bring this back from the edge. "I'm sorry."

"No." She began to cry, face in her hands, shoulders heaving. "No," she wailed. "No, I don't want to."

He put his arms around her again, uselessly. She'd crossed into a state from which no amount of comfort could retrieve her. She struggled to her feet. Turned away from him and wept into her hands.

3

THE SOUND WAS QUIET, pale and nearly still in the late afternoon. Eliot wore old shoes and walked at the water's edge. It was April, allergy weather. He'd come to the beach where he and Claire had brought the kids on summer days. Small, nice soft sand, almost no surf so it felt safe. He hadn't been this far from the house without her in months, maybe a year.

"Take some time," Holly had said at the front door. "Seriously. Take a few hours."

He could've done errands, but he'd decided on this expedition instead, trying to go with the spirit of the afternoon. Claire and Holly and Michelle having some special time together, like in the old days.

A wave came in and licked the side of his shoe. He continued past the pier, finally reaching the rocks that marked the end of the beach. If he continued over the rocks he'd reach another, smaller beach, full of grass at the water's edge, home to gulls. He couldn't locate in himself a desire to keep going or a desire to turn back. He, who'd been called Mister Decisive by Claire when they were younger.

His phone pulsed, and he jammed his hand into his pocket and pulled it out. A big nothing: prescription ready for pickup. He'd hoped for something significant, a text he'd need to answer, a reminder of a task he'd been meaning to complete.

At the house Claire and her friends were in the bedroom. The door was closed but he could hear music faintly. Bowie? He called out that he was home and headed for the kitchen. Their lunch plates had been scraped and left in the sink, which irritated him a little: Holly or Michelle could have unloaded the clean dishwasher and loaded their used dishes. But if they had, he'd probably be annoyed by their having put things away wrong.

It had been only an hour and a half. The evening prior, the four of them sitting over Eliot's ravioli with sage butter while the three women planned this afternoon, Holly said it should be long and luxurious, completely unrushed, because how often would Michelle be in town during Claire's last months? How often would the three of them get to be together again? Eliot had been tempted to hush her—why bring that up?—but Claire nodded along, happily in sync. "You know what?" she exclaimed as they finished their pasta. "We should go to the new place for dessert!" She turned to Michelle. "It's where that weird healthy coffee place was, remember? Where the coffee was made with coconut water? There's a new café there, they have this fantastic lemon cake." She pushed back from the table. "Come on, let's go!"

It was past eight o'clock, the end of a long day that had included a trip to the airport to pick up Michelle, Claire having insisted on accompanying Holly. Eliot said it was late, they'd barely arrive before closing; he'd be happy to make a lemon cake himself, how about that? The looks on their faces, the collective disappointment, made him feel bad, but he knew from experience the cost of an overfull day, how not just tired but also woozy and miserable she'd be on the following day. In the end, Claire and her friends holed up in the TV room with a box of Belgian chocolates Michelle had brought, and as Eliot cleaned up the kitchen he heard them talking and laughing, enjoying each other just as much at home as they would have had they gone out.

Claire, Holly, and Michelle. They were a threesome made of two duos, Claire paired with each of them separately before the summer the three shared an un-air-conditioned fifth-floor walkup in New York City. They were twenty-two and ranged, as Claire once said, from very timid (Claire) to almost adventurous (Holly). That meant Holly forced the other two out to bars and clubs on weekend nights, but they never stayed long. They went to the decaying piers on West Street and sunbathed. Holly met a stockbroker and had embarrassing sex with him, the guy surely unaware that afterward she went home and told the other two about his cringey bedroom talk. "Do you like my dick?" he'd murmured in Holly's ear. "Does that feel good on your pussy?" Ever after, when any of the three girls said she liked something, one of the others would find a way to quote the poor fool.

For a couple years the little group remained tight, all of them living in the same Manhattan neighborhood, occupying the centers of each other's lives. But Michelle left for a job in the South, and Claire started her PhD studies at Yale, and soon the ties loosened, especially once Claire and Holly met their future husbands and settled in the New Haven suburb where they'd grown up. After that the trio had to work to stay a trio, work performed mostly by Claire and Holly, it seemed to Eliot, while the main beneficiary was Michelle. They were so loyal to her, urging her to come to Connecticut for holidays, joining her on wildly expensive long weekends in Paris or London, which of course they enjoyed but which used up enormous amounts of marital capital (not to mention the other kind). Eliot didn't object to the trips even if Claire always came home exhausted by the pace of Michelle's tourism. No, Eliot's small grudge against Michelle had roots in a weekend so far in the past that he was embarrassed he still remembered it. Having just landed a big promotion, Michelle announced that she was hosting a thirtieth birthday weekend for herself in New York, a minireunion of the three friends. Eliot went along so he could help Claire with still-nursing ten-week-old Abby. It had been a long drive when Eliot, Claire, and Holly, plus the baby and baby paraphernalia, at last made it to the hotel Michelle had booked. Claire had to feed Abby right away, and fuck if Michelle wasn't pissed that Claire couldn't head straight out to the dinner she'd planned. "Well," she said peevishly to Eliot, who'd answered her phone call, "I'll need her to be in the lobby in no more than fifteen minutes or I'll have to change our reservation." It was petty of him, but he'd never forgotten it.

Finished in the kitchen, he went to the bedroom door and listened. No music now, and he couldn't hear voices. Without announcing himself he headed for the pharmacy and picked up the prescription. Josh was coming to spend a week, and he drove into New Haven, to a shop that sold Josh's favorite hard cider.

Holly and Michelle were gone when he got home. Claire was exhausted and when dinnertime came asked for scrambled eggs in bed but didn't eat them. Eliot pulled a chair close, and they sat in a companionable silence. After a bit she asked him to take the tray and bring her some hot water with lemon. She was all the way under the covers when he got back.

"Nice but tiring," he said. "Right? Hopefully you can sleep through the night. Should I bring your pills?"

"Not 'but.'"

"Huh?"

"I said not 'but.' It wasn't nice but tiring. It was nice, period." She spoke without lifting her head, the words muffled by how close the pillow was to her mouth.

In response Eliot simply nodded.

"Michelle's going to stay for a while."

"That's lovely."

"Or maybe go home and come back."

"Nice company for Holly."

"And for me too."

"Of course for you too."

Claire swept the covers aside and struggled to sit up. She wore an old-fashioned flannel nightgown, like a little girl on a Christmas card. Eliot didn't remember it, wondered if it was new, brought by Holly or Michelle.

"Bathroom?" he said, holding out a hand.

"Eliot. There's something I want to say."

"OK."

She took a deep breath. Let it out and stayed silent.

"What?"

Now she looked off in the distance. Her face as drawn as he'd ever seen it.

"What? Is everything OK? What is it, what can I do?"

She turned back, scowling. "You always want to do something."

Men and their endless desire to fix things. This was a song Eliot knew well. You weren't supposed to merely *correct* your tendency to disappear behind the newspaper on Saturday mornings, you were supposed to ask your wife to tell you more about how it made her feel. He imagined saying it was fine if she didn't have something for him to do, because he had things to do, household things, which—he did them all now, didn't he, didn't he?

This wasn't what he wanted, and he was briefly and furiously angry at her friends for leaving her in this mood.

"Never mind," she said. "Sorry. I actually will get up, since I'm halfway there. Can you reach me the walker?"

The nightgown dragged along the floor as she made her way to the bathroom. At the door she turned. "I'm fine by myself. Go relax, I'll call if I need you."

"What were you going to say?"

"Nothing, nothing. Foolishness."

"Seriously, what?" He knew he was pushing and knew he should stop. "I'm curious."

"I have to pee," she said. "Let's see if we can postpone that kind of cleanup for a little longer."

She would become incontinent. She would become bedbound, unable to chew, to swallow. The tumors in her body would grow and cause even more pain, and then even more and even worse pain. At one appointment Claire had asked exactly what would kill her, and Dr. Steiner had hesitated long enough that Eliot knew both that there was no certain answer and that the general answer was terrible. "We don't know," the doctor said at last. "It depends on the progression of your malignancies. But we do know how to keep you comfortable, I promise you that."

Holly and Michelle were back the next morning. Early, with

shopping bags. Just some little gifts for Claire: slippers, moisturizer from France. Eliot followed them into the bedroom and watched Claire light up at the sight of the gifts. The flannel nightgown, he learned, had been brought the day before by Michelle and had inspired the rest.

"You know what this is?" Claire said merrily. She was in the middle of the bed, sitting cross-legged, surrounded by wrapping paper. "This is death spa. Or maybe dying spa." She looked at her friends. "Death or dying?"

"Death," Holly said, just as Michelle said, "Dying."

The three of them burst into laughter.

Eliot retreated. He wasn't going to make himself scarce again today, but he wasn't going to linger and eavesdrop either. He sat in the TV room but couldn't bring himself to turn on the set midmorning. Do something, do something. Was this how it was going to be? Time to fill, his life to fill? He didn't want to fill it. Years earlier, when Claire had finished her initial treatments and her odds weren't great, she told him that she knew she was supposed to say she would want him to marry again if she died, but she didn't want to, she didn't want to have to say it.

He said, "To say it or to have to say it?"

"What's the difference?"

"If you don't want to say it, then you don't want it to happen. If you don't want to have to say it, then you want it to happen but don't want to condone it."

"Condone?"

"Discuss. Acknowledge."

"I don't want it to happen," she said. "I'm a selfish person." But when it came up again years later, she spoke about it as a given. Of course he would marry again. What was there even to discuss?

Eliot went out back. The apple trees were in bloom but it was still cool and he hadn't yet brought out the deck furniture. He sat on the top step. The yard sloped down to the woods, which were brightening with new leaves. The first time he and Claire left the kids alone for an evening, they came home to find eleven-year-old Josh trembling with fear over a list written by twelve-year-old Abby of the creatures that might be hiding in the woods, waiting for the right moment to attack. Claire felt terrible that she hadn't anticipated Abby's mild sadism or Josh's terror. For Eliot, it was nothing, a rite of passage. Of course Josh was frightened, but he'd survived and the next time would be easier.

Those years were not their best, Eliot and Claire's. Everything was about the kids, it had to be, but Eliot felt alienated. His main functions were to make money, fix things that broke, and follow Claire's orders. At her suggestion they went to a therapist who listened to this list and said it was interesting what Eliot had left out. "What?" Eliot said. He was truly in the dark.

"Well, you didn't mention enjoying your life. Enjoying your wife, your children."

Eliot wanted to crawl into a hole. Enjoyment could be his function? His purpose?

He assigned himself a correction. Working in the yard, he took pleasure in his body's strength. Watching the kids do sports, he enjoyed the camaraderie of the other parents, he was pleased by his kids' abilities to succeed with joy and fail with grace (sometimes). Instead of assuming he knew what Claire was doing, he watched what she was doing. How she put her whole body into fluffing cushions. How an issue at work took over her attention, prompted phone calls, emails, a dedication to her office community no less thorough than her dedication to family and friends.

"I think you were depressed," she said. Perhaps a year had gone by; they were in Maine for their annual vacation. High on a trail overlooking the ocean, the two of them alone because the kids were taking sailing lessons. He knew instantly what she meant.

"I guess so."

"You guess?"

"No, I was. I was." She wore a wide-brimmed hat, and he yanked it from her head and kissed her. "Thank you," he added.

A knock startled him. He turned, and Claire was at the back door. She beckoned, and he returned to the kitchen.

The rest of the house was silent.

"They're gone?"

"They're coming back later."

Eliot sagged inwardly but tried to maintain a neutral expression.

"Listen, Eliot," she said. "There's something I want to discuss."

He recalled the moment in her bedroom the night before: her wanting to tell him something, then not. Then erasing it.

"What?"

"I'd like them to be here with me."

"Them?"

"Holly and Michelle."

Eliot was puzzled. They'd just been over to the house, they'd been over the day before. Holly was over several times a week. Eliot didn't understand what Claire was saying, but he knew she was headed for something he wouldn't like. He was like a dog when it came to bad news: he was always on alert, ready to sniff out the tiniest bit of troubling information before it was spoken. This was according to her, anyway.

"What I mean is, I'd like them to take care of me."

"OK." He hesitated. "The more, the merrier?"

"Eliot. Instead of you."

He eased himself onto a chair. Claire so thin now, so frail, but in this moment also powerful and focused, her eyes narrowed, her mouth in a tight line. He had the presence of mind to record this image in his memory, to lock it up for later, so even in the moment, before she'd said anything more, he knew he was being asked to leave. He somehow knew.

4

CLAIRE WANTED THE END of her life to be like the end of Susan Simmons's. Susan, who'd been living alone for ten years when it became clear she had only a few months left. There was enough money for her to get home care, as much as she might need, but instead her nearest and dearest circled around. Three sisters, her closest childhood friend, two daughters. Some moved in, others lived close by and spent hours at the house. Susan's final two months were full of female energy, chatter, tears, laughter. Claire remembered Susan on a chaise under a soft blanket, her hand in a bowl of perfumed water one of her girls had brought in, step one of a manicure.

Claire paused in her account. They were still in the kitchen, but she'd taken a seat at the table and at some point Eliot had risen for a glass of water. He leaned against the counter and waited. There was a punchline coming.

"Her daughter asked her what color," Claire went on, "and Susan said, 'Pearl. I'll blend in with the gates.'"

Eliot was supposed to smile, but he couldn't. He was astounded by what Claire wanted. Aghast.

"It was amazing," she said. "I was over there every few days, remember? It was . . ." She shook her head and looked off, dreamy. "It must've started then, this wish, this yearning." She gave Eliot a pleading smile. "That's what it really is, a yearning."

Eliot couldn't stand this, not another moment. He said the first thing that came to mind: "You want your death to be pretty!"

She recoiled. "I do not!"

"Manicures? Soft blankets?"

"That's not it at all!"

"Then what is it?" He returned to the table and sat down. "Help me understand."

A weary look came over her face. "Eliot, you're going to have to start . . ." She sighed and shook her head.

"What?"

"Never mind."

"I'm going to have to start what?"

"I'm sorry about this. Really. I almost didn't ask. I knew it would hurt you, we all did. Even though—I swear, Eliot—this isn't about you. It isn't about anything other than . . . I just . . . it was so amazing at Susan's. We all worked together and cried together and . . . loved together." The dreamy look came back and she stared off, transfixed.

It was as if she were speaking a foreign language. As if she'd lived a secret life he was only now discovering. Secret and preferred. But he couldn't say that. He couldn't ask why his love wasn't enough. He said, "Why do I have to leave for this to work? Your friends can come over anytime. Hang out, give you—"

"Don't say manicures," she warned.

"Give you whatever you want."

Until the hard part started, at which point he'd step in. As he always had! Flooded with frustration, he rose and went to the back door. He needed a moment to cool off. He'd done everything for eight, almost nine years, everything—even if at times he'd done it clumsily. All those chemo nights, those hours and terrible hours. Just brutal. Holly and Michelle would need him for the bad moments, the difficult final days. Claire would need him. She couldn't see it now, but the whole idea was a fantasy about avoiding death. With her friends circling, lighting scented candles and bringing mugs of herbal tea, death would keep its distance.

He turned to face her. "Do you think this might be denial?"

She threw up her hands in disgust. "We all know how this is going to end! I made them think about it, really think about it. I made them imagine me in agony, moaning and crying. I told them about, you know—" She arced her hand over her belly: like a woman outlining pregnancy, though Claire was referring to ascites, fluid filling the abdomen until it was as distended as a balloon. She'd read about it in a chat room years earlier and it had lodged in her mind, terrifying. "They know . . ." she began. She paused and looked at him levelly. "They know I'll need morphine."

"Whose idea was it?"

"Mine! I mean, I told them about Susan's house and, I don't know, isn't there a moment when a rope is thrown, when it's still in the air? One hand has let go and the other hasn't yet reached out?"

"But who was throwing? Who was catching?"

"It was all at once! You know how we get sometimes!"

Eliot knew. Holly's then-husband Stuart had pulled him aside on a group vacation in the Caribbean when the kids were old enough to run around in a pack and the adults could relax. "Look," Stuart said, pointing to an outdoor bar where the three women had taken over a small table and leaned inward as if they were deciding the fate of the world. "What are they scheming about now?"

"Probably just which restaurant we should eat at tonight," Eliot said, and Stuart said, "Right, and oh by the way it's on a different island, we'll have to take a boat. Actually two boats and a plane, it'll be fun!"

Claire planted her hands on the table and pushed herself to standing. She gave Eliot a softer look, full of concern and remorse. "I shouldn't have asked, but I can't un-ask now. I mean, I can, but you're not going to forget this, you're going to know how I feel. What I want. So it's up to you, Eliot. Just please don't see it as anything more than it is. I love you. I love *you*."

5

JOSH WAS SCATTERED AND SENSITIVE, living paycheck to paycheck as he tried to make it as a musician. He earned money doing a patchwork of odd jobs that included babysitting twenty hours a week for twin toddlers, assisting a caterer at extra-busy events when additional staff was needed, and doing remote call center work when he was running low on funds. He lived with six other people, his bedroom carved out of the communal living room with a plywood wall and a curtain.

His flight arrived late Friday night. Eliot parked and went in for the sole purpose of getting to watch his son descend the escalator. The terminal was nearly empty, the baggage carousels inert under harsh lights.

Josh was chatting with another traveler when he came into view. He appeared young for his thirty years, partly because of his long hair and sloppy clothes, partly because of the earnest expression on his face. His companion was a middle-aged businessman, the two of them looking like father and son.

Then Josh saw Eliot. He gave the older man a quick pat on the shoulder and galloped down the remaining steps.

"Dad!" Josh flung himself at Eliot, wrapped him in a tight hug. He smelled of french fries and Dr. Bronner's peppermint soap, which he'd begun using in great quantities when he was a teenager. He pulled back and searched Eliot's face. "Are you OK?"

"I'm fine," Eliot said, but Josh was clearly convinced that Eliot was suffering. On the phone earlier that week, learning of Claire's wish, Josh had been speechless at first, then bitter. Eliot had jumped in with reassurances—he was OK, Mom was OK, everything would be OK—but clearly Josh was still rattled all these days later and cast quick, anxious glances in Eliot's direction as they headed for the exit.

"I don't get it," he said once they were in the car. "Why aren't you more pissed off? Why not just say no?"

Eliot's initial reaction to Claire's request had given way to a surprising stoicism, or maybe numbness. His outrage had faded, his hurt feelings. He hadn't decided anything, but he was no longer taking the request quite so personally. That was thanks to something Claire had taught him long ago: you felt wounded when you thought maybe you deserved it.

He knew he didn't deserve it.

He turned to Josh: so much tension in his face, in the way he held his body. "It doesn't really change anything."

Josh gaped. "It changes everything. It's not 'Till death or a few busybody friends do us part.'"

Eliot patted Josh's leg. "She's not asking for a divorce. It doesn't mean she doesn't love me or thinks I don't love her. Really. Look at it this way: If at some other point in our marriage she had asked to spend a few weeks with her friends, would I have gotten upset?"

"Dad. It might be a few months."

"Joshua."

Josh looked at Eliot.

"Honey, it could be weeks."

Josh turned and looked out the window. Claire had had a really bad day, very dizzy and in a lot of pain. Early in the afternoon Eliot gave her double her usual pain relief, but it wasn't enough. Out of habit, he called the palliative care doctor and had to wait hours for a call back. Only then did he remember he could use the hospice number for things like this. That this was the point of hospice.

"Abby's going to talk to Mom," Josh said.

Abby had been incredibly upset when she heard, telling Eliot that Claire didn't mean it, couldn't mean it: "It's so disrespectful." But when he carried the phone to Claire and put it on speaker, Abby was gentle. She suggested various half measures, Holly and Michelle having overnights at the house, Eliot going away for a week. He could visit the grandchildren, they'd love it! Afterward, Claire went into her room and wept, leaving Eliot thinking he should hurry up and decide if only to protect her from more conversations like the one she'd just endured.

"They've already talked," Eliot told Josh.

"No, again. This weekend. She's going to call while I'm here."

"You guys have to let whatever happens happen."

"This is because we care about you!" Josh exclaimed. "Do you not get that?"

Claire was asleep when they arrived but the house was ablaze, even upstairs, which meant she'd hauled herself to the second floor to turn on the lights in Josh's room. On his pillow there was a Hershey's kiss, her loving gesture of old when the kids had a bad day or aced a test or got home from sleepaway camp.

"Fuck," Josh said, eyes filling.

"That thing might be pretty old. Like decades old."

But there was a new bag in the kitchen, shoved between the junk basket and the milk frother. Eliot figured Claire had sent an SOS to Holly, asking her to run to the store.

In the morning Josh lay on Claire's bed with her, telling her about his latest gig, three nights at a bar in Wicker Park. His music had a folk vibe, influenced by Claire's beloved Joni Mitchell, the soundtrack of his childhood. He sang a new song for her, and she said it sounded more woke than folk, which made him laugh. Claire was the only person in the world who could say such a thing to him.

He wanted Louis' for lunch, so Eliot drove into New Haven and picked up a bag of burgers. Louis' burgers were uniquely ill-suited for takeout, the toast they used in place of hamburger buns soggy within minutes, but for Josh that was part of the charm.

Claire was up, and the three of them sat together at the kitchen table. It was like when Abby went away to college, Josh the only kid home for the first time in his life. Claire thought he blossomed in Abby's absence, came into his own: he told more stories at the dinner table, ventured opinions about the news of the day.

"Mom," Josh said. "I don't want to be an a-hole, but where's Dad even supposed to go? If you do your thing?"

The idea was that Eliot would move to Holly's house. The guest room there was comfortable—or, if he wanted, Holly would be happy to empty out drawers in the primary bedroom. Her house looked onto a pond. Wouldn't Eliot enjoy the view as summer came?

"Please stop," Claire said. "I don't want to talk about it." She smiled and reached for Josh's hand. "Is that OK, sweet pea? Can I just enjoy my boy?" She glanced at Eliot. "My boys?"

Eliot felt himself relax. Maybe she'd changed her mind, or was in the process of changing it. He suspected the proposal had grown out of confusion. Or out of brain lesions. Out of grief and terror. She could still take it back. He was prepared to pretend it had never happened, his wife of thirty-five years hadn't asked him to leave her to die in the care of others.

She rose and reached for her walker. "BRB," she said, moving slowly out of the kitchen. Josh shot Eliot a worried look.

"Bathroom," Eliot said. "Most likely. Bear in mind she usually spends most of the afternoon napping. Actually it's unusual for her to be up for lunch."

Josh bowed his head. He'd gone through a lot in the last eight years, his twenties in some ways defined by his mother's illness. Claire's initial diagnosis arrived just after he finished college, thanks to a routine mammogram she almost canceled. The family was in Chicago for graduation weekend, and there was a cool restaurant in River North that Josh wanted to try, the type of place you couldn't get into unless you went online at exactly 9 a.m. four weeks ahead of time. The menu was French Vietnamese, the chef a rising star in the culinary world, famous for his foie gras spring rolls. Josh was way too disorganized to get a reservation, but a friend had snagged one for his family only to have his parents decide they wanted to start the drive home to Seattle a day earlier than planned. The boy asked Josh if he'd like the reservation, and Josh presented it to Eliot and Claire as a thank-you for sending him to college. It would require them to push back their departure, but why not? Claire had her mammogram scheduled, but her doctor had dropped her back to once every three years; there would be no harm in waiting till later in the summer. Then the other boy's family decided to stay, the offer evaporated, and Claire got home in time. Saved by foie gras spring rolls, she used to say, when it seemed possible that she would be saved.

"Buddy," Eliot murmured.

Josh looked up and let Eliot see his pain, but just for a moment. "What about the ramp?" he said, shoving the last of his burger into his mouth and rising from his chair. He went out to the deck, Eliot trailing.

"It would be easy enough," Eliot said. "Entrance here, go to the back edge, swing around and land right there."

"I could help you."

"Oh, I'd hire someone. But I'm not sure it makes sense. I'm not sure how many times we'd use it."

"Dad. If Mom's going to die at home, do you really want her literally stuck inside the house for even a day? If she wants to go out? It could be June, July, it could be the most perfect summer day and the nicest thing ever to go for a walk around the block!"

Eliot's face warmed. "I wasn't planning on keeping her prisoner. I figured I'd carry the chair out, then carry her out to the chair."

"Sorry," Josh said. "It's just . . . it's like . . ."

"We want to make things as good as we can," Eliot said, "even though in the long view the effect will seem really small."

Josh nodded, and Eliot didn't have to finish the thought: the effect will seem small compared to the enormous fact of her death.

A little later something similar seemed to be on Claire's mind. Eliot told her that Abby wanted to Zoom later, and Claire flushed and said it wasn't important, this thing about Holly and Michelle; it didn't matter, obviously Eliot wasn't going to leave.

"I'm sorry," she said. "You must've thought I was out of my mind."

He was deeply relieved, but he took care to shake his head: no, no, not at all. Earlier in the day, contemplating the upcoming conversation with Abby, he'd recalled a fight he and Claire had when the kids were teenagers, when Claire was tortured over a road trip Abby wanted to take, driving all the way to Florida with two friends, none of them yet eighteen. Eliot felt fine about it: Abby was responsible, she'd check in every three or six or twelve hours, whatever was required of her. She had places to stay along the way. But Claire was deeply torn. It was yes one day, no the next; in truth, she was a wreck. At last Eliot expressed some frustration over her indecision, and she retorted that there was something cold about him if he couldn't understand her conflict: how she knew it would be fine, even good for Abby; and also how viscerally she resisted, recoiled at, the prospect of the anxiety she'd feel during the trip. Something cold about him or something wooden, unfeeling. It was one of the worst things she ever said to him, a sign of such deep alienation that the memory prevented him from acknowledging even a trace of irritation now.

"Of course not," he said, adding, "The heart wants what it wants." Which earned him a smile.

Abby's face was brightly lit against a nearly black background, her video setup ill-suited for nighttime. At the start of the call, the kids had been in the frame with her, shouting and waving, overamped at bedtime. Now she was alone. She had just finished explaining why what Claire wanted was impractical from a medical standpoint. Or if not impractical, inadvisable. Eliot had always been the point person. That should continue.

They were five minutes into the Zoom, and Claire had voiced nothing of what she'd said to Eliot earlier, nothing to retract the proposal. Eliot was on edge, wondering what was going to happen, wondering if she was just waiting for the right moment or if the earlier conversation had represented a passing second thought rather than a true reversal. Looking now at Abby's drawn face, he wished she were home with him and Claire and Josh, that the four of them were together. The two kids their adult selves but also not. Also more like their teenaged, even their childhood selves. Claire would let them dominate. She would be doubly mother, all mother, and they would overwhelm her with their kid feelings of privilege and primacy, wiping out any lingering trace of her desire to replace Eliot with her friends.

She coughed, and Eliot patted her back gently, thinking he shouldn't want her to be anything other than exactly who she was. He shouldn't want her to be dominated by anyone.

"I hear you guys trying to change my mind," she said. "I'm not the person with a decision to make."

Crushed, Eliot sat as still as he could, barely breathing. She wasn't retracting her request. She was doubling down.

"I can't change what I want," she went on. "I could say I've changed, but where does that get us, me telling lies at the end of my life? That's not what I want. I don't think it's what you guys want either. I think you'd look back and feel pretty bad about it." She turned and looked at Eliot. "You know?"

He forced himself to nod. About twenty-four hours after she first told him what she wanted—a twenty-four-hour period of profound shock and grief punctuated by dozens of little tasks having to do with running the household and the sickroom—she found him collapsed in front of the television and said, "Can I ask you a question?" Her face with a sallow cast, circles under her eyes. "How mad are you?" Eliot said he wasn't mad, which was true: he was sad, confused, a little embarrassed—but not mad. There was, however, something he should've already asked, but the answer was so obvious, but if he wasn't certain how she'd respond . . . "I should've already asked this," he said, "but would I be able to come visit?" And she burst into tears, unable in that moment to bear the rip she clearly felt she'd torn in his self-confidence.

Now, sitting between Josh and Claire, staring at Abby's image on his laptop, Eliot knew the time had come. There was a hot, agitated feeling in his rib cage. He waved to indicate that he had something to say. Josh stiffened at his side, Abby leaned closer.

"Everyone. I've made a decision. I'm going to do what your mother wants. Whatever you want," he said, turning to Claire and touching her face. "Truly, my love, anything." Saying the most private, the most intimate thing to her with the kids right there, watching and listening. He had an intimation of the next weeks or months, being unable to speak to her in the way he wanted, the way he always had when they were alone together.

He turned back to the screen. He squeezed Josh's leg, looked hard at Abby, and said, "I'll be five minutes away. I'll be here a lot, I'm sure. You kids will be here. Let's not make this a bigger deal than it is."

6

SO NOW THE THING that had struck Eliot as incredible was going to happen. He packed a suitcase, to get that out of the way. The day before returning to Chicago, Josh suggested a father-son hike at Sleeping Giant. They left Claire by herself, cell phone charged at her side, Holly alerted that she'd be on her own. Eliot assumed he and Josh would spend the whole time talking about Claire and his decision, with Josh coming up with some kind of Hail Mary to try to get him to reconsider, but as soon as they were on the trail Josh launched into a story about a conversation he'd had during his call center work.

"This guy, I swear, it was like he'd misdialed and meant to call a suicide prevention number. He was like, 'Yeah, I've just been having a really hard time lately.' I was like, 'I'm sorry to hear that. I'd be happy to help you with your customer service needs. Can you tell me what the issue is?' Because we have a script, right? And he was like, 'You sound like a good person. Do you have days where you just don't see the point?' I ended up on the phone with him for forty-five minutes. We get alerts when we haven't reached a resolution within a certain amount of time, depending on what kind of issue it is. They were beeping me and beeping me. I even got a flagged email from my supervisor."

"That sounds rough."

"No, Dad, that's the point. I felt kind of great about it. Like I think he felt better afterward. For real. I told him about deciding to stick with music. You know, after that one summer."

There was a bad period when Josh had no gigs and talked about giving up, getting what he called "a stupid job," which seemed to refer to anything with a salary and benefits that he might consider doing long-term. It was the summer Claire went back on chemo, after they found the lesions in her lungs. She told Eliot she thought Josh was bargaining, trying to ward off her illness by paying with his own unhappiness.

"Was he a musician?" Eliot said. "The guy?"

"No, but I could sense he had the soul of an artist. He was a manager at some company." Josh pronounced the word "company" as if it designated an obvious evil. "Anyway, do you think I'd be a good therapist?"

Eliot froze. Was Josh seriously considering embarking on a new career? One that needed a ton of training? Right now? Josh was in the lead and didn't look back, so he was unaware that he'd stopped Eliot in his tracks. Eliot's heart raced crazily. The trail was empty, no other hikers so far on this weekday afternoon. If he had a heart attack, Josh would have to run back down the trail, maybe run all the way out to the road before he got a cell signal or spotted a car to wave down. Was Josh capable of that?

At last Josh turned and saw Eliot several yards down the trail. "Guess not," he said sourly.

"No, no," Eliot said. "I was just surprised." He didn't know what else to say, what to add. Claire was so good at handling this kind of thing. So good at letting what felt fraught to Eliot unfold slowly—and become, in the process, less fraught. That he could do it at all was entirely due to her influence and guidance. She had given him his fatherhood. It wasn't just that she had given him children: she had given him his way of being a father. The greatest gift of his life, after the gift that was Claire herself. But alone out here, when she was so far away and so close to being entirely gone, he was lost. He said, "I guess . . . I mean . . . do you want to be a therapist?"

Josh rolled his eyes. "Dad, that's not the question I asked. Do you think that if I wanted to, I'd be good at it?"

"Well, sure," Eliot said. "Of course."

"Ugh, that is such crap, Dad!"

Eliot was baffled. "What do you want me to say?"

"See, this is why I get what Mom is doing. This. You don't even know."

"Know what?"

"Perfect!" Josh said with a harsh laugh. "There it is right there."

"There what is?"

"Dad. My whole life you're like this benign blob walking around. You're like . . . amenable. Except when you're not."

Eliot's pulse exploded: the heart attack he'd brought into being by thinking about a heart attack. But no, this was ordinary misery. Ordinary desolation. He turned and began to jog down the trail, paying close attention so he wouldn't land wrong on a rock or a root. He had to get to the car without mishap. There were no steps approaching from behind; Josh had stayed where he was. Eliot, the boring blob, was on his own, making a show of running away from someone who wasn't going to follow. Not boring, benign. The benign blob. He'd gone from quiet and witty to benign blob. What a life! What a shocking transformation! He heard voices for a moment, and then they were gone. He was approaching a switchback, and he feared he'd make the 180 and come upon a little family, a mother and a father and a boy and a girl, and the idea was so pulverizing that he left the trail and started up the mountainside, bushwhacking. Almost immediately he was winded. The terrain, the trees and rocks, the sudden, intense demand on his quads, his breath coming even harder until at last he stopped because you couldn't just climb up a mountain without a trail, for God's sake. Which . . . how fucking pathetically symbolic could you get?

Did he hear the voices again? No, it was a trick of his imagination. All was silent. No Josh in pursuit, no happy little family climbing up to meet him with a visual reminder of what his life should have been or had been. But had it? He wished he could ask Claire, but he'd stopped asking her questions like that, stopped asking her for reassurance. So long ago. He felt as if he couldn't breathe, as if his entire body were being squeezed, and he squatted and then sat all the way down. Moisture from the earth seeped through his pants so that in a moment, on top of everything else, his ass was wet.

Claire was with Holly when Eliot and Josh got home. They were watching a movie, both under a single blanket, like little girls on a sleepover. Josh waved at them and went straight up to his room, leaving Eliot to lie about the pleasant afternoon. He'd gotten so cold waiting for Josh in the shady parking lot that to warm up he said he was going to take a quick shower. But once he was closed into the guest room with its private bath, he went for the tub instead, filling it with water so hot that his feet and lower legs turned bright red when he stepped in. He didn't know when he'd last taken a bath. The tub was on the small side, his knees poking up above the water. But the immersion felt good. In childhood he had been moved from bath to shower on his seventh birthday, his father a great believer in milestones—like Claire, but in a masculine, programmatic way. Eliot's training wheels came off his bicycle on his fifth birthday. He became responsible for setting his own alarm clock at age ten. It was nutty in retrospect: his father's rigid timeline for his children's maturation, Eliot's mother's lazy or fearful abdication of responsibility for all such decisions. Josh and Abby had developed at wildly different rates. Josh at ten could no more remember to set an alarm clock than learn to drive. Josh at ten was cuddly and immature, still sitting on his parents' laps, holding their hands on neighborhood walks. He had been Eliot's little buddy, following him around on weekends wanting to watch—always watch, never help—as Eliot did his chores. Josh made up songs about raking, about hanging Christmas lights.

In the Sleeping Giant parking lot, when he finally appeared, he was painfully apologetic, telling Eliot he hadn't meant it, he loved Eliot, he was just in a bad mood for obvious reasons. "I'm an asshole. Really, Dad. Can we forget the whole thing? Please?"

"It's OK," Eliot said. "It makes sense that you're mad. It has to come out sometime, right?" He hoped this would build a bridge, forge some father-son communion, but he could see right away that he'd gotten it wrong, Josh with the furrow in his forehead that always accompanied disappointment.

"I'm not mad," Josh said. "I'm sad. There's a difference."

Eliot knew he shouldn't say more, but this might be his only opportunity. Plus Josh had brought it up. "What you said up there?

About how you get why Mom wants to do this thing. What did you mean?"

A long beat as Josh stared at the ground. At last he looked up and Eliot saw him decide to be kind rather than truthful. "Honestly, Dad, I was talking out of my ass. I don't get it, it's like the last thing I ever thought would happen." He paused. "Also, sorry, but I kind of don't want to talk about it anymore? Unless you're going to change your mind?"

And so they didn't—talk about it anymore. Though all of it loomed as they drove home with the reasoned voices of NPR filling the silence between them. Now, sitting in the bath—the water cooling off, not cold yet but no longer truly warm—Eliot wished he could tell Claire what had happened. He even knew how he would soften the intro, by first inviting her to guess what new career path Josh was considering. He'd keep the hard part off to the side, mention it but not dwell on it.

But no, he wouldn't tell her anything. Josh wouldn't want him to, and Eliot wasn't sure Claire would even want to hear it. Hadn't she essentially informed him that she no longer had the energy or appetite to talk to him, about the kids or anything else?

He thought of the earliest days of Abby's infancy, the stunning reality of having something square in the middle of his life that he thought about all the time—and wanted to think about all the time. Someone. He told Claire that he hadn't understood, when she was pregnant. Hadn't guessed. But she'd known, right? All along? And she said no, Abby in the world was entirely different from Abby in utero. She and Eliot were the same. And it was a good thing, because they would be obsessed together for the rest of their lives. Every giggle would interest them, every bruise; every misused word, book loved, game invented; every friend adored or feared, every heartbreak or victory, every hero revealed to have feet of clay.

You're like this benign blob.

Eliot remembered hearing about teenaged Abby's cutting commentary on Claire's abandoned PhD: "No offense, Mom, but you're not a very good role model." He and Claire had laughed and laughed at that. And there was an earlier time, when Abby was maybe four, when Claire told Eliot with something bordering on glee that Abby had yelled "I hate you" at her, after being denied something she wanted. Claire was over the moon that time, saying she could die happy because she'd managed to raise a daughter who wasn't afraid to express her true feelings. She meant in contrast to herself, a daughter who'd been raised to swallow hers. Claire had grown up feeling she was on Earth in order to make her parents feel good about themselves, a job all the more difficult because it was unconscious for all parties. A popular book among Claire and her friends had been *The Drama of the Gifted Child*, which Claire routinely and amusingly mistitled *The Tragedy of the Gifted Child*. A book whose thesis was the high cost of repression. It had loosened something in Claire, the realization that by resembling her mother, that by living up to her father's standards, that by giving both what they most wanted, she had fallen into a way of being in the world that she might not have chosen for herself had a choice seemed possible. She was ripe to share these discoveries, but when she and Eliot met, Eliot hadn't yet questioned anything about his upbringing. He hadn't *thought* of questioning it, had barely been aware that questioning your upbringing was a thing. At first she was gentle about his parents' foibles, but once the kids arrived she pressed him harder: She loved his father, but Eliot had to admit the old man was a sexist hard ass! Eliot had to agree with her—didn't he?—that being mindful about parenting was better than just automatically doing what your parents did!

The thing was, saying someone had to agree with you was rhetorical; it was an attempt at persuasion. Eliot had never really thought about this before. It was actually, as a conversational gambit, even a little bullying. "You have to admit . . ." "You have to agree . . ." Why not just say "Do you think . . ."? Or even "I think . . ." Because that's what it was, it was saying what you thought, but with the heavy artillery of a demand. Ready to step out of the tub, Eliot was pierced by the notion that for his entire married life he had pretended to agree when actually what he did, what he always did, was concede.

7

HOLLY'S HOUSE WAS HYPER-CONTEMPORARY, all steel and glass and exotic wood. She had gotten it in the divorce, Stuart a very successful TV writer who now lived full-time in LA. When the family built this house, Stuart was riding high on his hit series about a corrupt insurance company executive and his nefarious dealings with the owner of a nuclear power plant in the aftermath of an accident based on Three Mile Island. *Meltdown* had been the series people struggled to remember as they named the great anti-hero shows of the day. *There was that other one, the guy was an accountant or something?* As Stuart painstakingly explained to anyone who wanted to know why a guy making fifty million a year didn't see himself as a titan, there was a difference between a hit and a huge hit, let alone a hit and a megahit.

Holly, in typical Holly fashion, had named each room for one of Stuart's characters: the Malcolm H. Gruber Living Room, the Larry Hutchison Kitchen, etc. On a rainy day shortly after Josh returned to Chicago, Eliot carried his suitcase into the Carolina Hutchison Guest Room, named for the teenaged daughter of the nuclear power plant owner, a fan favorite for her generally malevolent outlook on life and her merciless mocking of her poor, benighted, capitalist monster of a father. After Stuart moved away, Holly went the extra ironic step of placing photos of the characters in the corresponding rooms: trying a little hard, in Eliot's view, but

Claire said Holly needed to change her relationship to *Meltdown*, take ownership of its place in her life, and the photos did that for her. This meant Eliot hung up shirts and dumped socks and underwear into drawers watched by a large picture of Carolina from the episode in season three when the scales fell from her eyes and she went from spoiled child to government informant. In this particular scene, a first meeting between Carolina and her handler at a random shopping mall, Carolina took very literally the idea that she was a spy and wore a trench coat and sunglasses as she waited in front of a Sunglass Hut sipping an enormous smoothie.

Eliot took a picture of the picture and texted it to Josh, adding: **Remember her?** During *Meltdown*'s heyday, teenaged Josh had liked to complain to Stuart that if Carolina was going to be given an awakening, Stuart should've turned her into an activist, not a snitch.

Eliot stared at his phone, willing Josh to respond. Josh had been back in Chicago for two days and it had been radio silence, not even a thumbs-up when Eliot asked if he'd gotten home safely. After Sleeping Giant Josh had avoided being alone with Eliot, and while the journey to the airport should've given them a nice hour together, he'd claimed he had to listen to a call center training thing and spent the ride with his pods in his ears.

He didn't respond to the picture of Carolina Hutchison.

Eliot had dinner club that evening, and he went into the kitchen to prepare. Each year he and the others chose a theme for their monthly meetings: one year it was chicken dishes from around the globe, another it was rice. The year devoted to barbecue involved recipes from every barbecue-notable state in the nation, with North Carolina getting two separate evenings. This year they had pivoted to dessert and were building menus organized around whatever recipe struck each host's fancy. For tonight Dan was making butterscotch pudding, and Eliot had the simple task of assembling a salad.

But where was Holly's olive oil? He opened cabinet after cabinet, and each failure to find it chipped away at his sense of purpose. Did he even want to go? What was he going to say when the others asked after Claire? At the last meeting he had told them about her decision to stop treatment, though he had framed it as their decision, his and Claire's. It had been, hadn't it? A decision made together? So much had changed in the last month.

He found the olive oil in a small pantry off the kitchen. There was a large bottle of the standard grocery store stuff and a small bottle of a high-end Italian import, and he helped himself to the latter. The motto at dinner club was that if you were going to make the effort, you should go for broke. The least Holly could do was underwrite Eliot's participation in this practice.

Dan was hosting at his Wooster Square condo. Eliot pulled up early, as he almost always did: anywhere, everywhere. He cut the engine and settled in to wait for the appointed hour. Claire was different—punctual but not punctual to a fault—and in certain eras of their marriage she had ribbed him about his conviction that if you weren't at least five minutes early you were late. Certain eras or certain moods: obviously a marriage had ebbs and flows, parallel lines and tightly woven braids. These were governed sometimes by time and sometimes by the vicissitudes of life events, relational ups and downs. Eliot remembered being in the car once with Claire, after dropping Abby at a friend's; Josh was off somewhere, not a concern. Claire said, "Let's go home and just look at each other and not talk." Eliot thought she was kidding, or that she was serious about not talking but kidding about looking at each other while not talking. But it turned out she'd read an article about the power of shared silence. Shared, mutually focused silence. Not the erotic power, the connective power. It wasn't her kind of thing, lifestyle or relationship journalism, but something had made her read it. He said, "What if one of us starts laughing or gets horribly bored with it? Aren't there pitfalls?" And she said that was the point, they'd find out how it was to react differently in real time, how his tolerance for that differed from hers. He said, "Don't we always react differently in real time? If we're going to react differently?" And she said, "Verbally, yes. This is a very specific examination of nonverbal behavioral differences." Then she thought for a moment and said, "On the other hand, we could just go home and fuck." Eliot laughed out loud now, remembering this. And then, as he locked up the car and approached Dan's door, felt a terrible melancholy descend.

Dan greeted Eliot as if they were midconversation. "So I tried two different recipes, I'm going to do a blind taste test and see what you guys think. Hang on, I'm not really in the mood for this." Leaving Eliot at the front door, he strode over to his stereo, playing what Eliot believed to be 1990s music. Dan always had something playing when guests arrived, and it was always louder than Eliot liked. A new song started, less melodic than its predecessor. It was more like what Josh called "noise," which oddly enough was a category, not a complaint. Eliot fished out his phone to check, but Josh still hadn't replied.

Dan beckoned, and Eliot followed him into the kitchen.

"How are things?"

"Fine."

"I mean . . ." Dan let his voice trail off meaningfully, and Eliot went with the narrowest interpretation of the question.

"It's just palliative treatments now. Stuff to make her feel better."

"And? How's she doing? How are you?"

"Nothing has really changed yet."

"Right."

About Claire's condition, at least, this was true.

The doorbell rang. Two of the others had arrived at the same time, and the final two followed not long after. Soon everyone was milling around, reheating things in the microwave, borrowing Dan's cutting boards to prepare garnishes.

Once they were seated, Mason—the oldest by more than a decade—announced that he and his wife had decided to move to Arizona, where one of their daughters lived. "I'm grateful to this group," he said. "I'll miss you all. You've helped me settle into my retirement." A physicist at Yale, Mason had stopped teaching only when the pandemic hit. For a while he continued to run his lab, but in the last year or so he'd stepped back from that as well.

They raised their glasses and toasted him. He was the first to withdraw, and Eliot wondered if his departure would be the initiating domino, if the group would still exist in a year's time.

Dan said, "I'd say you guys've helped me settle into my divorce if only I were settled into it."

"You're not?" said John, a high school English teacher. He was short and thickly built but very fit. He was Eliot's favorite, wry and warm, so warm that you didn't immediately get how private he was. Eliot respected the combination. He'd even tried to talk about it with Claire once, but her reaction shut him up. "Warm and private? Definitely sounds better than cold and oversharing!" As if Eliot were an annoying fly to swat away. Years earlier, the therapist had suggested Eliot say "Ouch" when he felt hurt, but he'd never been able to do that.

"Divorce," Dan said, "is a state that argues against the notion of 'settled.'"

Wally rolled his eyes. "Completely disagree. I'm very settled. I'll never marry again."

"You're not going to be alone forever."

"Maybe I'll live with someone again, but I'll never remarry."

"You say that now," Dan teased.

"And I mean it!" Wally had a short fuse and Eliot didn't like him much. When Wally hosted, the dinners never ran longer than an hour. His ex-wife was a friend of Holly's, and Eliot knew she had initiated the divorce.

Wanting to reroute the conversation, Eliot cleared his throat and said, "You've all helped me," then immediately wished he hadn't spoken.

"Damn," John said. "Sorry. I didn't even ask."

"I asked," Dan said, adding, "There's that modesty of character Jennifer loved so much. Fortunately there's butterscotch pudding we better get started on evaluating."

Relieved, Eliot rose and collected plates. The rule was that the guests helped with clearing but the host washed the dishes; it was personal, how spotless you kept your Le Creuset. When Eliot sat again, only John had returned to the table ahead of him.

"You like to hike, right?"

Eliot nodded, but the question made him think of Josh and he pulled his phone from his pocket. Still no response.

"Maybe we can go some weekend. Wadsworth maybe, or Seven Falls."

"Love to," Eliot said automatically, but why did John think he could leave Claire now, of all times? Did he somehow know what had happened? Could the news already be spreading, the very day of Eliot's departure?

"Saturday?" John said. "Pick you up around one?"

This was starting to feel pointed. If John didn't know, why was he making such a big deal about it? Pinning down a date so insistently, as if Eliot were in particular need of distraction? It was nice of him, but . . .

"This weekend's not great," Eliot said. "I'll text you with some options?"

"Of course."

Dan brought a tray of individual puddings to the table, half the ramekins white and half red. Everyone got one of each. The puddings in the white ramekins were the color of coffee ice cream, those in the red much darker. Dan explained that the darker ones had been made with brown sugar, while the lighter ones had required him to caramelize white sugar. "Which let me tell you," he said. "I sure hope the dark ones are better, because the light ones . . . I turned around for a second and next thing I knew the whole mess was black and smoking."

Mason looked puzzled. "But the cream lightened it?"

"I started over. And to tell you the truth, these are from my third try, because the second time I didn't go far enough and you could hardly taste the butterscotch at all."

"Why not add more Scotch?" Wally said.

"See that's the thing—there's no Scotch in butterscotch. Who knew, right? One theory for the name is that it comes from how 'scotch' sounds like 'scorch,' which is what happens if you cook sugar too long, as I learned. Others say it comes from the middle English word 'scocchen,' which means to 'score, nick, or cut,' like if you were making candy and had to cut it into pieces."

"That is such an excellent piece of research," said Piotr, pronouncing "piece" as "piss." Born in Moscow, he still had a heavy Russian accent despite having lived in the States since grad school.

"A third theory," Dan said, "is that the name's related to 'Scotland,' but I don't see how that makes sense given that it was invented in Yorkshire."

John beamed. "You know what I love about Yorkshire? We watch these shows, these cop shows, and the characters say 'I'm going down to pub.' Instead of 'down to the pub.' They drop the definite article. 'Will you put kettle on?' There's maybe a tiny 't' sound just before the noun. 'Will you put t'kettle on?' I love it."

"The simple pleasures of an English teacher," Dan said.

"Actually, they're very complex pleasures," John said drily.

Dan produced disposable sleep masks and had everyone cover their eyes and move their two ramekins around until they didn't know which was which.

Eliot dipped his spoon into one of his. The pudding was cool and silky. Luscious. The flavor reminded him of the hard candies his grandmother had kept in her living room in a crystal bowl, each candy wrapped in crinkly cellophane. Sucking on them caused a sudden surge in saliva production, so that you had to work to keep from drooling out of the corners of your mouth. Eliot and his brothers competed to see who could go the longest before crushing the candies between their molars. "Boys," their mother would admonish them when the chewing got noisy. She sent them to the kitchen to swish with hot water, to dislodge the bits of candy from their teeth.

The other pudding didn't compare. It was subtle to the point of bland. No surprise when Eliot took off his mask to discover that he preferred the darker of the two. Everyone did, though in no time there was nothing left in any of the ramekins.

"What have we learned from this?" Piotr said. "'Don't waste your time caramelizing sugar'?"

"What is brown sugar?" Wally said. "White sugar with molasses added?"

Mason said, "So butterscotch pudding is really molasses pudding?"

"No, you have it backward," Dan said. "Molasses is what you have left over when you refine sugar. You don't add molasses to white sugar to make brown sugar. You subtract molasses from brown sugar to make white sugar."

"Really?" Eliot said. "Is that true?"

"Your mind is blown," John said.

"It is. And on that note, I should get going."

Eliot hadn't been thinking of leaving, but once the words were out he was on his feet, eager to be gone. He retrieved his salad bowl and moved toward the door. "I didn't realize what time it was. Sorry, sorry, don't let me interrupt. See you all next time."

"Eliot!" Dan called out.

Eliot turned.

Dan put his palm to his upper chest: a gesture somewhere between terror and love. "Good luck."

A moment of stillness, and they all did the same, put their palms to their chests. Eliot's eyes swam as he called out his thanks.

The night was cool and damp, early May and perfumed by blossoming fruit trees up and down the block. Eliot got in his car but didn't start the engine. He wondered if John had simply wanted to be friendly or if word was spreading. Eliot didn't want to think of people gossiping about him and Claire. *What does that say, that she wanted him out of the house for her final months?* Why couldn't it say nothing? When he was back home after dropping Josh at the airport, Claire had asked him to lie down with her, to hold her, and with their faces inches apart said she couldn't do it unless she knew he understood it wasn't a verdict on him or their marriage. "It's wanting A," she said, "rather than not wanting B." "I know," he said, and she cupped his jaw and looked into his eyes—not unlike a mother, he thought now, who was proud of her newly mature, sensitive son.

It was out of his way, but he drove by the house. Most of the lights were on. He didn't know which rooms Holly and Michelle had taken and wondered if Abby and Josh knew or cared. Sheer curtains covered the living room windows, but he could just make out a figure moving through the space, heading to the back of the house.

He got out of the car and quietly closed the door. The gate creaked as he pushed it open. Either Holly or Michelle had failed to bungie closed the garbage can, and he corrected that before continuing to the backyard. He made his way down the fence line to the woods, where he had a clear view into the kitchen.

Michelle was at the sink, rinsing dishes and setting them in the dishwasher. Her first visit following Claire's initial diagnosis, she was so awkward and uncomfortable that Claire got Holly to take her away. Eliot remembered a whispered conversation while Michelle was in another room, Claire telling Holly to make up a story about needing Michelle at her house, how with Stuart gone she was really struggling. Or was she supposed to say that with her youngest gone to college she was struggling with her newly empty nest? Some reason invented having to do with Holly needing Michelle more than Claire did. All to spare Claire Michelle's anguish. "She can never know," Claire said, impressing on Eliot how important it was that this fib be kept a secret. Eliot imagined making his way to the house now and saying to Michelle: Listen, there was a time when she wanted *you* gone.

Claire entered the kitchen, moving slowly. Holly was just behind her. They sat at the table and in a moment Michelle joined them, setting down a plate of something. They were talking, but of course Eliot couldn't hear them. Still, he could tell it was a muted conversation, muted in tone. Something about the way their bodies moved, the angles of their heads. They reached for whatever was on the plate as they spoke. It contained something sweet, judging by how quickly Holly reached for more. Holly was the kind of person who couldn't eat one cookie: she had to keep going, it was a compulsion. "Sort of like Stuart googling his own name," she said one long-ago evening when something prompted her to try to explain her speedy consumption of a plate of gingersnaps. At which point Stuart without missing a beat said, "The only difference is that you can't *see* a swelled *head*." The hush that fell over the table after that. At least fifteen years ago, and Eliot had never forgotten it.

Now, in the kitchen, Claire lowered her forehead to the table.

Was she upset? The very thought made Eliot's heart rate speed up. The hidden part of caring for someone who was sick: monitoring her emotional state, trying to reduce stress, to protect against painful news. Claire herself said crying made her feel terrible physically. Headache, exhaustion.

She lifted her head, and Eliot realized she was laughing. Holly and Michelle seemed amused too, so maybe he'd been wrong about the muted tone.

If only he could hear them. There was a vent in the garage that carried sounds from the kitchen, but he wasn't sure he could get into the garage without making any noise. Besides which: What was he thinking?

His phone pulsed. Abby, sending a picture of the kids holding a sign that read COME VISIT US GRANDPA. Abby texted Eliot several times a day. She described memories of ways he helped her when she was a child, as if having been a good dad meant he didn't deserve to be sidelined as a husband. He gave the photo a heart and crept as quietly as he could to the gate, then strode to his car.

No lights on at Holly's house; he hadn't thought of it. He used the flashlight on his phone to navigate the concrete path and its intermittently placed pairs of steps. He turned off the alarm using the four digits of Claire's birthday, wondering if it was Holly and Stuart's original code or if Holly had changed it after Stuart left. Or even recently. Maybe she'd changed it for Eliot.

He tried to read in bed but it was still early, so he got up and roamed around the house. Holly had left food in the refrigerator for him, which pissed him off. He dumped a bowl of broccoli and rice salad into the garbage, followed by a platter of chicken. She seemed to have missed the fact that he did all the meal prep at home these days, that he didn't need feeding.

He found the tail end of a basketball game to watch. Susan Simmons had planned her own funeral, but that was one thing Claire didn't want to do. It wasn't about her, she said, it was about the rest of them. "You and the kids, it's for the three of you." Was that going to change as well, and Eliot would hear that it had all been decided by Claire and her friends and he had nothing to do but attend?

Josh had already said he wanted to sing something, maybe a song of his own. Eliot remembered an end-of-session talent show at the kids' summer camp, Josh seated on a stool with a soulful, earnest look on his face, performing a song he'd written, his voice sweet and still high. It was dusk, mosquitoes coming out of the woods and making a beeline for the captive audience. In love with her son's innocence, Claire squeezed Eliot's hand so painfully that his wedding ring left a mark.

Eliot found his text thread with Josh. Five different messages to which Josh hadn't responded. He typed **Benign blob needs a signal.** But that would just put Josh on the defensive, and he deleted it. He killed the TV and got back into bed. Carolina Hutchison in her trench coat stared down at him from the opposite wall.

Buddy, please, Eliot typed into the thread. He sent it before he could reconsider, turned off the bedside lamp, and held his phone in the dark.

8

"DAD, JEEZ, IT WAS no big deal. I've just been busy."

"OK."

"Like, we just spent a week together."

"OK."

"I thought I answered."

"OK."

"Dad! You're being so needy! Abby says we have to take care of you as much as Mom, but isn't that later? I mean, aren't you just waiting? Aren't we all waiting?"

It was morning, and Eliot was on Holly's patio with a cup of Holly's coffee lightened by a slug of Holly's organic heavy cream. The pond *was* lovely, no other property visible though there were a few houses nearby, veiled by trees. Eliot wondered if Holly ever got spooked, being out here by herself. Right after Stuart left, Eliot and Claire spent hours with her, bringing over dinner, sitting in front of the fireplace and trying to match her mood, agreeing that Stuart had been difficult when Holly was angry, agreeing that he'd been kind and supportive when she needed to mourn. She blamed Hollywood the monolith rather than Stuart's ambition, as if no one could have resisted the intense lure of glamour and fame. Since the end of *Meltdown* Stuart had gotten exactly one program going, a short-lived zombie show that was denied a second season. He pitched and pitched, schmoozed and schmoozed. He helped various friends sharpen their pilots but was too proud to be anyone's number two. He had to be The Guy. Which meant he had to be in LA even more, which meant he had to renounce the quiet life he'd spent a large portion of his earnings building.

"Dad?" Josh said. "I'm sorry."

Eliot said, "I think we are all waiting, yes."

"You're not being needy. I'll try to be better about texting."

"I'm only needy if you don't answer."

"I know, that's what I mean."

"No, you only think of it as needy if you don't answer. My guess is if you just sent me a lol or a thumbs-up or whatever, it would change the way you feel about me reaching out."

"Whoa, Dad, therapist vibes."

Eliot chuckled. "I wanted to tell you, I think you'd be a great therapist."

"You don't have to say that."

"But it's true, I think you'd be great at it. I hesitated on the hike that day because it's a long path. A lot of training."

"Did you tell Mom?"

Eliot hesitated. He couldn't tell Josh the real reason he hadn't informed Claire, his sense that she didn't want to get into things with him anymore—he couldn't without talking to Josh about the situation, the reason he was here on Holly's terrace. And Josh didn't want to talk about that.

"I didn't want to take that from you," he said at last. "It's yours to tell her or not."

There was a silence, and suddenly Josh was sobbing.

"Buddy, what?"

Always a wailer as a little kid, Josh keened into the phone, crying, "No, no, no." Eliot made consoling noises, told Josh how sad it was, how much Claire loved him. At last the weeping subsided. Josh said, "Hang on," and from a distance blew his nose. He came back and said, "Sorry."

"Don't be sorry."

"You know what I was thinking? My housemate Loreen? Her parents split up when she was like eight or so, and she said one of the worst moments was when her dad let her stay up really late and eat a shit ton of candy. And she was like, 'Is this OK?' And he said, 'Your mother and I don't make decisions together anymore.'"

Eliot waited.

"So I was thinking . . . you and Mom won't talk about me anymore. After she dies."

"That's so painful."

Josh sniffed again but didn't cry. Eliot wondered if he'd made a mistake, not telling Claire. Had he misread her? The thing was, telling her would have ended up including the cruel things Josh had said to him. *You're like this benign blob.* She would have comforted him, and that would have been unbearable.

He made her favorite soup, avgolemono, bright with lemon. He didn't want to deliver it in Holly's Tupperware, so he went out and bought a container of his own. He texted ahead of his arrival so the women wouldn't be startled when he came in.

Claire was asleep. Holly gave him an overly long hug, her arms wrapping tight. He'd been gone all of twenty-nine hours.

"Eliot. How are you, how'd you sleep? I hope the woodpecker didn't bother you. Did I tell you about the woodpecker? Outside my bedroom? Noisy little fucker but maybe you were in the Carolina room. Anyway . . . she had a rough night. She was up for several hours just feeling . . . 'off,' she said. Her back hurt. She went to lie down a bit ago." Holly looked into Eliot's eyes. "Do you want me to wake her for you?"

Eliot couldn't believe this. Did he want Holly to wake Claire for him? Next thing he knew she'd be offering to show him where the bathroom was. "No, Holly, I don't want you to wake her."

Holly's eyes widened. "Should I not have said that? Shit, I'm sorry."

"I'll put this in the fridge."

He made his way to the kitchen. A catalog of women's athletic wear lay open on the table: Michelle's for sure. She was always training for a half-marathon or signing up for a cycling trip through the mountains. Eliot once asked Claire if she would describe Michelle as a force of nature, and Claire said not at all, if anyone was a force of nature it was Holly. Michelle was the opposite, an incredibly well-made, intricately constructed machine. "And what are you?" Eliot responded playfully, and Claire thought for a moment and said, quite seriously, "I'm a ploughed field. Strong enough for the force of nature not to destroy me, cultivated enough to provide a smooth operating surface for the machine." Could any of that explain why Claire's friends were in the house with her and he was not?

An old feminist slogan came to Eliot: *A woman needs a man like a fish needs a bicycle*. Claire had hated it, thought it missed the point entirely. "I don't *need* you," she told him. "I *want* you." So the point now was: she didn't need Holly and Michelle, she wanted them. Instead of him.

Holly had entered the kitchen behind him. She went to the fruit bowl and grabbed an orange and a lemon, saying, "Have you ever done salmon where you sort of immerse it in olive oil and then layer on citrus slices?"

"Can't say I have."

She peered at the knife block, and Eliot was perversely glad when she selected one of his older knives, which he knew had grown dull. She set the orange on its end and carefully sliced off a strip of peel, impatiently pushing her hair behind her ear when a lock fell in front of her face. Her hair these days was a dark, unnatural red, verging on burgundy—quite different from the reddish blond of her youth that for years she'd tried to replicate. During the pandemic she'd let the gray grow out, and when she decided to "try" again—this was how Claire and her friends talked about all manner of niceties, from wearing makeup, to dieting, to dressing up—her hairdresser talked her into this more dramatic shade. According to Claire, Holly wept when she got home from the salon, but she'd grown to like it and now asked for it every time.

"Why are you looking at my hair?"

Eliot feigned confusion. "What?"

"You were looking at my hair."

"No, I wasn't."

"OK." Holly rotated the orange, about to slice off more peel, but instead she set the knife down and leaned forward conspiratorially. "I wanted to tell you," she said in a low voice, "Abby called last night and kind of yelled at me."

Eliot didn't feel like doing chummy right now. "I don't believe that."

"Maybe she didn't yell, but she was upset."

"What did you expect?" he said. "Seriously?"

"This was all Claire!" Holly cried. "A hundred percent! We tried to talk her out of it!"

Eliot strode out of the kitchen, but Holly came after him and begged him to stay and talk. Worried their voices would reach Claire, they retreated to the TV room, where Holly teared up as she described the afternoon when the idea first appeared, the day he went to the Sound. She said it was like something came over Claire; Holly hadn't seen her so lively in ages, talking about Susan Simmons as if she'd been a guru rather than a retired piano teacher with nice tulips in her yard. Susan had been such a guide for Claire. For Claire and for others in the support group. Susan was magnetic. She was wise.

This was pretty much what Claire had said to Eliot, but now he had the presence of mind to be puzzled. He'd spent a fair amount of time with Susan Simmons: a perfectly nice person, but not in any way magnetic. Shy and wounded, more like. Someone who didn't "try," that was for sure. Frizzy gray hair (when she had hair). Birkenstocks in the old style, before they started making them silver. Baggy pants, droopy sweaters. And it wasn't as if Claire had always thought of Susan in such an idealizing way. More like the reverse. "Susan's got to get out more. I'm not blaming her for her lack of energy, but I think she'd feel better if she made an effort." Something like that. Radiation was harder on Susan than it was on Claire, though she had a slightly easier chemo regimen, without the worst of the stuff Claire had to endure. But unlike Claire, she lost the ability to have an orgasm, a detail Claire reported after swearing Eliot to secrecy. One night, about four years in, Eliot and Claire saw Susan at a restaurant sitting across from an elderly man.

Eliot figured she was on a date, but Claire said no, the man was her mentally ill half-brother, whom none of Susan's three sisters saw anymore. Susan had dinner with him once a year, keeping a promise to her long-dead father. Maybe that was "magnetic," though in Eliot's memory Susan look somnolent at the restaurant, and she and her half-brother left shortly after Eliot and Claire arrived.

"So what do you think?" Eliot asked Holly.

"About the Susan thing? She saw something she wanted. She put all this magic on it. The idea occurred to her and it flipped a switch."

"It occurred to *her*."

"Eliot, my God. I'm telling you, we had nothing to do with it. We were shocked. I mean, we didn't let her see that. But this was the last thing we wanted. Because of you. I can't imagine how you feel."

"Maybe you can but don't want to."

Holly grimaced. She stared at her hands and sighed. At last she looked up and said, "Do you think it's denial?"

"I do."

"And the Susan Simmons thing..."

"I keep thinking 'pretty.'"

"She wants a pretty death."

"Right."

"Nothing pretty about puking up a bunch of red wine."

Eliot was taken aback. "She threw up last night?" Had she been drunk, laughing at the kitchen table while Eliot watched from the backyard?

"She tried to clean it up herself."

"How much did she have?"

"Half a glass?"

Eliot frowned, and Holly's demeanor changed. "Please don't tell me she shouldn't have wine. What the fuck difference does it make?"

"Her head already hurts most of the time."

"She *wanted* it."

Eliot looked down. His feet aligned perfectly along the outer curves of an ivory circle in the mostly gray-blue Nepalese rug he and Claire had bought at a store in New York. When he was a boy and taken to his grandmother's house, to help pass the time and to keep from squirming, he stared at what she called her "Oriental carpet," intricately patterned in tones of green and tan and brown, and occupied himself by selecting one color after another and looking for its match in the front yard. The darkest green went with the fir tree. A lighter, brighter green corresponded with the birch leaves. A pale tan was the same color as the house across the street. This got him through many a dreary afternoon.

The bedroom door opened in the distance. There was the sound of Claire's cough, dry and chesty. The gentle scuff of her slippers.

She appeared in the doorway, looking wan and bedraggled. Then she saw him and smiled happily. "Honey, what are you doing here?" She came to the couch and let him help her sit, then leaned close for the kind of kiss they used to give each other at the end of the day.

"Brought you some soup."

"Avgolemono?"

He nodded. "You OK? Holly said it was a tough night."

Claire looked at Holly, who quipped, "I put it in the log. I guess he has access."

"Guess so," Claire said with a small smile. She turned to Eliot. "How was dinner club? Did you have fun?"

Eliot described Dan's puddings, the blind taste test. It was the kind of detail she enjoyed. He had no idea how long he should stay.

She said, "Did he do one in a bain-marie and the other with cornstarch?"

"The difference was in the type of sugar."

"But how did he cook them, how did he thicken them? Did he do them in a bain-marie or did he use cornstarch?"

"I don't know. Is there a big difference? They were thick. Pudding-ish."

"There's a huge difference. Pudding made with cornstarch is grainy." Claire looked at Holly. "Remember that stuff your mom made? I feel like maybe it was pineapple flavored?"

"Oh, my God. It was so disgusting. But wasn't that a mix?"

"No, she stirred it on the stove. And it had a skin on top, remember?" Claire shuddered. "She was going for 'comfort food,' though I don't think we called it that then. It was during the period when, you know . . ."

"She had her breakdown," Holly put in. "God, was that a time." She turned to Eliot. "I would get home from school and it was my job to help her do one thing every day. Some days it was walk around the block. Other days it was go to the store. 'One thing,' doctor's orders. Then my father would come home and it would be like: OK, back to normal, you're not clinically depressed once six o'clock hits, you've got to make your husband a drink."

Eliot knew how to have this kind of conversation, the long look back at growing up in the 1960s. He said, "My mother made my father a drink every single weeknight of his life. And on weekends he made her a drink."

"Same drink?"

"On weekdays she had sherry—she'd pour herself maybe two ounces. On weekends he'd make her a martini. Always bourbon for him."

"My father drank gin," Holly said. "Beaucoup gin. As I've discussed endlessly with both of you."

Holly's father had died of cirrhosis when she was in college. In the years leading up to his death she spent a lot of time at Claire's house. She adopted Claire's parents and they adopted her. When Claire's father died, it was Holly who fell apart. This was about a year after Stuart moved out, a hard time for her in general. She was a wreck, much more a burden on Claire than a comfort to her.

"What else?" Claire asked Eliot. "Any gossip?"

"Mason's moving to Arizona."

"Really?"

"The rest of us agreed maybe this is a good ending point."

"Eliot, no! Why? Five people is plenty. Or you can recruit someone to take his place. You don't want to stop, do you?"

Her distress made him feel bad that he'd lied, though he knew he'd lied to provoke it.

"Surely there are other guys who'd be interested," she went on. "Holly, didn't you tell me Gretchen's husband was jealous and wanted in?" Claire touched Eliot's hand, her rings having become so loose that she'd stopped wearing the diamond and had applied a lump of melted candle wax to the inside of the wedding band to keep it from falling off. "Fight for it. I'm serious. You'll need it when I'm gone."

Eliot said, "I like those guys, but if I never saw any of them again I'd be fine."

"You're missing the point, Eliot."

Resentment roiled through him. Even now, even on the brink of death, even after signaling that she was in some essential way finished with him, she had to correct him. All their life together she'd done this. He rose and moved to the door. He turned back and said, "Then I guess the point will be missed. Soup's in the fridge. It'll keep for a few days, or you can always freeze it."

9

A FORMER COLLEAGUE PHONED ELIOT for advice. She'd done well enough at the firm, but she didn't see a partnership role in her future and was thinking about getting out. Could she pick Eliot's brain?

He agreed to meet her for a drink at a restaurant in Middletown, a half hour from Holly's but he was glad for the long drive. When it came to time-consuming errands, he was like a horribly parched, dehydrated guy crawling through the desert. A half hour's drive? Equivalent to a tall drink of water. An hour? That was a liter of Gatorade.

Her name was Melinda but she went by Cindy, Eliot didn't know why. When they were settled on barstools she said, "Did you ever think of leaving for an industry job?"

"Everyone thinks about it. Kind of built into the work. What sector are you thinking? You're mostly telecom, right?"

"I can't remember how long it was before you made partner, once you were a principal."

The answer was twenty months, but Eliot didn't want to make her feel bad. "The question is what you want your days to be like. Maybe you'd like to stop traveling so much."

"I've flown twice in the last month," she said sourly. "I like flying." The bartender had just delivered their drinks, and she took a sip of hers and muttered, "God, is there any vodka in this thing?

Excuse me!" She waved the bartender back. "Can you top this up for me?" She took a big swallow and held out the glass for him to take. "Now there's plenty of room for you to give me my money's worth."

Embarrassed, Eliot looked away, used the mirror over the bar to watch the hostess yawn extravagantly. The bartender moved off with Cindy's glass, and Cindy caught Eliot's gaze in the mirror, held it until he turned to look at her.

"What?" she demanded.

"Nothing."

"I'm still a ball-breaker. Go ahead and say it."

Eliot shrugged.

"Ball. Breaker. Or are you too much of a gentleman?"

He was silent a moment, considering his options. "How about if I answer a question with a question? In what way would it help either of us if I said it?"

Cindy scoffed. "You're so fucking prudent. So careful. How does she even deal?"

The bartender came back with her drink, filled to within an eighth of an inch of the rim. He set it down carefully, but Cindy lifted it so clumsily that it spilled, dousing her hand and the napkin. It came to Eliot that she'd begun drinking earlier in the day.

"Oops," she said. "Now I'm making a mess." She waved, but the bartender was already setting a stack of napkins in front of her. She wiped up the spill, took a long swallow. "So how does she?"

Eliot had lost the thread. "How does who?"

"Carol. Deal with you. How's she doing, anyway? Didn't she have cancer or something?"

"It's Claire," Eliot said. "And she's dying."

Cindy was midsip, and she choked a little, coughing. "Eliot, I'm sorry. I'm such an asshole, I'm sorry." She coughed again, her face red.

"Is it telecom you do mostly?" he said, hoping to get her back on track so he could be on his way. "I know we worked together on—"

Cindy coughed again, patting her sternum.

"You OK?"

"Definitely," she said, but she coughed again, twice. Then three more times, each cough harder than the last. By now the bartender had come over. "I'm fine," she said waving him away. "Fine."

"You don't seem fine," Eliot said.

"There it is," she said with a smirk. "The only guy I know who can take an undeniable fact and turn it into a deadly weapon."

Eliot wasn't following. "A deadly weapon?"

She snickered. "You've heard of killing with kindness? You kill with boredom. You kill with the obvious. We used to laugh at you, did you know that? You'd end a meeting saying"—she dropped her voice into a stern baritone—"'We've got some work to do.' You'd walk out of the conference room and we'd be all: 'You've gotta hand it to Eliot, he sure knows how to motivate a team!'"

Eliot set his drink down and made his way to the exit. His face was on fire. He turned back, and she was cringing or possibly laughing into her hand. But wait, he hadn't paid. He handed the hostess some bills and gestured at the bar. He was unable to speak.

He didn't bother stopping at Holly's for clothes. He drove until he hit I-95 and merged into southbound traffic. He opened the window for some air and was immediately assaulted by the throbbing, buffeting sound known as the Helmholtz Resonance, a fact of physics imparted by Mason one evening when Eliot happened to give him a ride to dinner club. Eliot lowered the other windows, interrupting the effect but causing a deafening roar of ordinary road noise.

He could make it to Virginia by midnight. One at the latest. But what was he going to do, ring the doorbell? For some reason he was dead set against calling ahead. He had to show up unannounced. *Here I am!* He should have gifts to give the kids in the morning and wondered if there'd be anything suitable at a service station. *Here's more candy than your parents will allow you to eat!* The idea of Abby saying yes to any candy was laughable. She was a health nut. Claire always said they shouldn't fault their doctor daughter for being diet- and fitness-oriented with the grandchildren, but Eliot never wanted to fault her. He wanted to tease her.

He thought of Josh's housemate, the story about the newly divorced father letting his daughter eat a lot of candy. *Your mother and I don't make decisions together anymore.*

Tears crowded Eliot's eyes, but he was damned if he was going to let them fall. He was coming up on an exit, and though he didn't know where he was he took it, pretty sure he hadn't made it even to Bridgeport. He saw an enormous Walmart, found the entrance to the parking lot, and stopped under a light. Hundreds of cars were parked. Hundreds of people were shopping.

He'd checked in every day since he dropped off the soup, sometimes by text, sometimes with a quick visit. It seemed as if nothing had really changed. Claire slept a lot. Hospice had called him one afternoon to touch base. They worked with families too, the man said, and it was his job to notice if someone wasn't OK. He'd heard Eliot had moved to a friend's house. Was he OK?

A wave of nausea swept over Eliot, and he opened the car door and leaned out. Nothing. No "upset vomit," as Claire called the moments on TV when someone got bad news or saw something gruesome. Never to be confused with the "pregnant vomit," employed to telegraph how many thousands of TV pregnancies. Claire had told Stuart that if he ever wanted to write a pregnant character, he should have her take a sip of coffee and find it a little off-tasting. Then he should have her discover, maybe a week later, that the smell of sauteed garlic was gross. "That sounds like really dramatic TV," Stuart said.

Eliot found Stuart's number on his phone. They hadn't spoken in several years, close to a decade. In some way Stuart was the last person he should call, but maybe that made him the best.

"Eliot, Jesus," Stuart said by way of hello. "I've been meaning to reach out. How are you? Sorry, idiotic question. You're terrible."

"Well, yeah," Eliot said, "but are you talking about—"

"Let me count the ways, right? Sam told me. I guess Josh told him, then he called Holly and she confirmed that the three witches are together again. Or the two witches are helping your lovely wife through her final days."

So it was out there. Circulating. Holly's son Sam was Josh's best friend, or had been when they were kids. Sam was quick, sometimes a little churlish—a lot like his father. And like his father very social. He could've told any number of other kids, who could have told their parents. Holly was probably telling everyone.

"Yep," Eliot said.

"Fucking fuck."

Eliot had always liked Stuart but they'd never been real friends, despite how much time the families spent together. This failure had been a grave disappointment to Claire and Holly, which was maybe why Eliot and Stuart kept each other at a distance. Though also: Stuart was very artsy. In addition to being a major cinephile, he read poetry and went to see art nearly every time he was in New York. He read poetry *about* art. Eliot felt like a caveman in comparison. A caveman with a knack for strategic planning.

Holly'd had a lot of complaints, but one thing you could say about Stuart: he was very kind to children. His own, his friends', it didn't matter. Eliot had always admired this. Stuart would be the guy on the floor helping with a LEGO build, the adult herding a dozen kids outside to play Red Light, Green Light. When it came out that he was having an affair in California—that one part of why he was spending so much time in LA was a hugely ambitious TV producer named Lori Mensch—it was no surprise that she had a five-year-old who saw his dad only twice a month. Stuart was playing stepdad. "To a little Mensch!" Holly chortled, but it turned out "Mensch" was the woman's maiden name, and the story didn't even have that punchline to make Holly feel better.

A large family approached the minivan next to Eliot's, and he leaned out to close his door. In the process, something tumbled from his pocket. "Oh, fuck, hold on," he said to Stuart, placing the phone on the dashboard so he could reposition himself to retrieve whatever had fallen. He reached and succeeded only in pushing it away, something small and metal. He had to get out of the car to retrieve it. A key, the key to Holly's back shed, which he'd needed to access that morning in order to find the fertilizer she'd asked him to spread on her flower beds. He got back in the car, and just then the minivan's security system got triggered and its emergency alert started bleating.

"Michael, you idiot," the approaching woman shouted at her husband, her voice nearly drowned out by the honking alarm.

Eliot managed to get his door closed and picked up the phone. "Sorry," he said to Stuart.

"Where the hell are you?"

"A parking lot."

"Any particular parking lot? What's going on? We haven't gotten to the part of the conversation when you tell me why you're calling."

Eliot thought of the lonely days at Holly's house. The horrible half hour with Cindy, essentially confirming Josh's assessment that Eliot was a benign blob. He said, "I was driving. And then, I don't know, I thought of you."

"How's the house, anyway?" Stuart said. "I never liked that thing. I thought it was cold, but Holly had to make her statement. So you're just hanging around waiting for the nicest woman in the world to die while my busybody of an ex-wife stands guard? When was the last time you were in California, why don't you come visit?"

"Visit you?"

"I take your point. But the invitation's there, Eliot. Come out, we can reconnect. Or connect, how about that as an ironic twist?"

"I can't see leaving right now," Eliot said. "But thank you."

10

ELIOT DROVE BY THE HOUSE every few days. He told himself he was checking on things, but he didn't even slow down. Maybe he was checking to make sure the place was still standing. No deadly fire had leveled it. No *Wizard of Oz*–style tornado had lifted it from its foundation. Everything was the same except he wasn't pulling into the driveway.

At the supermarket one day he bumped into a neighbor who said, "Eliot! I figured you were out of town!" Because of his absent car. He mumbled something about a complicated engine problem, return trips to the shop, and feigned absorption in an array of pasta shapes until she got the message and moved on. He imagined her telling people that she'd bumped into him and he'd seemed really overwhelmed, poor guy.

This neighbor had been a stalwart through Claire's illness. She'd brought over meals, even offered to spell Eliot for a day so he could get some rest. She told him more than once that he was doing an amazing job, prompting Claire to say later that no one would have complimented a wife in the same way. A wife was expected to be a caretaker. For a husband, doing the work was the same as being amazing at it.

Had Eliot been good at it, though? Let alone amazing? He was back at Holly's after the supermarket, putting away the relatively few groceries he needed for this time-out life, and he thought maybe not. Maybe he'd been adequate. Merely adequate. Was that the real reason Claire wanted Holly and Michelle?

What was caretaking, anyway? Could you separate caretaking as a whole from the sum of its parts? Helping, soothing, driving, phoning, cooking, listening, tending, waiting, learning, remembering, deciding, forgoing. A lot of forgoing.

Some people said "caretaker" and some "caregiver," which—of course, given the difference between "give" and "take"—sounded loftier, more emotional. It sounded deliberate, sensitive, thoughtful. A caretaker was someone who looked after your property while you were away.

"You know what you are?" Claire said to Eliot one day, long before she was ill. "You're a trouper." He was about to head off to Brussels for work, a week-long trip for on-site meetings and workshops at the insurance company that was his main client at the time. He said, "Sure, OK. But is that a compliment?" And she said, "It's not not a compliment. Why does it have to be one or the other? I was thinking of it as a description."

So maybe being a caretaker was a description, while being a caregiver was a compliment. Eliot figured he'd been the former.

At Sleeping Giant with Josh, Eliot had realized he was wearing boots from another century, and he decided he should get a new pair. One lovely day toward the end of May he took himself off to a cavernous outdoor goods store, where a twelve-year-old filled him in on recent changes in hiking footwear. Maybe the kid wasn't twelve, but he was twenty-two at most, short and powerfully built, like a wrestler. He disappeared and returned carrying a stack of six boxes. "This is our bestselling performance trail runner," he said as he opened the first box and withdrew a shoe rather than a boot. Eliot was about to correct him, but the kid was already opening the next box, which contained boots, and it seemed easier to let him talk up each pair than interrupt.

It turned out Eliot preferred the lower-cut options anyway. They were lighter, more comfortable. There was one pair of boots he was tempted by, but they were over two hundred dollars and quite stiff. "Really," the kid confided, lowering his voice and putting his hand on the shoes Eliot liked best, "unless you're backpacking with a load over forty pounds or climbing in snow, these are all you need."

"Sold," Eliot said. "But can I ask—what's a 'performance' shoe?"

"That's what these are! They're going to help take you to the next level. Support your performance."

"But I mean . . . don't all shoes do that? Or aren't they supposed to?"

"This shoe's designed for it!" the kid said.

None the wiser, Eliot made his way to the front of the store and got in line. A moment later, a gray-haired guy appeared behind him, smiling with amusement. "I overheard you back there, asking about 'performance' shoes."

"How to feel ancient in one easy step," Eliot said. He was about to go on but hesitated, unsure he wanted to have a real conversation. If he stopped now that would be it, but if he kept going they'd have to have a whole "Hey, nice chatting" thing once Eliot had finished paying and was ready to leave the store. And if *that* happened, they would inevitably see each other in the parking lot and have that whole coda. If Eliot had been with Claire there'd've been no choice, she'd've chatted away and learned all about the guy's wife and kids before they'd even reached the register. She always joked that Eliot was a miser with chitchat, and Eliot that she was a spendthrift.

He said to the guy, "If I'm buying 'performance' shoes, what are the other ones called? Bad shoes? Ineffective shoes?"

The guy held up a pair of pants.

"Don't tell me. Performance pants?"

"Technical pants."

"Technically pants," Eliot quipped, "but some people prefer to think of them as . . ." He couldn't finish his joke. Embarrassed, he shrugged, but the guy picked it up.

"Some people prefer to think of them as a way to divide the men from the—"

"Old men," Eliot said along with him, and they both smiled.

"Going hiking in Switzerland," the guy said. "In July. These pants are going to make me so agile."

"While wirelessly connecting you to Swisscom."

The guy nodded at Eliot's box. "Headed anywhere special?"

Eliot always took his hiking boots to Maine, but the last couple of summers he hadn't used them, Claire not up to more than a stroll into town. And of course this year there would be no Maine. The deposit had been due right around the time of Claire's last PET scan, the test that presaged the decision to stop treatment. Had they even discussed sending in the deposit anyway, in case by some miracle she was still alive in August—alive and energetic enough for a trip? Eliot didn't think so. A few days after the scan results came in he found her going through the plastic bin she called her "Maine box." It contained old shorts and sweatshirts that she reserved for their annual trip, river shoes for walking on rocky beaches, a packet of falling-apart trail maps carefully stored in a Ziploc. "Baby," he said, wishing he'd been there to help her or stop her. "It's OK," she said. "I'm just sad. I love it there."

In the store, the guy with the technical pants was waiting for Eliot to respond. "Just time for a new pair," he said.

The line moved slowly, allowing Eliot to learn that the guy was four months into a retirement devoted to travel and fitness. After Switzerland in July, he and his wife planned to spend November in Patagonia and were contemplating a trip to Egypt in early spring. Leaving the store, Eliot tried to remember how he had viewed retirement before Claire's illness. It was still far off in those days: he and Claire talked about travel as an abstract goal; they joked about how Eliot would have to find volunteer work or do pro bono consulting with nonprofits, anything to keep him from following Claire around the house the way her father followed her mother in their later years. Claire's father had been an engineer and after finally retiring in his seventies made a study of his wife's habits and told her how she could become more efficient at the housework she'd been doing very competently for forty years. He took over the grocery shopping and before departing for each trip rewrote the list so that the items were in the order in which he would encounter them as he pushed his cart up and down the aisles. Every day at eleven thirty he tracked Claire's mother to wherever she was hiding from him—or "hiding"; she always had some reason for her location, the light was better for knitting in such-and-such room, she'd gone into some closet or other and discovered that it really needed sorting—and he asked her what she was planning to serve for lunch. Teenaged Abby was outraged by her grandfather's behavior, but Claire said it was working for both of them and he shouldn't be lectured about it.

The retirement question changed when Claire was diagnosed. It was no longer what would the two of them do after they stopped working but would they have that time together at all. With the lung metastases, it became evident that if they did she'd likely be unwell. During Eliot's last weeks at the firm a colleague said something vaguely sympathetic about the unfair or unfortunate kind of retirement Eliot was headed for, such a gross misunderstanding of Eliot's feelings that it helped him realize he was fine with the life he was approaching, grateful he could afford to stop working and devote himself to his wife.

And now he wasn't even doing that.

Eliot saw Holly's car zip past and pull into a parking spot at the end of the row. Michelle got out of the driver's seat and started toward the store.

"Michelle!"

She was a rusher—Claire's word—and Eliot could see a trace of impatience in her expression as she saw him and registered a slow-down in her errand. "New shoes?" she said, nodding at his bag. "Same."

"How's everything going?"

"Good. Really good. We're going to the beach this afternoon."

"The beach?"

"It's on the bucket list. Baby bucket," Michelle added, touching thumb to thumb and forefinger to forefinger.

"Cute," Eliot said, but he thought first that he would've been happy to take Claire to the beach and next that she wouldn't have asked him because in truth he wouldn't have been happy—even if he'd been willing, he wouldn't have been happy. He would have worried that she'd exhaust herself walking on the sand or fall on the uneven surface.

"Are you running again?" Michelle asked, gesturing at Eliot's bag.

"They're trail shoes."

"You'll have to tell me where to hike around here. One of these days," she added as she glanced at her watch. "I should get going now."

Eliot didn't plan what happened later, but without letting himself know where each step might lead he drove by the house at two thirty, securely within any window you'd define as "this afternoon." And indeed, Holly's car wasn't there. He continued on, turning at the corner and turning again into a semiprivate, largely hidden cul-de-sac, where he parked his car and reflected for only a moment before getting out and locking up. He walked home, looking around to see who might be outside, which neighbors in which yards. It was deserted.

He let himself into the garage. No danger of Holly parking inside; a year or so earlier Claire had chosen a new couch for the living room, and Josh had asked that the old one be stored, in case he moved out of his shared house and had room for it. The winter had been so mild that Eliot had never needed the space for parking, and the old couch was still there, covered by a tarp—waiting for Josh to claim it or, more likely, for Eliot to get someone to haul it away.

He didn't have a book, but he had his phone, as long as it didn't die. He took the plastic off the couch and lay down. Endless quarter hours dragged by. He read an in-depth article about permafrost. He looked at Josh's social media accounts, mostly notices about gigs he was playing. At one show he was opening for a group called The Melindas, which reminded Eliot of the evening in Middletown, drunk Cindy and her cruelty. Yet somehow he felt embarrassed? The moment was still hot in his memory, painful.

He found his text thread with Claire. He scrolled backward, looking for texts that were more involved than just **Can you pick up some OJ?** He went back, back, back, his gaze falling for some reason on a text from her saying **Instead of a birthday gift for Abby, maybe we send her and Isaac somewhere great. London? And we babysit?** Other texts in the vicinity suggested that one had been sent during one of Eliot's final work trips, when he had to spend several days in Houston even though her updated chemo regimen was underway and very hard. His response to her text confirmed this. **Sure but wait till I get home and we can figure it out together. Bet you're wiped. Any nausea? Holly said Steiner came in during the infusion.** Out of curiosity, Eliot looked for the same date in his text thread with Holly, who generally took Claire to chemo when Eliot couldn't. **He's sort of like a really nerdy rock star,** Holly had said of Steiner. Eliot had responded **Yeah but they can't GIVE away tickets to his shows.** This was so unfamiliar Eliot would have argued that he'd never written such a thing. Reading it, he felt a little like a pleased father, charmed and a little surprised by a child's wit.

Deeper into the past on the Claire thread was a photo she'd texted him, of a letter he'd sent her. This was even more surprising than his text to Holly. "Dear Claire," Eliot had written on March 8, 1988. "OK, here's your letter."

> The thing is, I saw you yesterday and I'm going to see you tomorrow, so what am I supposed to write about? I get that I'm missing the point, the point is Can he write a letter? (Remember that movie where the maniac football fan made his girlfriend pass a quiz about his favorite team, to prove they were compatible?) The answer is yes I absolutely, positively can write a letter. "Dear Mom and Dad, I am at camp. It is fun. We rowed to the island for lunch. We had peanut butter sandwiches and bug juice. Love, Eliot." Is that the kind of thing you mean?
>
> Dear Claire, dear Claire—if we lived before telephones and were separated for months on end, maybe I would write you long letters about how much I missed you and the weather, though perhaps not in that order. Or I'd pose philosophical questions, or I'd try to reveal the contents of my tormented soul. Here's a philosophical question: is the soul the contents? Or is it the container? I love your neck. I love your ankles. (I seem to have a thing for joints.) I love when you have sweat stains on your clothes and get flustered. I love your hair. (I think women want to hear that men love their hair.) You know what I really love is

Apparently it continued on the back, but she'd sent a picture of the front only. Eliot's handwriting was hard to read on his phone; he kept having to enlarge the image. He didn't remember getting the text containing the picture of the letter, let alone writing the letter in the first place. Claire's text said **What a pill forcing you to write me a letter.** Eliot wanted to say More like a genius. It took all he had not to tap Reply and compose a years-late response.

A car pulled into the driveway. The women were back. What the hell was he doing? He should go into the kitchen right now, be there when they entered. Just borrowing a pan haha.

He heard car doors closing, voices.

"That was so nice." Claire.

"You always loved the beach." Michelle. "Remember when you guys visited me in North Carolina and we went to the Outer Banks?"

"Aren't those beaches like falling into the ocean now?" Holly.

"I think it's more that the ocean is rising over them." Claire again.

"Still the pedant of the group," Holly said, and they all laughed.

Their voices faded as they headed for the front door. Then silence. Eliot had no idea if they'd even go into the kitchen. It was 3:40. Could be hours before anyone thought of dinner.

He waited. His exit was through the side door, out the gate, and along the fence. He'd have to move quickly to avoid being seen through the living room window. Of course now he needed to pee. How long was he going to wait? And what if they saw him through the living room window despite his speed? This was a disaster in addition to being a violation.

A sound from the kitchen came through the vent. He crept closer to hear better. Some creaking. Water running. Someone was alone in there. Was that more steps?

"Oh my God." Spoken in a low voice he could barely make out, though he could tell it was Michelle who'd spoken. "Oh my God, oh my God."

"Shhh."

"She's in the bathroom. Somehow in the house it's not as obvious how sick she is."

"It was kind of shocking."

The refrigerator door opened. A glass was set on the counter. The sound of pouring.

"Ugh, this orange juice is turned." Michelle.

"Orange juice doesn't turn."

"It so does. It gets that kind of fermented taste?"

"Dump it."

"Can we save the chicken for another night and order . . . wait, shh, here she comes!"

Silence as they waited. How many times had Eliot listened for Claire's approach? Here she comes, here she comes. Usually welcome, even deeply desired. Sometimes tolerated. Very rarely dreaded.

"Hey, you," Holly said.

Michelle said, "You don't want to lie down?"

Claire said something Eliot couldn't hear.

Holly chuckled. "Sam does that all the time. I'll text back 'No, I can't believe it!' Half the time I never find out if he thought 'it' was terrible or great."

"I wish he'd get back together with Alison." Claire's voice was distinct now. Alison was Josh's postcollege girlfriend, a lovely person whom Claire and Abby both adored. Eliot too, but it had been obvious to him that Josh wasn't ambitious enough for her. Or not ambitious: driven. Or not even driven: serious. And forward-looking. Alison was going places and Josh was happy to hang.

"Honey, you've got to get over that," Holly said.

"Why?"

"Yeah, why?" Michelle said.

"Because it's killing me?" Claire said lightly.

"Haha."

Michelle said, "Maybe you want to die with a sense of who he might end up with. A hint."

"I don't know," Claire said. "I could've said I wish he'd meet someone soon, if that was the case."

Holly said, "You want to die with a sense that you know the woman he's going to end up with."

"That makes sense," Michelle said.

"Because he's already internalized a sense of the two of you together. You and Alison. So after you were gone he'd still feel your stamp of approval."

"Could be," Claire said. "It's so funny. Eliot never thought she was right for him."

Eliot's attention sharpened. Had he hidden in the garage so he could hear them talk about him? His failings?

"Oh, you mean the career girl stuff?" Holly said. "How she was climbing the ladder at—where did she work?"

"Wasn't it a nonprofit?" Michelle said. "Not that that precludes climbing ladders. Quite the contrary."

Holly said, "Wasn't that just his way of wishing Josh was more ambitious?"

"No," Claire said. "Definitely not. I mean, he worries about

Josh's future, yes. But he thought they were mismatched. He worried Josh would feel lesser or picked on. Over time."

This was true. Over the years Eliot had sometimes babied Josh, which Claire didn't love. She didn't want him to be like his father . . . but she also didn't want him to be the polar opposite.

He waited, wondering if she'd start in on his faults, his shortcomings. He sort of wanted her to. But Holly said, "Good for him."

And Claire said, "Right?"

There were footsteps. A cabinet opened, and water ran into a glass. Holly said, "Hey, do you guys want to watch the last episode of that show?"

"Which one?"

"I was afraid you'd ask. From the night before last. The one about the people in . . . fuck, where did they live? Some mountainy place. Jesus, kill me now."

"Oh, I know the one you mean. With what's-her-name. She always reminds me of Carolyn Johnson."

"Carolyn Johnson, oh my God."

"I just want to take a two-minute shower first."

"We'll allow you three. And try that sandalwood stuff."

And then silence. Within seconds Eliot knew they'd all left the kitchen. Claire and Michelle headed for the TV room, Holly to take a shower. And Eliot none the wiser, except—

They were just themselves. He'd been listening to them talk for decades.

11

HOLLY CALLED EARLY ONE MORNING and told Eliot that Claire's head hurt worse than it ever had before. Eliot asked to talk to Claire, but Claire's speech was so slow and slurred that he couldn't understand her. Holly got back on and said she hoped Eliot didn't mind her calling, she just felt he should know. Hospice had urged her to give more Vicodin and an additional sedative, and this seemed to be helping, but it was hard to say. "The thing is, she was fine last night. Or, you know 'fine.' Exhausted and kind of spacey. And her back really hurt."

"And her head, obviously."

"Actually that didn't really start until around four this morning."

"Did she call for you?"

"Oh, we take turns sleeping on her floor. I was already there."

Eliot pictured this, Holly in a sleeping bag on the bedroom floor. He'd always kept a baby monitor in the guest room so he could hear if Claire called out. The idea of Claire's friends on her floor vindicated the whole plan.

Though he would have slept on her floor. Not well, but he would have done it.

He asked if he should stop by, and Holly was silent for a long beat and at last said later would be OK, around five, five thirty. She'd switched his question from "should he" to "could he." The idea that she thought she had the power to grant or withhold permission irritated him. He'd agreed to a hike with John, but he texted and said he couldn't manage it after all. He set about making a batch of blueberry scones, Claire's absolute favorite when made with wild Maine blueberries, but the huge, tasteless supermarket berries he had in the fridge would suffice, and he thought the result would please her.

Before his cooking class, Eliot would have agreed that you couldn't confuse scones and biscuits, that they were certainly different, but he couldn't have characterized the difference, let alone accounted for it. Now he knew. Scones were dense and crumbly, biscuits light and flaky. Scones often had things added to them. (Could you put blueberries in a biscuit? You could not.) Most important was that scones contained eggs. As he assembled his ingredients he thought that when dinner club was finished with desserts they should focus on breakfast pastries. There were croissants, brioches, muffins, buns . . . He would mention this at the next meeting. They could spend a year having breakfast for dinner.

Or maybe not. Maybe he'd keep open the possibility of urging the thing to fall apart. He had options, destructive and otherwise.

It was nearly six when he got to the house. In keeping with his reluctance to deliver food in Holly's Tupperware, he had gone out and bought a basket and a flowered cloth napkin at a little gift shop he'd never before given a second look. Once he'd arranged the scones in the basket and covered them with the napkin, he felt self-conscious about making such a deal about the presentation, and he spent a few minutes trying them on a generic paper plate he found in Holly's pantry—a paper plate she could never be certain originated in her kitchen. But on the plate the scones looked crowded rather than plentiful, so he put them back in the basket.

Michelle opened the front door while he was still getting out of his car and watched as he made his way up the walk. Not smiling. Looking, in fact, a little put out.

"Hey, you," he said.

"Everything's fine here."

"Great."

Voices came from the TV room. Eliot found Holly and Claire with the shades drawn, watching an episode of *Meltdown*. "Memory lane!" he exclaimed, setting the scones on the coffee table. "Stuart low on money?"

"He gets like a quarter of a cent when someone watches it," Holly said.

"No, I know. I was kidding."

Claire turned to Holly. "Can you pause it?"

Holly paused it. Claire gave Eliot a look he couldn't decipher but figured was a muted cry of pain. Over the years they'd developed a shorthand of looks: it made her feel less awful, not having to say she felt bad but not having to hide it either. He sat next to her and put his arm around her, but she resisted being pulled close. She may even have stiffened a little under his touch.

"You OK?"

"We're watching this." Her voice was neutral but the statement was clearly an objection.

"Oh, sorry. You asked Holly to pause, I thought you wanted me to—"

"I just didn't want to miss anything," she said, her voice trailing into a cough.

"Got it." Eliot didn't know what to do. He pushed the basket closer to her. "Made you some blueberry scones."

She pulled back the napkin and said, "Fancy basket." She looked at Holly. "This isn't yours, is it?"

Holly shook her head.

Claire gave Eliot a questioning look. It was almost worse that she didn't actually ask where he'd gotten it. He found himself lying: "John brought me some rolls in it. You know those kind of hot cross bun things? He got them in Boston."

"John Harvey brought you hot cross buns. From Boston. In this basket." She was the picture of disbelief, which just made him more resolute.

"That's what I said."

She broke off a piece of scone and put it in her mouth. "Yum," she said dutifully. She repositioned the napkin and pushed the basket away. "We'll have them later." She reached for a blanket and settled back into the cushions. "Thanks," she added.

Eliot looked at Holly, but he couldn't read her expression. Obviously he had misunderstood and was unwelcome. Had Michelle been watching out for him? Had she been stationed at the door to dissuade him from coming in? The idea made him feel sorry for her. Part of the threesome but situated at its edge.

He said, "Guess I'll get going."

Holly raised the remote, but Claire held up her hand and said, "Wait."

Holly waited. Eliot waited. Standing near the door, Michelle waited.

"What?" Claire asked Eliot.

"What do you mean 'what'? You wanted to say something else, right? Or 'say something' period, since you haven't really said anything at all."

"God, Eliot."

"What?"

"I just meant 'Wait till Eliot leaves.' For her to hit Play."

Eliot swallowed, already trying to not mind what she'd said, to chalk it up to pain, fatigue, illness. He thought she might even apologize. The scene Holly had paused showed the two leads, Malcolm and Larry, at their favorite meeting place, a picnic table outside the local A&W. Malcolm always had a root beer float. Eliot said, "I remember this one. It's the one where Larry finds the dead animal when he's jogging." He looked at Holly. "He wrote it after you guys had that gross mess in your yard. At the old house?" He turned to Claire, to bring her into the conversation. Trying to show he didn't mind, wasn't bothered. "Sam and Josh found it, behind the shed? A dead raccoon?"

Thrilled, Holly looked at Claire and they both burst out laughing,

"No!" Holly exclaimed. "Eliot, no, we're not laughing at you. It's just that a couple days ago . . ."

"Oh, my God," Michelle said, joining in the laughter.

"Let me tell, let me tell." Claire coughed hard and patted her chest. "We were in here watching TV, around nine or ten one night. All of a sudden we hear this screaming. Serious, serious screaming. It was super close by, so Holly opened the blinds, and—" Laughter caught her up again, and she coughed and fanned her face.

"Holly opened the blinds . . ." Eliot prompted.

"There were two raccoons out there. Standing on their hind legs, one right behind the other, fucking and absolutely screaming."

"It was unbelievable," Holly said. "Never seen anything like it. Just right out there by the fence screaming their heads off."

"Sorry I missed it," Eliot said. He needed a joke, but all he could come up with was: "Should've filmed it and posted it on what's that website, Animal Porn."

"Is that real?" Holly turned to Claire. "Is that a thing? Or is he kidding?" She paused and pretended thoughtfulness as she added, "I know so little about porn in the animal kingdom."

"Let him have his sexy secrets," Claire said, and they were all still giggling as Eliot left the house, his heart in splinters.

12

IT POURED ON THE FIRST OF JUNE, a cold rain that was incongruous, given the plentiful signs of early summer, soft flowers everywhere, tender leaves on trees. Eliot watched the surface of the pond, nearly colorless, tiny dots widening into circles and disappearing. Abby and Isaac and the kids were due soon, and Abby had asked Eliot to be at the house when they arrived, "so the kids won't be confused." He was waiting for her text. This was to be her family's goodbye visit: unofficially, but Eliot doubted she would bring the kids again, once Claire had declined further. She'd come by herself.

Would she be surprised by the difference since April, would she think Claire was sicker? Eliot wasn't sure. He thought Claire was more tired, groggy, quiet. That her breathing was more often labored, her cough nearly constant. But was she much worse off than during Abby's previous visit?

A week earlier Claire had broached this very subject with Eliot, asked if he thought Abby should be prepared in some way and if so how. Eliot was at the house with her, eating a takeout dinner he'd brought, Holly and Michelle having left shortly after his arrival. He was surprised by the question. Claire had always been the captain of what to say to the kids. He told her he wasn't sure, didn't think there were any major headlines, and she was quiet for a moment, then said she agreed, she thought it was mainly in how tired she was. She'd hardly touched her food, and she pushed her plate away and said she wanted to lie down and would Eliot go with her.

The bedroom felt different. Closer, more cluttered. There was a host of newly framed photos: on the dressers, the windowsill. Mostly the kids, but there were several of the two of them, Eliot and Claire, including a snapshot someone took at their wedding that Eliot had forgotten entirely. Instead of the two of them close together in the frame, it was a picture of Eliot looking at Claire standing alone in the distance. He recalled Claire joking that the picture should be captioned "'What have I done?' thought Eliot." And he said, "No, it's 'Now I've got her,' thought Eliot."

She lay on top of the quilt and pulled a throw blanket over her legs. "Will you lie down with me?"

He kicked off his shoes and lay next to her. She moved onto her side and backed herself against him, the inside spoon. She reached back for his arm and pulled it around her. Her body entirely familiar, even in its almost skeletal state. He held her closer. Somewhere outside there were children's voices, kids enjoying the evening daylight before bed. Eliot remembered those days in his kids' lives, he and Claire sitting on the porch while Abby and Josh ran around, how he felt pulled in opposite directions: part of him wanting the lovely outdoor time to go on and part of him wanting it to hurry up and be over so the kids could be put to bed and he and Claire could have some freedom . . . until the next morning arrived and it all started up again.

"This is nice," Claire said.

It was. But now that she'd said it, he became aware of how much tension he was holding in his body. It took a real effort to release it. He tried the technique taught to people in the grip of anxiety: Focus on one part of the body and inhale to the count of three. Hold to the count of four. Exhale to the count of five. Left leg, then right leg. Left arm, then right arm. After a few minutes of this he began to feel heavy, then almost sleepy.

"Eliot?"

"Right here."

"I'm sorry about the other day. When you brought the scones. I felt like shit and I took it out on you. I'm sorry."

He stroked the side of her head. "It's OK. But thanks for saying it."

"They felt you didn't trust them."

"Holly and Michelle?"

"They didn't say so, but . . ."

"I thought I was supposed to come."

"Poor Eliot. I know this isn't easy."

He didn't want to agree, to say it wasn't easy at all, to acknowledge his unhappiness. But he had to make sure she wasn't having second thoughts. The worst thing would be if neither of them was happy but for different reasons couldn't say so. He said, "It's good, though? It's still what you want?"

She found his hand and squeezed it, saying yes.

Abby texted when they were half an hour out. It was still raining, and Eliot found an umbrella in Holly's closet and ran to the car. Claire was up, uncharacteristically sitting in the living room so the kids could see her the instant they entered the house. Her leg jiggled with excitement. At the slam of car doors she reached for her walker and pulled herself to standing. The front door burst open, and the kids ran to her with Abby behind them calling out, "Be careful! Be gentle with Nana, please!"

They each took a side, Sonia clasping one of Claire's legs while Noah grabbed the other, both filled with excitement.

"Guys!" Abby said, but Claire waved her off, clearly determined to enjoy her grandchildren. They were five and three, curly-haired, miraculous. They hadn't known Claire healthy, and sometimes Eliot envied them the innocence of not knowing what had been lost.

Isaac entered carrying a few duffel bags, and Eliot went to help him. Isaac was tall and reedy, his legs spindly below his shorts. He was "very chill," according to Josh, which made him a great husband for not-at-all-chill Abby.

"Here, I've got those," Eliot said, but it was too late, Noah had spotted him and run over. Eliot lifted him high, Noah's favorite Grandpa game, then lowered him until their faces were aligned and they could move onto Noah's second favorite Grandpa game, rubbing their noses together.

Once the kids were settled in the kitchen with Claire and bowls of ice cream, Abby asked Eliot to step onto the deck. It was still wet from the rain though the sky had cleared dramatically and turned a piercing blue.

She said, "Oh my God, Dad, why didn't you tell me?" And there it was: to Abby Claire was obviously six weeks closer to death. "What are they saying?"

"Hospice? Last time they were here they said 'weeks to months.'"

"As opposed to three to six months."

"I guess."

Abby sighed. She had a long neck and very pretty collarbones. Claire had always encouraged her toward low necklines, but Abby as a teen and young woman had been very modest. Her T-shirt today had a deep V, and Eliot wondered if Claire had noticed or if such observations vanished under the stress of feeling so unwell.

"Sorry Josh is being such a dick."

"He's not," Eliot said, surprised. "We're fine."

"Hilarious. He's convinced you're still very upset with him. He's worried you told Mom what an asshole he was at Sleeping Giant, and Mom's not telling him she knows because she doesn't want him to have to feel guilty for creating strain in the family."

Eliot chuckled. "That's the most convoluted thing I've ever heard."

"Surely not."

Things did seem fine with Josh. Eliot texted with him several times a week, their pattern from before the fraught visit. The last few days, with Abby and her family due, they'd been trying to figure out when Josh should return. Josh wanted time with Claire before she was much sicker, but he also wanted time with her at the end.

"I wanted to tell you," Abby said. "An OB I know? She said this"—Abby waved her hand at the kitchen door, evidently indicating the house and all it contained—"reminded her of how there are death doulas now. And they're usually women, like childbirth doulas, offering this kind of woman-to-woman connection during a life transition. I thought that might make it feel better for you."

Eliot didn't like the idea of Abby talking to colleagues about his banishment. "I . . ." he said. "I mean . . ."

She seemed to recognize his discomfort. She'd brought a glass of water outside and drained it now, saying, "Guess I should see what's going on in there. We're probably not too far from a tantrum or two." She headed for the door but turned back. "Hey, I heard you might visit Stuart?"

Eliot barked out a laugh. "Oh, my God, that's nuts. We're so tangled up with that family. I can't believe that got back to you—especially since it's not remotely true. I spoke to him. So you and Lucia still talk? I thought you guys had drifted."

"I talked to Sam. He thinks the whole thing is weird."

Eliot didn't want to hear what anyone else thought. He got to his feet and headed for the grill, saying, "Shall I barbecue? I could run out for stuff now, or if tomorrow's OK I can shop in the morning."

"Don't bother. The kids have turned against 'striped food' for the moment, so that would just mean extra work feeding them. What were you planning on doing tonight?"

"Nothing. I mean . . . I don't live here."

Abby gaped at him, and he realized his mistake. When she said she wanted him at the house when she and her family arrived, she meant *by the time they arrived*. She meant *for the duration of their visit*. Did Claire have any idea of this? Did Holly and Michelle?

"You have to sleep here," she said. "I told you that."

"I don't think you did."

"I a hundred percent did. I told you I don't want the kids to be confused. I told you that."

"Why should it confuse them? They know about sleepovers."

Abby buried her face in her hands.

"I'll talk to them. Holly and Michelle," Eliot added quickly, before Abby could warn him off talking to his grandchildren. "They can go to Holly's."

Abby looked up. "Are you sure they're not already planning to? Maybe they got the memo and only you didn't?"

Holly and Michelle had indeed gotten the memo and only Eliot hadn't. They were on their way to Holly's car and Eliot was following: not exactly to complain but because he was still confused. Or maybe to complain. Maybe exactly and for the sole purpose of complaining.

"We thought you knew," Holly said.

"It's just three nights," Michelle added.

"He's upset about not knowing, not the plan itself." Holly turned to look at Eliot. "Right? You're not saying you'd rather be going back to my house tonight?"

But Eliot was distracted. For years a root had been pushing upward at the sidewalk, and now there was a crack. When had that happened? Surely not since his departure, though it was a neat correlative to his disrupted life.

"Eliot?" Holly said.

"We're sorry," Michelle added. "We should've made sure we were all on the same page."

"There are way too many pages for that," Eliot said. "In this encyclopedia."

Later, after a dinner hastily thrown together with staples, Eliot returned to the sidewalk for a closer look. The crack was long and deep, suggesting it had happened a while ago. He didn't know how he'd missed it. Decades earlier he'd called a concrete contractor out to look at a similar problem, and he knew from experience that a repair would be a pain. Something for later. When he was back in the house and alone.

With the cleared clouds, the temperature had risen at least ten degrees, and it was going to be a nice weekend. Abby and Isaac would take the kids on outings, returning for stories with Nana, for meals and bedtime. Claire had looked exhausted all through dinner but somehow found the energy to participate until at last the kids were finished eating. As soon as they were released, she too left the table.

The kids' last visit had been at Christmastime. Claire still on chemo then, still cycling in and out of feeling a little better and feeling a little worse, though it was clear that "better" already meant less than it should, and with "worse" it was hard to distinguish between certain chemo side effects and the consequence of having cancer spreading through her body. During the visit Abby had the idea that the kids should do things with Claire that they'd never done before, things that would stand out in memory so that Claire herself might stand out, so that she might be remembered by her grandchildren. Abby came up with making popcorn garlands for the tree, not a family tradition and therefore quite suitable until it became evident that the kids were too little to handle the needles and Claire too exhausted, despite Dr. Steiner's careful timing of her infusion schedule, with an extra week off so she could enjoy the holiday with the family. Eliot and Abby ended up doing the whole thing, staying up late one night, bleary-eyed and bleeding from tiny pinpricks to the pads of their fingers made by the needles when they jammed them too hard through the popcorn kernels.

"Dad!"

Abby was at the front door, calling for him. He made his way up the walk, feeling the afternoon's roughhousing with the kids deep in his legs and in his lower back.

"What's up?"

"They want you."

"Mom already kiss them?"

"She's in bed. She had a really long day."

"I'll bet if you go in there she'll say she wants to."

"She's asleep, Dad. I'm not going to wake her just so she can kiss them good night."

"Isn't that why you're here?"

Abby bowed her head. Eliot reached for her shoulder, and she flinched and said, "No, I can't do this right now, I really can't." The final words emphatic, her gaze fixed tight on Eliot.

"I'm not asking you to," Eliot said. "I'm not asking anyone to do anything."

The weekend was tiring for Claire. No matter how much Abby and Isaac urged the kids to be gentle with Nana, they were noisy and ferociously active. Eliot divined from the way they competed for Claire's attention that they had been schooled, at least to some degree, in the importance of this weekend. He pictured said schooling, Abby and Isaac applying the current methods of manipulation to the ancient art of getting children to do as you wished. The picture led him to think about the ways he and Claire had attempted to control Abby and Josh when taking them to see Claire's parents or, particularly, Eliot's. Their methods had included a certain amount of bribery, which was very much out of fashion these days.

Over the years Eliot and Claire had talked a lot about how the repetition of the older girl plus younger boy configuration in Abby's family made it easy for the generations to blur, for Eliot to call Noah "Josh," for Claire to assign a memory from Abby's childhood to Sonia's young life. It was almost impossible for the generations *not* to blur. Apparently this was true even for Abby: over the weekend she told Eliot that she was concerned about Sonia's bossiness, worried that Noah would be squelched, that Sonia wouldn't leave room for him. Eliot stifled his amusement until she burst into laughter and said, "Shut up, shut up!" He pulled her close and kissed the side of her head.

They left after lunch on Monday. Claire went straight to bed, saying it was probably the last time she'd see the kids but she was so tired she just felt numb. He helped her get settled, her face pale and drawn, her arms in her short-sleeved top thinner than he'd ever seen them. "I feel like I'm abandoning Abby," she said. "It's so important to have a mother while you yourself are mothering."

"I'm so sorry, love," he said, stroking her head. "I know she's going to miss you, we're all going to miss you so much. But I also know she'll be OK—and that's thanks to the mother you've already been to her."

He lowered the blinds before gently closing the bedroom door. He didn't know when Holly and Michelle would return and feared it would be soon, that Claire would text them and tell them she was ready. But a little later he found her phone in the kitchen, on top of a notepad on which she'd written "Can't find long cord for my charger." This was an odd way for her to communicate, but he looked fruitlessly around the house and at last ordered several chargers and some extra cables. He texted her a screenshot of the order to see when she was reunited with the phone and also wrote "Ordered Sunday afternoon" on the notepad. He stripped all the beds and was starting laundry when he heard the front door.

"Hello?" Holly called softly.

Eliot hurried out to intercept them. He put his palms together next to one ear and tipped his head to the side.

They had grocery bags and headed for the kitchen. They asked about the weekend, and Eliot showed them pictures on his phone, including a lovely one of Claire sitting with a grandchild on each side as she read aloud from a picture book.

Holly said, "It must have been so hard when they left. Last week she told us she almost wished they weren't coming, so she wouldn't have to say goodbye."

Eliot thought of Claire's exhaustion as she got into bed, her numbness.

"It was a way for her to tell us how sad she felt," Michelle added.

"I get it," Eliot said.

He told them he had some chores to do. Over the course of the weekend he'd become aware of a squeak from one of the bedroom doors upstairs, and he found some WD-40 in the garage and quieted it down. He put a new clamp on the dryer hose, having noticed that it wasn't venting as well as it should. At last, Claire still resting, he headed back to Holly's, but once he arrived he realized he'd left his shaving stuff at the house, having made the reverse trip on the first evening, after everyone was in bed, to gather the same items.

He would need milk for his morning coffee, so he went by way of a minimart at a gas station and took a few extra minutes to fill the car. All of this meant he'd been gone about an hour when he walked into the house again. He heard sounds from the TV room and approached but stopped short of the open door. Claire was crying, but so too were Holly and Michelle. He backed away, made it as far as the living room, and crept close again. Holly crying was a sound he knew well: her sobs involved a series of stutter breaths, followed by heart-wrenching wails. He'd never heard Michelle cry before. Quiet sniffs.

Holly spoke softly. Something she said made Claire cry harder, and Eliot retreated. He couldn't get his shaving stuff without going past the TV room, but he couldn't reveal that he was in the house. They thought they were alone.

13

PIOTR HOSTED THE NEXT DINNER, which meant he was in charge of the main event, a dessert that contained three different chocolate elements: two layers of chocolate cake, a chocolate buttercream frosting, and a glossy chocolate glaze. When everyone arrived they found the cake displayed on Piotr's desk in the main room, stationed between a letter opener and a stapler. The arrangement looked like something on display at a surrealist art museum.

Piotr and his wife lived in a third-floor apartment in an old house near Yale. Ksenia was Russian too, and always very involved in helping Piotr get the place ready. They pushed mismatched tables together and laid a patchwork of cloths on top until the whole was covered, if somewhat bumpily. There were always candles and flowers, even if the latter was just a bunch of daisies in a drinking glass. Ksenia hung around and greeted everyone, then holed up in the bedroom. The only bathroom was en suite, so when you needed to go you had to disturb her, a circumstance that led to a lot of aching bladders and more than a few rushed after-dinner visits to the back alley.

Eliot had brought the entrée, a simple preparation of chicken thighs roasted with garlic and lemon. Accustomed to Claire's tiny appetite, he had overcompensated on quantity, and as the dinner wound down he realized he'd have at least eight pieces to take home.

"What I learned about buttercream," Piotr said as he sliced the cake, "is that there are French, Italian, and Swiss buttercreams that all involve cooking egg whites or egg yolks to a certain temperature, you add sugar in a certain, careful way, and you beat it and only then add carefully sized bits of soft butter, little by little. And then there's American, where you dump a box of powdered sugar into a mass of butter and attack it with a mixer!"

Everyone laughed, and Dan said, "French, Italian, Swiss, and American? What about, I don't know, German?"

"Have I told you guys," John broke in, "about the annual language conference? Very proud people all of them, each thinking his language is the best?"

"His or hers, please," Dan said.

"It's easy enough," Wally said with a frown, "to make fun of people insisting on inclusive language, but as the father of daughters . . ."

"Daddy's a feminist, huh?" Dan teased.

Exasperated with them both, Eliot shot John an apologetic look and said, "The annual conference?"

"So they're at their annual meeting," John said, "and the Englishman says he'll settle the matter of which is the best language for good. He says, 'Take the word "buttuhfly." You can feel in the word the quick flahpping of the wings.' The Frenchman says, 'Zut alors, zee French word "papillon" gives so much more, you *feel* zee flutter, you see zee quick, darting rhythms.' The Italian says, "No no, my friends, it is only in *Eeetahhhhlian*, with our beautiful word "farfalla," that you get, along with the fluttering and the beautiful sight of the flying creature, also the exquisite colors of its wings." And the German cuts him off angrily and says, 'And vhat iss wrong mit "Schmetterling"?'"

Everyone laughed. Eliot was enjoying himself, the sniping notwithstanding. He felt guilty about having wished the group would dissolve. Maybe he hadn't wished it, maybe he'd just imagined it.

"Sorry, Piotr," John said. "I interrupted. *Is* there a German buttercream? A Russian?"

"The German kind uses whole eggs," Piotr said, "and doesn't hold its shape."

"That's a disgrace the Germans shouldn't tolerate," John said. "There isn't room for such sloppiness in post-Nazi Germany. And your people? Is there a Russian buttercream?"

The bedroom door opened and Ksenia poked her head out. "It's vile. Absolutely revolting." The door closed again.

"I guess that answers the question of whether she can hear us," Dan said.

Piotr said, "She's correct, I'm afraid. It is disgusting. And very Soviet, really."

"How so?" Eliot asked. "What's in it?"

"You will have to google," Piotr said. "I'm too ashamed to say."

At the end of the evening, Eliot and John stood out front talking. John was at the end of his school year, madly grading papers and looking forward to the summer he and his wife would spend in Vermont. With Mason gone as well, the July meeting would be small, just Dan, Wally, Piotr, and Eliot—and Eliot knew he might be at Claire's deathbed by then. Or in mourning.

"I hope you'll stay in touch this summer," John said.

"You must mean about Claire."

John nodded.

"The situation is strange," Eliot said. "It's turned into 'a situation,'" he added, surprised to find himself heading toward a confidence.

"What do you mean?"

"I had an idea you knew. Paranoia, I guess. You don't know? You haven't heard anything? I was asked . . . well, I was told . . ." Eliot wanted to explain, but he also, desperately, needed to pee. He couldn't just drop his bombshell and run. "Would you mind holding this for one second, while I . . ."

"Go see a man about a horse? Let's both go, you can hold my broccoli and then I'll hold your chicken. Whoops, that sounds like—"

"I never let another man so much as look at my chicken," Eliot said as they hurried to the alley.

They took turns standing behind a dumpster and pissing at someone's fence. Returning to the street, Eliot explained what had happened, how he found himself living in a strange house while his wife enlisted her friends to stay with her. It took a while to explain the whole thing, and as he went along he found himself including side stories, the painful hike with Josh, his odd three nights back at the house with Abby and her family. By the time he'd finished, he and John were sitting on the curb, forearms resting on their raised knees.

"So what are you thinking?" Eliot said. "Dumb? Passive?"

"I'm thinking you love her. Of course you went along with it. It's not even a question. It's her dying wish."

Eliot nodded. A pair of young guys on bicycles rode by: unhelmeted, fearless. Another moment and, as if by agreement, Eliot and John got to their feet and brushed off the seats of their pants. "Take care, man," John said. "Reach out. Or don't, no pressure. Either way, I'll be thinking of you."

Home at Holly's, Eliot put away the chicken and sank onto the couch in front of the TV. He thought of Ksenia poking her head out to comment on the conversation, her quick, ready appearance. When Eliot last hosted, Claire stayed in the bedroom, didn't even come out to say hi at the beginning. Afterward, he lay in bed with her for a while, but he was already sleeping in the guest room and didn't let himself drift off. "How is it for you?" she said suddenly, after they'd been lying silently for quite some time. "That you have these friends without me?" It was a strange question given how long the group had been in existence: Claire knew them all, knew their wives. Eliot pointed that out, and the change in her position, a slight movement away from him, told him he'd said the wrong thing. She'd been looking for him to say it was OK, it was good. Washing the dishes half an hour earlier, knowing she'd be close to sleep by the time the kitchen was clean, he had viewed the moment of joining her as tricky in the way that stepping into a rowboat could be tricky, a careful and delicate shift in balance. "It's OK," she said. "You can go now, honey. I'm really tired."

Now, alone in a house not his own, Eliot turned off the TV. Piotr's cake had been good, not great. He had swapped in American buttercream because he hadn't given himself enough time and the recipe for the Swiss had been daunting. Sitting in front of the darkened television, Eliot pulled out his phone and googled buttercreams. It took a few tries but at last he found a reference to

Russian buttercream, made with butter and . . . a can of sweetened condensed milk? Eliot took a screenshot and texted it to John. Moments later he got a barfing emoji in return. **Passing out now,** John wrote. **Nice talk tonight. FWIW I totally get it.**

He meant Eliot's having acceded to Claire's wish. Women like Abby's OB friend, maybe even Abby herself now, saw it as a wish that grew out of sisterhood, out of the idea of women as natural nurturers. Natural nurturers and maybe also natural friends, easy friends, practitioners of easy intimacy. Women didn't look each other over and wonder who could bench-press more. ("Dad," Josh would say to that. "The 1950s are calling. They think you should get back there stat, it's way too dangerous for you here.") Eliot saw it differently, and it seemed John did too. They took a step back, Eliot and John; they took the longer view. The why of it didn't really matter. It was her dying wish. End of discussion.

14

"THREE TO SIX MONTHS," the hospice woman said. "That's based on what we've seen in other people at Claire's stage of disease. It's very individual."

Eliot was sure he hadn't heard right. "Sorry, did you say 'three to six months'?"

"It's an estimate."

"But did you say 'three to six months'? Is that what you said?"

They were talking on the phone, a call hospice had made to Eliot, to check in. It was a hot day, very humid. Eliot was on Holly's patio, and he moved under the eave, where there was a strip of shade. It was he who'd brought up the timeline.

The woman hesitated. Laurie, that was her name. She said, "It could be two. It could even be one. Things can change quickly. But that's our best guess."

He couldn't speak.

"Eliot?"

"I'm just really confused. It was 'three to six months' when we started, two-plus months ago. And Geoff, a while back—quite a while back, I think—I could have sworn he said it was 'weeks to months.'" Eliot thought the guy's name had been Geoff. Hoped it had.

"Right," Laurie said. "It's always a range."

"But 'three to six months' is a *longer* range than 'weeks to months.' Isn't it? Wouldn't you go from 'three to six months' *down* to 'weeks to months'—not up? And then days to weeks, and hours to days? I'm confused is all. I assumed the estimate would have gone down, but now you're saying it's about where it was two months ago."

"Eliot. I think this has been very distressing for you. Being far away from her."

Eliot was not interested in this. "It's ten minutes."

"I've never seen this before," she said carefully. "A spouse being relocated. I know it's Claire's choice."

A flash of Meryl Streep, and Eliot burst out laughing.

"What?"

"I just had the thought that *Sophie's Choice* was 'which child would she select to live.' Claire's choice is 'which person would she select to help her die.'" It wasn't funny, but Eliot was laughing, almost giddy. Claire's choice: The Nazis had asked, and Claire had chosen her friends! Eliot was off to the gas chamber! "Sorry," he said. "This is inappropriate."

"Nothing is inappropriate."

This too struck him as funny, and he choked back more laughter.

"Eliot, have you ever done this work?"

"No," he said, reining himself in. "I was . . . in business. Consulting."

"I don't mean professional hospice work. I mean the work of helping someone die."

Eliot's parents had died in a car accident when both were in their eighties. A shock but also a mercy: no illness, no suffering. Claire's father suffered a massive, fatal heart attack. Only Claire's mother had been ill before dying. He said, "When Claire's mother was at the end of her life we all visited, but I don't know how much help I was."

"Dying is a lot of work. It requires a lot of help. I hope you don't feel . . . pushed aside. There's work for you to do too, is what I'm trying to say."

Eliot pressed something on his phone to make it beep and told her he had to go. He had been tempted to point out that a sick, isolated person alone in an apartment in a big city, or alone in a remote cabin in the woods, or alone on a desert island, would die just as surely as someone with a lot of help. Maybe it was good to have help. Helpful to have help. But could you really say dying *required* help?

Oh, he was in a state. He stripped down to his underwear and waded into the pond, fronds of submerged grass twisting around his lower legs. When the water was deep enough he dove the rest of the way. He swam to the middle of the pond, about a hundred yards, the water much colder at the center. It felt amazing. He floated on his back for a while, staring into the great blue of the sky. It was so humid he could practically see the air, a haze of moisture. Not very much of his adult life had been spent alone, really alone. There wasn't another person in sight. He took a deep breath and went under, letting himself go down down down into the darkness. He gave a kick and shot upward, breaking the surface of the water, gasping.

He'd brought a kitchen towel to the patio earlier, to lay on the teak table before putting his lunch down. He used the clean side to dry himself a little before going into the house.

He showered off the pond smell, dressed, and on impulse went into Holly's bedroom, which he'd treated as off-limits so far. Known as the Janet Hutchison Suite, the room was watched over by a large picture of Janet, the Lady Macbeth of *Meltdown*, played by a stunningly beautiful actress who disappeared into the character's conniving malevolence. The photo was from the pilot. As the wife of the plant owner, Janet was leading a group of schoolchildren on a tour through the plant's public area, talking about the safety of nuclear power. She stopped at a display of energy sources through the ages and pointed out a photo of grimy men emerging from a coal mine. "We don't want our daddies to have to work this hard, do we?" went her mock-worthy, oft-repeated line.

The bedroom was enormous, a testament to Holly's belief at the time the house was designed that she would spend the rest of her life as a rich married person, or maybe a married rich person. In any case, both married and rich. At the sleeping end of the room, in addition to bed and bedside tables, there was a walnut bench from the 1970s that Eliot had heard cost over fifty thousand dollars. At the other end, a living-room-size seating area had been arranged in front of a fireplace with a floor-to-ceiling blackened-steel surround.

Eliot opened the drawer of one of the nightstands and found a slender turquoise vibrator and a book with a bookmark. He opened the book and scanned the page. *He looked at her with bland curiosity. "Take off your blouse," he said. She unbuttoned the buttons and let the top slip from her shoulders. "Your bra. I want to see your nipples." He seemed almost bored. Certainly in no hurry.*

Oh, Holly. Embarrassed for her, Eliot put the book back and closed the drawer. He entered the walk-in closet, where she'd fanned out her clothing to occupy the copious space, though one bank of slanted built-in shelves was empty and must once have held

Stuart's shoes. Holly's shoes were on similar shelves, the top one of which held a collection of very high heels that appeared all but unworn. There was a label on the shelf that read FUCK ME SHOES in Sharpie, though it had been liberally doctored with a ballpoint pen in a way Eliot couldn't read from a distance. He moved closer and found that Holly had edited the label to read YOU'VE GOT TO BE FUCKING KIDDING ME SHOES.

The bathroom was finished in concrete, giving it the feel of a barracks, though a barracks with double sinks set into a black marble countertop, a freestanding cast-iron soaking tub, and a double-size walk-in shower.

Holly was so alone here. Eliot imagined her in the tub late at night with maybe some candles lit but essentially surrounded by darkness. She'd been so desperately sad after her separation. On a few occasions Eliot came over on his own to keep her company. This was pre-cancer: one time Claire was out of town, another time she was busy with something. "You're my friend too," Holly said on one of these occasions, leading to a mix-up about her meaning. "*You're* my friend too" vs. "You're *my* friend too." Or even "You're my *friend* too." Something to do with where the emphasis lay, what she was actually saying. They laughed trying to untangle it.

Claire once told Eliot that maybe he and Holly should get together once she was gone. This was before it was a foregone conclusion that she would die, so it wasn't so fraught a notion, given that the opportunity might never exist. Also, she said "should," not "could." If it was "should"—ordained—then it wouldn't have to do with anyone's wishes, anyone's desires.

Eliot returned to the nightstand. The book in the drawer had a sober cover—no bodice ripper, this. Navy blue with a narrow white line framing a box that contained the title and author. No one Eliot had ever heard of. The first few pages established that it took place in London. He turned to the bookmark again. *He said, "Put your finger there. No, don't put it inside. Just like that. Pointing." He moved away from her. Leaned against the wall and studied her. "Now move it up and down."*

Jesus, Eliot could see how this might work. He took the book to his room and lay on the bed with it. It had been weeks, maybe months, and once he'd read a little more, he brought himself off in moments. He'd had the foresight to grab a towel beforehand, and when he was done mopping up he tossed the towel toward the bathroom. Now what, fall asleep with the book in his arms?

He went outside and drove to the house. Holly's car was in the driveway. A day would come when Holly would drive the exact same route to check on him. *You're my friend too.* Would *she* want to? Would *she* think they should? He would have to make sure to pretend to desire her before saying no, it was too weird. Or no, it was too soon. Having spent the last almost-nine years in sexual limbo, he could more easily imagine sexual death than a resumption of a full sexual life. Almost nine years, ten by the time he was ready—would there be anything left to resume? Or would it have to be a second start? A beginning so different from his actual beginning that he'd feel himself a different species. He was a little hard again thinking about this.

A knock startled him. Michelle was on his flank, in running clothes. His car was still running, and he powered down the window and said, "Hot, huh? I went for a swim in the pond."

"She was asleep when I left," Michelle said—not unfriendly but not exactly friendly either. "If that's what you were wondering."

Was he supposed to be wondering something? "Hang on," he said as he again reached for the window power button. "I'm coming in, I need my trunks for next time."

He followed her to the door, her hot pink runner's tank top stuck by an oval of sweat to the center of her back. Her thick black hair was in a ponytail. Claire had always envied Michelle's thick hair, especially once hers began to fall out with the first chemo.

Holly appeared immediately, coming in from the kitchen. She saw Eliot and said, "She's asleep."

"I told him," Michelle said.

"I need some things," he said and without another glance headed for the guest room, annoyed that he'd allowed himself to become annoyed. They weren't saying he shouldn't be here.

And he did need some things. His trunks, sure, but also shorts, his Tevas. Should he be thinking past summer? You had to be expected to die within six months for hospice to begin. If Claire's six months had begun in March, that would mean death by October. But if she could still be six months off, as he'd heard on the phone earlier, it might be as late as December.

He couldn't talk about this with anyone. It sounded too much like he wanted her to hurry up. But that wasn't true. He just wanted to know.

He found Holly and Michelle in the kitchen, Holly chopping something. He decided on a reset. A friendly conversation.

"So how is she? Can you fill me in?"

"Sleepy," Holly said. "Exhausted."

"Sicker," Michelle said. "So tired and out of it. Coughing. Her back's been hurting and she hardly eats."

"Laurie?" Eliot said. "The one with the purple glasses? She

called earlier and told me three to six months. But I could've sworn that guy Geoff said weeks to months before Abby was here."

"The last thing we heard," Holly said, "was one to three months. That was from Ifeoma. The Nigerian one."

Eliot sighed. There was no consistency. "Do you ask yourself why it matters so much? Like, why the fixation on time?"

Holly and Michelle exchanged a glance.

"What?"

Michelle said, "We've talked about how, with our living situations affected, it's sort of inevitable that we'd be watching the clock more."

"The calendar," Holly said. "You especially," she added with a glance at Michelle.

Michelle nodded. Eliot didn't know what arrangements she'd made, to be away from home for so long. A house sitter? He couldn't imagine embarking on an open-ended abandonment of everything familiar. Though something like that had been imposed on him. Or he'd agreed to it, anyway. A time-out life. A nowhere existence.

"Does she . . ." he began, but he stopped, unsure he should ask.

"What?" Holly said.

"Talk about me not being here? Does she ever say she'd like me to come over more?"

A look passed between Holly and Michelle, containing an urge on Holly's part and a warning on Michelle's.

"Guess not."

Holly fiddled with a pen lying on the counter. "It seems like she thinks it's a good amount." She hesitated. "Maybe slightly bordering on"—a quick glance at Michelle—"maybe very slightly bordering on too much."

"Too much?"

"She didn't say that," Michelle said.

Eliot swallowed. "But she said something like it?"

"Not really," Holly said. "I think it's more that with you likely to pop over anytime, it's not quite the . . . different thing she wanted."

It served him right for asking. "So she wants me to come less."

Michelle shook her head. "She definitely didn't say that."

"We weren't talking about you," Holly said. "We were talking about it."

"It?"

"Death. Dying."

Eliot remembered Claire joking around: *This is death spa. Or maybe dying spa?* That morning in April when Holly and Michelle came in with gifts. Sitting cross-legged on the bed in her flannel nightgown. The three of them laughing.

"She's disappointed?" Eliot said. "It's not what she wanted? Not as much fun or whatever? I mean . . . not fun but meaningful?"

"She thought she would be going through more," Holly said. "Emotionally. Anger. Sadness. Looking back. But she's not."

"It's strange," Michelle said. "She hasn't said so, but from my perspective, it's almost like she doesn't have time for that."

"Interesting," Holly murmured.

"But what did she say about me?" Eliot said. "During this conversation about 'it.'"

"It was just . . ." Holly began, but she stopped herself. "Eliot, honestly. You're obviously struggling. I hate that, hate it. You've made a big sacrifice, which"—she glanced at Michelle—"we both think is exceptional, but also not at all surprising. Given the person you are, the husband. And on top of all of that you've been really good about not letting her know how you feel."

"Please tell me what she said."

Holly sighed and looked at Michelle, who shrugged, seeming to agree that there was no choice but to tell him.

"She was saying that there are times she feels close to something, kind of like remembering a name you forgot, it's on the tip of your tongue. It's so awful when you can't remember and so delicious when you get it."

"So it's something she wants."

Holly nodded.

"And?"

"She said it's like she's almost there sometimes, and then something happens to keep it away. Like you come in."

15

THE HOUSE WAS IN BEVERLY HILLS, behind a stucco wall covered with bougainvillea. The street was wide, each front yard enormous. Stuart's was among the smaller places, not small but no bigger than the houses in the Connecticut neighborhood where he and Holly had spent the first years of their marriage, two blocks from Eliot and Claire.

Eliot thanked the Uber driver and wheeled his bag up the brick walk. Through the fretwork of an iron gate, he saw a brick-lined patio lush with plants, and beyond that an arched front door. Stuart was on his way home but stuck in traffic, and he'd texted Eliot the codes to get inside. Like his ex-wife, Stuart used important birthdays to access his home: Sam's for the gate and Lucia's for the front door.

Mi casa es su casa were the final words of Stuart's text, and Eliot headed straight to the kitchen, having consumed little other than almonds and a damp airport sandwich since he left Holly's house nine hours earlier. In the fridge there were four enormous glass bottles holding an array of juices in colors ranging from green to yellow to orange to pink. He poured himself a tall glass of the yellow stuff and gulped it as he found cheese, charcuterie, olives, melon. He located crackers in a cabinet, a bag of focaccia on the counter.

Stuart's wife, Carmel, was a dentist whose practice was in the Valley, and Eliot had already heard that she wouldn't be home until after seven. (Carmel was Stuart's third wife. On the phone call arranging the visit, Eliot had learned that Stuart's marriage to Lori Mensch had been a short-lived nightmare.) Carmel had plans for three of the five evenings of Eliot's visit, so it would be just Eliot and Stuart most of the time. "We'll shoot the shit," Stuart had said, "like old times."

Josh had been in favor of the trip, Abby very much against. "You know what's going to happen if you go," she told Eliot. "Mom's going to decide she wants you back at home. Then what'll you do?"

"I'll fly home, sweetheart," he said. "I'll be home in half a day."

"But what if she needs you faster than that?"

"To do what? Chest compressions?"

"Dad! What if she *wants* you faster than that?"

"Then she'll have to wait, and I'll feel very bad. But after some time goes by I'll get back and then I'll be with her."

"I don't see why you don't come down here. It's so much closer."

"Northern Virginia is indeed closer," Eliot said, "but it's not a much shorter trip to drive there than to fly to California."

"Or, you know," Abby said. "You could wait until after."

Eliot savored the salty prosciutto, chasing each piece with a chunk of cantaloupe. Finally the front door opened, and in a moment Stuart was in the kitchen doorway. He'd shaved his thinning hair and wore his beard trimmed down to stubble, and he looked as fit as you could in your sixties without seeming like you spent all your time at the gym. A trace of softness at the middle, toned everywhere else.

Eliot had been consuming his snacks hunched over the countertop, and he set down a piece of bread and went in for a hug.

"I wouldn't have recognized you," Stuart said, looking Eliot over as they pulled apart.

Eliot had put on fifteen or twenty pounds in the last decade, but he still had a full head of hair, if more salt than pepper at this point. "That bad, huh?"

Stuart rolled his eyes. "I meant you look changed. Like a different human being lives in your body."

"Great idea for your next show."

"OK, Mister Deflection. Let me show you to your room."

Stuart carried Eliot's bag down a long hallway to a pair of French doors that let onto a second brick-lined patio. Across the way was a freestanding structure, also white stucco and covered with bougainvillea: an in-law unit or guesthouse. Eliot felt a brief pang that he'd be alone under the guesthouse roof. It had been a long time since he'd slept in the same building as another person. He'd sort of been looking forward to it.

Stuart said, "You want to shower or something? Let's meet up again in an hour. I've got a couple emails I need to write."

Stuart, it turned out, was busier than he'd expected to be, or busier than Eliot had expected him to be. Eliot had a lot of time to himself, and he walked around Beverly Hills each morning and napped each afternoon, enjoying the slight befuddlement of waking to bright light and a hanging ruff of scarlet flowers just outside his window. There was a little coffeemaker in the room, as if he were a guest at an exclusive hotel and had been upgraded to one of the individual cottages sprinkled across the lush grounds, and he was sipping coffee after one nap when he got an email from John. "Don't know if you're a poetry person, but I just read this and thought it might speak to you." He'd sent a link to a poem about a man at a woman's deathbed. Eliot skimmed it. He wasn't particularly a poetry person, and when he slowed down it was almost too painful to read:

> *In the hard light and hum*
> *of the room to which I've come*
> *to stay, I watch the clock*
> *and wait, and hour by hour*
> *begin to disappear.*

He typed a response: "I'm not really—but then again I'm not not, so thanks for sending." But that was silly. "Beautiful," he wrote instead, and he sent it before he could reconsider.

One day he borrowed Stuart's car and drove to the beach. In Venice he window-shopped, slowing in front of stores displaying things Claire might like. He went into a home goods place and asked to see a matte white vase in the window. It had a handmade look, curvy and asymmetrical. Eliot's work had sent him to cities all over North America and Europe, and he always brought Claire something, often no more than a small bowl or pair of candlesticks, other times a handbag or an item of clothing he knew would look good on her. He was a great gift-giver, she always said. Turning the vase over in his hands, he felt a tidal wave of grief approach, and he set the thing down and hurried from the store. Outside, he grabbed a parking meter and emitted a wail that made a woman walking past him stare and pick up her pace. Still holding the meter, he slid down to a crouch, utterly wrecked. He tipped his head back and roared, or thought he roared; his sense of reality had vanished. His heart raced, and he wondered if this was a panic attack, except he wasn't scared so much as distraught.

He couldn't live without her.

He lowered his head to his knees and tried to slow his breathing, and after a few moments the world returned, traffic, pedestrians, the smell of waffle cones from a nearby ice cream shop. He thought: OK, that's that. Of course he was going to flip out. It was surprising it hadn't happened sooner. Maybe the emailed poem had infected him. The idea that as he waited to lose Claire, it was he, the person he believed himself to be, who was disappearing.

On the last evening Stuart took him to an impossibly hip restaurant with no-frills wooden tables and steel chairs. The lighting was industrial, the music 1980s new wave, which made Eliot and Stuart, during lulls in the conversation, bob their heads to the beat of songs they'd last heard when they were in their twenties.

They talked mostly about Stuart and his work, more because Eliot kept asking questions than because Stuart had only one topic, though Eliot remembered this about Stuart, a tendency to monopolize. But the fact was, he was a good storyteller. Thus his career.

At one point he noticed Eliot staring at his shaved head and said, "Nothing looks older than a balding-but-not-bald head. Male-pattern baldness is the opposite of an aphrodisiac. It's a turnoff. A buzzkill. For business, I mean, not for actual sex. See, what we're doing most of the time in this business, basically all the time, is a form of dating. Every phone call, every lunch, every meeting is a date. You haven't been on dating apps yet but I guess you will eventually—sorry—and you'll find that at the end of every cup of coffee or glass of wine you basically have to say 'That was fun, let's get together again.' Even if on the inside you're shuddering. So, every Hollywood meeting ends with some version of 'Hey, if this project doesn't happen let's find something else to work on together!' That's the equivalent of 'goodbye' at a Hollywood meeting. As unlikely as consummation ever is, you've got to act like you're ready to do anything, jump into metaphorical bed with anyone. And you've got to look the part. No male-pattern baldness. No . . . 'tonsure,' is that what it's called? The ring of hair? None of that. Newsflash, right? 'All they care about in Hollywood is looks,' who knew? Well, I want to tell you that in truth: *all they care about in Hollywood is looks*. It's like the end of *Casablanca*. What's going to matter in this town is the impression you make, and if you let yourself go it's going to fucking kill your career—maybe not today, maybe not tomorrow, but soon and for the rest of your life."

Eliot felt his belly bulging over his belt and leaned back to take the pressure off. "You're my love" Claire always said when he talked about losing weight. "You look perfect."

"Holly hated coming out here," Stuart said. "She hated that she couldn't not participate in the glamfest."

"That she had to 'try,'" Eliot said.

"Yes! She had to 'try'! Like it was an on-off switch. She was either a slob in sweatpants or spending tens of thousands of dollars trying to look like a celebrity. We talked about moving out here after we got the second season of *Meltdown*, did you know that? I mean, try living close to the center of the primary bread-winner's industry, what a concept! We could've gotten a nice house in Santa Monica, sent the kids to whatever fancy school the studio head's wife or whoever could help with. Lucia was into it. She was—what?—twelve, thirteen? She was in one of those phases of hating her friends. I remember Holly telling her, 'If you hate the girls in Connecticut just wait till you meet the girls in LA.' Like, she couldn't even let me have one kid on my side in a battle I was never going to win. What? What's that face?"

"I was just remembering how worried Claire was that it would happen, you guys would move."

"Because she'd lose her best friend."

"I don't think it was that self-centered. I think she worried that Holly would be miserable."

"A damn good bet any day of the year. Sorry, divorce bitching. It's not even true."

Their server arrived with dessert menus. Stuart held up his hand to stop her, but Eliot nodded, and she set one in front of each of them.

Stuart said, "Listen, I apologize. I didn't mean to malign her just now."

"Holly?"

"Claire. Saying she worried about us moving because she'd lose her best friend. Calling her self-centered."

"It's OK."

"Do you feel like Holly is the love of Claire's life? Not in a lesbian way, just—her emotional center, her home? Her main person?"

"I never thought that," Eliot said. "I am. Or, you know, I was. She would tell me 'You're the love of my life.'"

"'You're the love of my life, but could you please try harder to . . .'"

Eliot smiled perfunctorily. "Did you feel that way? That Claire was Holly's?"

"I wouldn't have said so then. Carmel got me thinking about it. Last night, when we were getting ready for bed. She said women who have intense best-friendships are more intimate with their friends than with their husbands."

"Let me guess, Carmel doesn't have intense best-friendships."

"Touché," Stuart said. Then: "She likes you."

"I like her. She's a lot of fun. She's got a nice, wry sense of humor. Not what I expected."

"No?"

"Well, 'dentist' lands pretty hard."

"Are you OK with what they're doing?" Stuart said. "Really OK?"

He meant Holly and Claire. Or rather Holly and Michelle and Claire. But really: Claire. Claire's choice. What Claire was doing.

"I wasn't going to say no," Eliot said. "So I made myself OK with it."

"Why not say no?"

Eliot shrugged. "It's her dying wish."

"Carmel asked if you have low self-esteem."

"If the question pisses me off that means yes, right?"

"I haven't talked to Holly," Stuart said, "but Sam told me this is all because of some friend of Claire's who had like a Connecticut version of a female drumming circle to usher her to her death? Something like that?"

"Susan Simmons."

"But that's the story?"

"She lived alone and became, you know, terminal. Her sisters and daughters came to take care of her, some friends. Claire found it really meaningful."

"So she was one of the friends."

"Via cancer. They met in a support group."

"What did she mean by 'meaningful'?"

"I don't know." Eliot thought for a moment. "Maybe it was more 'special' than 'meaningful.' It put her in this mood, almost... exalted. Like how you might get after, I don't know, an amazing concert."

"Like it was an aesthetic experience?"

Eliot shook his head. He was doing a terrible job of explaining. All he could do was repeat himself: "It was her dying wish."

And yet. What was it Holly had said about Claire? *She thought she would be going through more.* Was she actually, secretly, disappointed?

"What's weird," Eliot told Stuart, "is that Holly's not sure it's working, that Claire's getting what she wanted."

"That kind of makes sense," Stuart said. "Claire loved being at her friend's house, the community, because she was offering care, participating in the kindness. She assumed she'd feel the same if she were on the receiving end. But who knows if this Susan woman felt anything like that. You know? It's a tall order, to feel exalted while you're dying."

Eliot shrugged and fell silent. He regretted the conversation. The server was passing, and he flagged her down and ordered the butterscotch pudding, curious to compare it to Dan's. He hoped

Stuart might order something after all, but Stuart simply handed her his menu, untempted. He had his career to think of.

"So, your new show," Eliot said. "Or your let's-hope-it-happens show."

But Stuart was looking over his shoulder. Watching the server: an attractive young woman wearing a thin dress that clung to her body. Earlier Eliot had noticed that she wasn't wearing a bra and had struggled each time she approached not to stare. Stuart turned back and said, "Let's go out."

"Out?" Eliot knew what Stuart meant but feigned stupidity. "Aren't we out already?"

"Out out," Stuart said. "A bar or something. Isn't that why you're really here? That's why we put you in the guesthouse, by the way, I kind of forgot that actually. In case you needed privacy. Sorry, I've been really busy or—"

"You think that's why I'm here?" Eliot said. "Why I came out here? To get laid?"

"Calm down, I'm kidding."

"Are you?"

"Dude, relax."

Eliot looked around. The restaurant was packed, normal conversation nearly impossible given the din of voices and music. No one else over forty except a few men with thousand-dollar haircuts, each accompanied by a very young woman in a very revealing dress. Eliot had had enough. Enough of Stuart, enough of LA. He said, "Never mind. Let me try to cancel my dessert. Early flight tomorrow, we should get going. This is on me, obviously."

"Eliot," Stuart said.

"What?"

"Have your fucking dessert."

Eliot reached for his wallet, pulled out a credit card, craned his neck for the server.

Exasperated, Stuart pulled out his own wallet.

"I insist."

Stuart shrugged, put his wallet away. He said, "You can say you changed your mind, you know. It's your house. She's your wife. Fuck if I'd put up with that."

16

CLAIRE ALWAYS THREW a good dinner party. She made sure the guests would like each other and seated them carefully, not saying anything beforehand but confident a pair of Oregonians would discover the link, or that a twin would learn that the guy with whom she thought she had nothing in common was also a twin. Eliot thought that not telling them in advance was a form of torture, but Claire said it was more like a game that no one knew she too was playing. The last of these dinner parties was a month before her diagnosis. Later, in the years between the initial treatments and the metastases, she sometimes invited people over, but it was different, quieter, less festive. "I'm no longer a hostess," she said to Eliot at the end of one such evening when friends had come over to eat and watch a documentary. "I used to be a hostess, but now I just sort of let people in the door and have food available." Cancer had taken something from her that was not energy or verve or ambition. It wasn't happiness or even contentment. It was an essential part of her that she couldn't name. She could only miss it.

Flying home from California, Eliot thought about this in light of Stuart's comment the first day, that he looked like a different person. Had Claire's cancer taken something from him or given something to him? An albatross to carry. The albatross of grave responsibility. Once, crossing the street near the hospital, on his way back to her with a milkshake she'd asked him to fetch, he was nearly hit by a car making an illegal turn. It was a matter of centimeters, of microseconds. He twisted his ankle leaping out of the way. The cup flew out of his hand. What went through his head was: I can't die right now, Claire's waiting for me.

Midmorning on his first day back he bought flowers and drove to the house. Reports while he was away had been in keeping with reports from the days before his departure. She was often so sleepy or drugged that she hardly seemed to be there, but at other times she was alert, able to smile, chat, laugh; ask for a cool drink or a bite of fruit. She texted him rarely these days, but on the trip he'd gotten a sweet message one evening, accompanying a picture of a very old photo, fading at the edges, of a much younger Eliot lying on a chaise with a tennis hat covering the top half of his face. He recognized the club where he'd learned to swim as a boy. He was smiling in the photo, so he must've been awake under the hat, was possibly posing for the picture like that—or refusing to pose for it. **This is how I think of you,** Claire said in her text. **Quietly happy like this.** She ended the message with a heart emoji. If it was also true that the photo was a picture of Eliot unable to see . . . *this is how I think of you* . . . well, he was certain she hadn't meant that.

He entered the living room, blinds closed against the high-summer light. It took a moment for his vision to adjust. Claire was on the couch, not sitting up but not quite lying down either. She was slumped sideways. He had the impression she'd been set down that way, that someone hadn't taken care to arrange her in a good position. Her eyelids were heavy, her mouth gaping a little.

"My love?"

No response and he hurried over. She appeared to be sleeping with her eyes slightly open. Or was she . . .

He found her wrist and felt for her pulse. Steady enough.

"Why are you like this?" he said gently, like a parent talking to a baby somehow turned around in its crib. He gathered throw pillows to make a better nest for her, eased her head down, lifted her legs onto the couch. "There, that's better."

He took the flowers to the kitchen and laid them on the counter. "Hello?" he called softly. Would they have left her alone? Gone out somewhere? Holly's car was in the driveway.

The TV room was empty and he returned to the kitchen, found a vase, and arranged the flowers. Only after he'd been in the house a good five minutes did he hear a voice. He went to the back door, shuttered against the sunlight. They were on the deck. Sitting under the shade umbrella, drinking iced tea from tall glasses and looking at their phones. He opened the door.

"Eliot!" Holly stood up quickly. She was wearing an incredibly short dress, or maybe some kind of nightgown. "What the fuck?"

Taken aback, he said, "I could say the same to you."

"What are you talking about?"

"You dumped her on the couch and came out here?"

Holly grabbed her glass and headed toward him, saying, "I can see my ex-husband had a lovely effect on you," as she swept past him into the kitchen. He followed, trailing as she made her way to the living room. She circled the couch so she could get a good look at Claire. She said, "Seriously, what are you talking about?"

Eliot moved so he could see too. It was Claire napping. That was all: just Claire asleep, a sight he'd seen thousands of times. Her eyes were closed now.

Holly pulled a pin from the back of her head, and her hair fell to her shoulders. Impatiently, she gathered it up again and refastened it. "What are you talking about 'dumped'?"

"Nothing," Eliot said. "Sorry, she just looked uncomfortable."

"She's got tumors all over her body, what do you expect?"

He left the house and returned to Holly's, where he puttered for a while: started laundry, took a little time to look at headlines, checked his investment accounts. Isaac had asked his opinion of a job offer, and Eliot wrote him a considered email. By midafternoon he'd run out of things to do and decided to go back to the house, to see if he could catch Claire awake.

Holly was full of apologies. She'd been surprised to see him, that was all. She hadn't expected him so soon after his return. She hoped, she really hoped he'd had a good time. He'd have to tell her all about Carmel, the kids were definitely up and down about her.

Claire was in bed, sitting up but bleary and coughing a lot. She smiled at the sight of him. "There you are! How was it? Tell me everything."

"My love." He was so happy to see her. He kissed the side of her head, then the back of one hand and the back of the other. He wanted to shower her with kisses. "First tell me how you feel."

She sighed and coughed. "Not so good. I'm OK, but earlier. I'm drugged. Sorry."

He pulled a chair close. He held her hand as he told her about the trip, Carmel, the house.

"It's funny," Claire said.

"What?"

"He ends up in a conventional Spanish-style house and Holly's in the architectural marvel."

Josh was coming in a few days, and they talked about his latest news, a gig with crushingly tiny crowds. On the phone with Eliot, Josh had said you couldn't even call them crowds. "Crushingly tiny people," he said. "No one over five feet tall."

"It's OK," Claire told Eliot. "He's going to be a therapist."

Eliot was taken aback. "He told you?"

"It's my prediction. I've always thought that when he got past this dream he'd find his way to helping people somehow."

Eliot was surprised by this. "You think he'll get over music?"

"I think he'll get past it."

That was a nice way to frame it. Claire dozed a little, woke, asked him to help her lie flat. When she was comfortable he kissed her forehead and left the house, assuming he'd return in a few days, but when he woke the next morning he realized he was finished. Done. He packed up, started Holly's dishwasher, and drove home. He was going to be the one to usher Claire out of life. It was his job, his burden, his privilege.

17

CLAIRE WAS IN BED, clammy, her hair in sweaty curls against her head. She'd been achey and feverish earlier, but ibuprofen had brought her temperature down. Eliot placed a cool washcloth on her forehead. "Thanks," she said, her voice faint and hoarse, the word barely distinct.

When she seemed settled he gathered up a few tepid washcloths from earlier and rinsed them in the bathroom sink. He carried a plate of uneaten toast to the kitchen.

The front door thudded closed, and he went to greet Josh, just getting home from the grocery store. It was the Fourth of July, and there were fireworks popping around the neighborhood.

"Crowded?" Eliot said.

"Bearable."

They unloaded the bags together. Eliot was going to grill for the first time since the previous Labor Day. Holly and Michelle were joining them, a thank-you dinner for taking care of Claire. They'd each visited since moving out nearly a week earlier but hadn't come together.

Eliot and Claire hadn't talked about it much: neither his having been gone nor his having returned and sent her friends away. This had surprised him, especially at first. He'd expected protests, special pleading—from all three of them. But when he walked in with his suitcase, Holly emerged from the kitchen and hardly batted an eye. He'd been rolling possible jokey announcements through his mind—"I'm baaaack" or "Party's over"—but right away she said OK, as if he'd slowly worn her down over days or weeks and she was conceding as much from exhaustion as anything else. She said, "She's asleep. Can we stay till she wakes up and tell her ourselves?" Eliot had pictured himself alone at Claire's bedside, how he'd help her up, and only once she became aware that they were alone in the house gently tell her he'd sent Holly and Michelle away. But he said yes. Claire would want a moment with her friends. Later, when Holly and Michelle were gone and he tried to explain himself, Claire waved him off, said she understood. He tried again at the end of the day, and again she waved him off. She was telling him to let it go. They were back to how things should be, and he'd come to view his time at Holly's as an aberration, the product of a decision he wanted to forget. He was embarrassed that he'd said yes, dying wish or not. The wish hadn't made sense. Stuart was right: it had been based on an assumption about Subject and Object, giver and receiver. The Claire of the equation vs. the Susan.

On the deck, Eliot scrubbed the grill rack until it gleamed, using a special cleaning device with steel bristles that worked like magic. One of his first turns hosting dinner club, he grilled salmon that fell apart when he tried to turn it over. Now, along with the cleaning tool and a handsome spatula-and-tongs set, he had a fish grilling basket, a vegetable grilling basket, and for Christmas three years running had received a copy of *Backyard Grillmaster*, twice from Isaac.

He went inside to put together a marinade for the swordfish he'd gotten Josh to buy. He glanced at his watch, checking to see if it was time for more pain medication. Claire's back and legs hurt nearly all the time, and a couple days earlier Stacey from hospice speculated that the cancer had spread to Claire's bones. "She can have a bone scan if you want," she told Eliot at the front door. "Hospice doesn't mean no testing."

"But we wouldn't treat it, so what good is the knowledge?"

"We can use radiation for symptom control. For pain reduction."

Eliot was horrified. He didn't think Claire would want to submit to more radiation no matter what. The cost was too high. Just picturing the waiting room at the radiation center washed him with misery. Day after day, week after week, sitting there by himself while Claire gamely followed the tech back to the machines. At least with chemo Eliot had been permitted to sit with her during her treatments.

"We'll think about it," he said to Stacey. "Thank you."

She touched his shoulder. "Take care, Eliot." And as he watched her head for her car, he got the feeling she was glad he was home.

He'd asked Josh to buy potatoes for a warm potato salad with vinaigrette he'd first made for dinner club, but there wasn't much time left and he decided to skip it. Josh had already shucked eight ears of corn. There would be burgers, the swordfish, a salad, and of course s'mores fixings because Claire believed no outdoor cooking was complete without s'mores. In other words: plenty. Eliot had been texting a little with John lately, and he took a picture of the crowded kitchen counter and sent it along with a stupid joke: **Enough food to include the British if they've gotten over their loss and would care to join.**

He'd told John about moving home. Other than sending a

wildly expensive bottle of Japanese whiskey as a thank-you, Eliot wasn't sure he'd ever be in touch with Stuart again.

"There she is!" Holly said when Eliot pushed Claire in her wheelchair onto the deck. Holly's tone had the false brightness you'd use when speaking to a child who'd been sulking in her room.

Until half an hour earlier Claire had been asleep and was still very tired. Seeing Josh and her friends, she lifted her hand to wave, but she didn't seem to have the strength to get her elbow off the armrest, so the wave was small. Eliot wasn't sure anyone else had seen it.

Josh jumped up to move a chair out of the way. "Hey, Mom," he said sweetly. Claire's expression when anyone appeared in front of her was one of pleasure, but it was a general rather than a specific pleasure, the exact opposite of how she'd always greeted her children. Eliot saw how this bothered Josh and how he tried to hide it with good cheer.

Holly, Michelle, and Josh were all drinking margaritas Holly had made.

"Clairie?" Holly said, holding up the pitcher.

Claire coughed and shook her head. Then, worried, she looked around. "Do I have my water?"

Eliot had installed a cup holder on the back of the wheelchair. He found the water bottle and gave it to her.

She brought it to her mouth, but the bottle was closed and she had to lower it again and release the cap before she could drink.

Holly said, "How do you feel today, honey?"

"Hanging in," Claire said, her voice raspy.

Holly blew her a kiss. "Been missing you."

"I'm going to miss you," Claire said. "All of you."

The others received this as it should be received: lovingly, appreciatively, sadly. Not Eliot. He was gravely disappointed in Claire. Painfully disappointed and surprised, and then just terribly, terribly sad. Not long ago—though before the brain mets—Claire told him that she found it pitiful when people said they'd miss things after they were dead. Eliot recalled the moment in detail: They were entering a shop where she often bought cards and small gifts. She said, "People say they'll miss springtime. Or their dog, or mint chip ice cream. They'll miss lying in a hammock with a book." She stopped and looked up at him. "Missing things," she said emphatically, "is an activity undertaken by the living."

"So it's denial."

"Of course it's denial."

"Maybe they're just saying they love those things. Springtime or the dog or what have you."

"That's kind and no doubt true," she said. "But you'll never hear me say I'll miss something after I'm dead. I promise you that."

Over dinner Josh entertained the women with stories of his weird work life. He'd helped cater a the-divorce-is-final party that featured a series of stations where the honoree's friends could play carnival-style games directed at the ex-husband: throw rotten tomatoes at a picture of him, dunk a life-size replica of him into a tank of water. "Oh, and the couple I babysit for?" Josh said. "With the twins that just turned three? They're constantly overpaying me, by the way. 'Here, Josh, let's just make this an even hundred' when they owe me, you know, sixty dollars. I mean, I get that they think that the more they pay me the safer their kids will be, but still. Anyway, they both have these crazy intense jobs, like Dad's." He turned to Eliot, seeking confirmation. "You know, the grinding work weeks, the insane travel, how tired and grumpy you were on the weekends?"

Eliot looked at Claire. She wore a blank smile and didn't seem to notice his glance. The grinding work weeks, how tired and grumpy he was on the weekends? There was some truth to it, doubly painful given that Eliot had been bothered by the same things in his father.

"But every Wednesday at four they leave work and meet at this stretching place. You know about these stretching places? Like a gym, but just for stretching, someone stretches you? There are single sessions and partner sessions. And they get home on Wednesdays like so blissed out. I've been really curious about the whole thing, and last week I finally went in and asked for a tour. Turns out it's basically a fancy spa."

"Why so curious?" Holly said.

"Yeah," Michelle said. "And did you tell them you were going?"

"Of course not! That would be an invasion of their privacy like crazy."

"It's a public place," Eliot pointed out.

"But I was only interested in it because of them." Josh turned to Holly. "I just wanted to know, like, what was the vibe? Was it going to be techno, or—"

"You thought it would be kinky," Holly teased.

"I did not!"

"Partner sessions. You did."

Michelle said, "What *was* the vibe?"

"Soothing. Singer/songwriter, mellow instrumentals."

"Oh, I see now," Holly said. "You wanted a gig. Maybe you should write some stretching songs."

"Stop," Claire said.

Everyone froze. Claire was staring down at the table, as if the effort of holding up her head was too great. For a moment Eliot thought maybe he'd been hearing things and she hadn't spoken, but she went on: "Leave him alone."

Holly looked chagrined, and so did Josh. He was a little old to have Mom coming to the rescue.

"I'm sorry," Holly said softly. "I was just kidding around."

"Would you kid one of the girls that way?" Claire said. "Abby, or either of yours?"

"You're right, you're right." Holly took a big swallow of her margarita. She looked at Josh with a pained expression and said, "Sorry, Joshy."

"It's 'Josh,'" Claire said.

Somehow they recovered, but after that they focused on eating. Eliot made busywork for himself, back to the kitchen for more butter, to the garage to grab another bag of hardwood for the fire. Claire tried to eat an ear of corn but kept setting it down, and at last Eliot got up and sliced the kernels into a small bowl.

It wasn't long before she was ready to lie down again. They hadn't gotten to the s'mores, and Eliot hoped she wouldn't notice the marshmallow bag on the kitchen counter and change her mind.

He needn't have worried. She seemed dazed as he wheeled her through the house. In the bedroom he helped her out of the chair and stood by as she held on to the bed with one hand and with the other tried to get her pants off.

"Here, let me help with—"

"I can do it, El."

She peeled the pants off laboriously, pushing at one leg and then the other until they were puddled around her feet and she carefully stepped out of them. Still wearing her top, she sank onto the bed and let Eliot help her the rest of the way, swiveling her legs up onto the mattress, putting pillows in place so she could lean back.

"Thanks for doing this," she said.

He kissed the top of her head. "Of course."

"Dinner tonight, I mean. Having them over." She looked up at him from her pillows. "It was nice. I've missed them."

Eliot bowed his head.

"Eliot, it's OK." She reached for his hand. "I promise. I'm sorry about everything. I know it hurt you."

He held up his hands. "Do I look hurt? I'm fine. Better get back to the company."

An hour later Eliot and Josh were in the kitchen cleaning up when Claire cried out. Eliot hurried to the bedroom: empty. She cried out again, and he found her lying awkwardly on the bathroom floor, having fallen. No walker: like an idiot he'd failed to station it at her bedside. He crouched behind her, tried to lift her from her underarms, but she screamed in pain. At first he thought he must've hurt the sore area where her breast had been, but she said, "My leg, oh my leg." She was in anguish.

Josh was in the doorway. "What should I do? Call nine-one-one?"

"No! Hospice. The number's in the kitchen."

Josh raced off, and Eliot tried to roll Claire onto her back, but any movement was excruciating.

"Get away, get away, no!"

"My love. I'm so sorry."

A wheaty smell reached him, and a moment later he saw a pool of urine under her bare legs. She began to weep. "Kill me. Please kill me."

Josh reappeared and said someone was on the way. He knelt by Claire while Eliot found Vicodin and water. Whoever arrived to move her, it was going to hurt terribly, so Eliot should do it now, get her off the floor.

But to hear her scream again. To hear her beg again for it to be over, for him to end it. Plus what did he know about how to safely move someone after a fall? He pulled a towel from the rack and folded it under her head for a pillow. He told Josh to get her throw blanket from the bed. More Vicodin. Josh held her hand and Eliot kept his palm on her shoulder. Should he try to reach Abby, far away on a long-planned vacation? But no, this was not the end, this was a bad fall. His fault, for failing to leave the walker within reach.

Outside, a staccato of pops, kids across the street setting off fireworks.

"Remember Juno?" Claire murmured. "He always got so scared."

Eliot froze. Juno had been Claire's family's dog when she was growing up. He died the winter she turned sixteen. When Abby and Josh were little they begged Claire for Juno stories: his fondness for Claire's mother's bathrobe, which he chewed to pieces; his tricky maneuvers when there were strips of steak fat in the garbage can.

Josh squeezed Claire's hand and said, "You always helped him through it, that's what I remember. He always went straight to you for comfort."

At last the doorbell sounded. Eliot left Claire and hurried to greet whoever had come. He was crushed to find Stacey standing on the front step. How was this soft, 140-pound woman going to do any better than he had? He'd expected a team of men, a stretcher, a method to immobilize Claire in case she'd broken something. Had she broken her leg, her hip?

In the bathroom Stacey kneeled at Claire's side. "Hi, Claire. I'm so sorry you're hurting."

"Can you help me?" Claire was less panicked now, working hard to be a good patient.

"That's why I'm here," Stacey said. "That's why we're all here."

She told Eliot and Josh to get more pillows, and somehow, rolling Claire from side to side despite her moans of pain, she maneuvered Claire onto them. Moving slowly and carefully, inches at a time, stopping, resting, continuing, they were able to lift Claire's cushioned body and get her to the bed. Stacey advised Eliot to bring a sedative. Was the leg broken? It was hard to say. They'd know a lot more in the morning.

She left and Eliot was terrified again. You couldn't just do *nothing* about a broken leg. He decided to call 911, then decided no, the whole point was not to do that. He imagined calling Steiner, telling the operator that it was an emergency. Steiner, or whoever was on call for the holiday, would say they couldn't help. Or the operator wouldn't even connect him. There would be operator triage. This was not an oncology emergency, it was a hospice emergency, but Stacey had come and gone. She'd said this was within the realm of hospice-managed events. And now here they were: Claire in agony with a possibly broken leg and Eliot unable to help her.

18

FOR TWO DAYS NOTHING HAPPENED. Claire was drugged, surfacing into pain as the Vicodin ebbed, drifting off when the next pill kicked in. Her leg hurt so much that it definitely might be broken. If so, it might be broken because of the fall, but the fall might have happened because of bone metastases. Then again, if there were bone metastases, that could account for the leg pain. There'd been back pain too, after all, hadn't there?

A little, Eliot said.

No, Holly said. Quite a lot.

Claire was too drugged to respond.

Hospice was in and out, but the hospice doctor didn't arrive until the third day; the holiday weekend had slowed things down. She examined Claire and said that contrary to what people sometimes expected during hospice, she recommended an X-ray, for several reasons.

One: knowledge alone, the comfort of learning what they were dealing with.

Two: the discovery of which avenues were available for pain relief. People who sustained fractures during hospice sometimes received stabilizing treatments to reduce pain and regain mobility.

Three: the option of further studies. An X-ray might not clearly reveal bone metastases, but it might lead to a bone scan that would. People with bone metastases during hospice sometimes had radiation for symptom reduction.

And Eliot was back at the horror of more radiation.

Abby was due that evening, after a thirty-nine-hour journey from a campsite in the Canadian Rockies. Three flights, seventeen hours waiting in airports, all following a seven-hour car ride with a pair of children who'd been promised two whole weeks with Mommy and Daddy never looking at their phones.

Josh drove to Newark to pick her up. It was midnight when they finally pulled in, Eliot asleep in an armchair by Claire's bed. Abby wanted to see her mother right away, but Claire was so heavily drugged there was no hello.

Eliot made them sandwiches. They sat at the kitchen table, the three of them, Eliot and his kids. Abby listened to his summary of all that had happened and said without hesitation that Claire should go in for the X-ray. Until then Eliot hadn't been sure how he felt. Now he saw he'd been waiting for her to say no X-ray so he wouldn't have to.

"We'll all go," she said. "We'll get a nonemergency ambulance for Mom, and Josh and I will meet you there. OK?"

Eliot nodded. An X-ray was just an X-ray. It was just information.

"I'm so glad *you* were here when it happened," she went on. "I mean, they would have called you, but . . ."

She broke off talking. She meant she was glad Eliot had been back, that it hadn't been Holly and Michelle dealing with Claire's fall, and Eliot's face warmed as he felt himself longing for more: more relief on her part, more praise. Embarrassed by this yearning, he said, "Josh was here too," as if he wanted to straighten out a misunderstanding.

"Yeah, dude," Josh said to his sister. "I was here too."

Abby cracked a smile. "Could you guys *be* any more avoidant?"

"I'm not being avoidant," Josh said.

"'Enabling,' then. You're enabling Dad's avoidance." Abby turned to Eliot. "Dad. I'm so glad you're back home. So glad you're here with Mom, where you should be. Now you say 'Me too, sweetheart. Me too.'"

Eliot was silent for a moment. Timing was everything, right? He held her gaze, held it, held it. And said: "As am I, sweetheart. As am I."

Radiology was jammed—a lot of summer vacation mishaps—and Claire had to wait, lying on a gurney with Eliot and the kids at her side. The pain wasn't quite as bad, and with less narcotic in her system she was clearer than she'd been in days. She said, "If it's a fracture they can splint it, right? Or even put a plate in or whatever, so maybe I can walk a little in the time I have left?" She looked at Abby. "Right?"

A plate meant surgery, and Eliot was aghast. Her body couldn't take that! And even if it could, she'd need so much physical therapy afterward that the whole idea was absurd. His father'd had a hip replaccment when he was in his seventies, and the PT was so hard he nearly gave up. And *he* was in good health.

"It would help with the pain too, Mom," Abby said. "You'd be surprised—parents after their kids' fractures have been stabilized can't believe how much of a difference it makes."

At last the X-ray tech came and wheeled Claire away. Eliot went to the far corner of the waiting area and collapsed onto a chair. A few seats down, a little boy cradled his arm while his father cradled him. Beyond them an older woman coughed fitfully and patted her sternum.

Abby and Josh remained at a distance, conferring about something. Finally they parted, Josh heading off somewhere while Abby came to sit with Eliot.

"Listen, Dad. I can tell you're reluctant to consider treatment. But if we're looking at a pathologic fracture, there are—"

Eliot held up his hand. "Please. Please. I can't deal with speculation. I don't want to figure out a decision tree. OK? Can we just wait?"

"Of course."

"I mean, how much would you put her through? To make three more weeks incrementally better?"

Abby frowned. "Where are you getting three weeks?"

"They said one to three months a few weeks ago."

"The woman this morning said three to six months."

"That's impossible!" Eliot cried. He'd come very close to shouting, and he worked to steady his voice. "That's impossible. They said that at the beginning."

"Then tell me how much remaining time would make you in favor."

There was a water fountain on the other side of the waiting area. Eliot took his time heading over, bending for a drink, bending for a second one. As he straightened and wiped the back of his hand across his mouth, he thought there might be no better drink of water than the one from a drinking fountain, and that the feeling of your hand sliding across your face, dragging water with it, was part of the pleasure. He thought of staying at the fountain, drinking and drinking.

"Six weeks," he said when he got back.

"It could be that," Abby said. "It could be more than that for all we know."

Eliot sighed. A moment later Josh reappeared at the far end of the waiting area. He was talking on his phone and beckoned Abby to join him. He handed her the phone and she glanced at Eliot and headed out of sight.

It was Holly: Eliot was certain. Holly had chosen to call the kids instead of him. He was losing her too.

He closed his eyes. He'd slept fitfully when he could sleep at all. Through most of it Claire had been so heavily medicated that she was hardly there. Her relative clarity this morning had been a surprise, a lovely yet heartbreaking surprise. Rumbling through the subterranean areas of his mind was an idea struggling to emerge. When it did, it made him want to drop to his knees. He'd been missing her.

Claire had early bone metastases in her spine and in her left leg, where she'd been experiencing pain, exacerbated now by the fall. She didn't have a fracture, but her femur was compromised and likely to fracture in the future. The treatment options and combinations were numerous.

Finished at last with all the imaging, she waited on the gurney while Eliot called another nonemergency ambulance to take her home. He sent the kids ahead so they could take delivery of the hospital bed Claire finally needed. It was nearly six o'clock when the ambulance guys wheeled her into her transformed room, and she was so exhausted Eliot wasn't sure she registered the change.

Josh had to get back to Chicago for a gig, either that or cancel. Abby felt awful about Isaac and the kids, who'd also cut short their vacation and were home now in sweltering northern Virginia. Both were in favor of a pair of interventions described by the hospice doctor: an injection of a bone-strengthening drug plus a procedure with the unlikely name of cementoplasty, which introduced medical cement into weakened bones in order to stabilize them, reduce pain, and help prevent fracture.

Eliot didn't know what he thought.

After the kids left, he had a long conversation with the hospice director, who said the treatments on offer were meant to protect Claire's remaining quality of life, not try to extend it. Together, the interventions could bring about real pain relief, and the downsides were few, especially if they did the cementoplasty on the leg only, rather than in the spinal column as well. The procedure might make her achey for a few days, nothing worse than that.

Eliot suspected this was an understatement, the equivalent of "you'll feel a little pinch." Besides which: the treatment might help Claire get back on her feet, but what was the point of that if the other metastases were going to consign her to bed soon anyway? Not to mention death.

He said, "I don't know how to help her decide without knowing better what kind of time she has left and what it'll be like."

"I understand."

"I don't mean to complain," he went on, "but it's been really confusing." He tried to recount the things he'd heard from different hospice staff, and the things Holly and Michelle had heard, but as he spoke he found he couldn't quite retrieve what had been said and when and by whom. Maybe it hadn't been as confusing, as apparently contradictory, as it had seemed.

The director listened very sympathetically. She said that going forward everyone on the team would work hard to be consistent. "My best guess is a month or two."

"So that's 'one to three months'?" Eliot said.

The director hesitated for a long moment. "Bargaining is universal," she said at last. "Everyone does it."

"I'm not *bargaining*."

"Are you sure?"

Maybe he was then.

Holly and Michelle brought dinner. Eliot helped them carry trays to Claire's room, and the three of them sat in chairs ringing the bed. Though groggy, Claire tried to eat the healthy fish and vegetables her friends had prepared but gave up and asked Eliot for a milkshake.

He was out of ice cream and went next door to see about borrowing some. The house was somewhat newly owned by a young couple named Laura and Jay—amusingly, because the previous owners had been an old couple named Laura and James.

Young Laura invited Eliot in while she checked her freezer. She and Jay had three small children, and the house was full of pleasant chaos. The formal dining room had been given over to the kids:

in place of Old Laura's heavy wooden table and chairs, the breakfront displaying her Spode collection, Young Laura and Jay used the room for a plastic indoor climbing structure and a pair of art easels.

Young Laura reappeared. No ice cream in the kitchen, but she had a deep freeze in the basement, did Eliot want to wait while she checked?

He waited. Old Laura had been only slightly less crabby than James, among the crabbiest people Eliot had ever met. Claire felt sorry for them. She believed they had become crabby over decades of isolation and loneliness, with no children to occupy them, vex them, please them, care for them. Claire planted annuals in their front yard every spring, invited them to holiday celebrations. When James got sick Claire helped Old Laura arrange his medical appointments and home healthcare. When it was Old Laura's turn, Claire did all the arranging. She was ill herself as Old Laura failed. Dragged herself from chemo to sit at Old Laura's bedside.

"I can't vouch for its freshness," Young Laura said, reappearing with a frost-covered half gallon, "but it's all yours if you want it. Strawberry."

Eliot hurried with the milkshake. In the bedroom, Claire was more alert, listening intently as Michelle talked about a former colleague who'd taken a position at a Silicon Valley biotech company.

"She lasted seven months," Michelle said. "Hated the culture. *Hated* it. She knew there'd be a different ethos, but she was shocked by how slippery and self-deluded the people were. So much doublespeak, she said. So much talk about saving the world with their oh-by-the-way highly profitable technologies."

"Was it California itself though?" Holly said. "Not the company?"

Michelle shook her head. "She's staying out there. I'm going to visit and we're going to climb Half Dome."

"Sam and his friends tried Half Dome," Holly said. "Only two of them made it, not including Sam. He couldn't hack the last part. You hold on to cables as you climb a sheer rock face."

"I've never been to Yosemite," Michelle said. "Even if I don't do the summit, I'll be excited to see the park."

"Send pictures," Holly said lightly, then she looked at Claire and said, "Oh, shit, sorry."

Claire said, "Maybe I'll still be hanging on."

Michelle shook her head. "I'm not going anywhere till after."

Eliot had been wondering why Michelle was still around, some part of him hoping she was just slow to gather the energy for packing and the trip back to Atlanta. It had made sense that she was taking her time: It was July, who wanted to be in Atlanta? But apparently it was not foot-dragging. She had decided to stay till the end.

"Eliot," Claire said. "I want to do it. All the stuff, the injection, everything. Do you mind?"

Did he mind? Mind if she undertook something that might make the rest of her life more comfortable, better, happier? Of course not, provided it could be guaranteed. But there was no guarantee. The recovery could be difficult; the whole thing could end up making her remaining time worse. He thought it was too risky. But to say that when obviously she wanted to do it . . .

"I know it's silly," she said, "but I want to be able to walk to the bathroom again."

"Hashtag goals," Holly said, and the three of them looked at each other and laughed, Claire right there with the other two. Eliot rose to carry dishes to the kitchen, hobbled by a thought that had landed in the center of his mind: *Don't leave me for them again.*

19

THE BONE-STRENGTHENING INJECTION happened first. The shot itself took no time. From parking the car to returning to the garage, the whole thing occupied twenty-five minutes, most of it devoted to waiting out a possible severe allergic reaction.

Two days later they went for the cementoplasty, technically an osteoplasty, since it was being done to her leg and not the bones in her back, which would have been vertebroplasty. The procedure happened at a medical specialty called interventional radiology, not to be confused with radiation oncology, the locus of Eliot's recent dread. While Claire was being worked on, Eliot researched the two medical fields on his phone, wondering which would be the higher-paying career and which the more rewarding. Thinking about this made him remember a guy at a tech company outside of Boston, Tony Palmieri: bright, ambitious, a go-getter. Eliot's team spent fourteen weeks on the project, most of it on-site. One evening Eliot and his colleagues had a client dinner with Tony and a few others, and Eliot ended up in a heated debate with Tony over the question of what "rewarding" meant, whether it should be thought of as the same thing as "remunerative" or as very specifically not including "remunerative" in its defining characteristics, the view held by Eliot. Afterward Eliot told Claire about the argument, and Claire said Tony was to be pitied, didn't Eliot see? A man who couldn't imagine a reward other than money? Eliot said he couldn't pity someone making $500k a year at the age of thirty-five, and Claire with an amused look on her face said Eliot's view proved that his position was a lot closer to Tony's than he thought. It was the kind of embarrassing gotcha Eliot sort of enjoyed, providing the gotcha-ing was done by Claire. Anyone else and he hated it.

Home after the osteoplasty, Claire complained of intense pain. Eliot tried to make her as comfortable as he could, but as he'd feared she seemed worse off than before the procedure. She was in agony or drugged into slumber. The whole thing seemed to have been a waste of time, of energy, of *her* time, which was different from general time and critical. He said as much to Holly, and she said he was being way too quick to write it off. In a week, who knew? Claire could be back on her feet.

Days went by. Claire went from bed to wheelchair to toilet to wheelchair to bed. One evening Eliot found her holding her head and weeping. She confessed she'd hoped her headaches might ease up. "I'm messed up, I'm so confused, I'm an idiot."

"It was magical thinking," he said. "I understand."

"Ellie." She looked at him in agony.

"What?"

"Don't be mad at Holly."

He was taken aback. "I'm not."

"Let her be your friend. She just wants to be your friend."

"God, you mean as opposed to—"

"No, no. Jesus, not that. I was never serious about that. I mean it's important to her, and I can tell you she's a really good friend to have." Claire was no longer upset; she'd moved into the role of cleric.

"I do know that already. Also, you make it sound so one-way, like all the good would be flowing from her to me."

"I'm sorry," she said, but she didn't deny it.

Calls came in from faraway friends. Claire didn't have the energy to speak to most of them, so it fell to Eliot to answer the calls or not, give updates or not. When he didn't have the energy to talk he sent an email, copy and pasting from the previous email, sent to the previous caller. Word spread, and Eliot imagined a map of the country with tiny lights going on: clusters of brightness, pockets of impending grief. The largest was in the Bay Area, where Claire had several cousins. Eliot remembered their first trip out there together, timed to coincide with a wedding. They'd been dating for maybe eight months at that point, and it felt momentous: flying together, staying in a hotel together, his introduction to her extended family. Once the festivities were over they spent several days exploring, Claire the tour guide, since she knew her way around. On the last day she took him to a small beach they reached by driving up a twisty mountain road and down the other side to the ocean. Craggy sandstone cliffs crowded the beach, empty on a weekday in March. They'd brought sandwiches, and they spread out their jackets and sat on them, eating and enjoying the view. Gulls flew overhead. The air smelled, not altogether pleasantly, of seaweed. Then voices broke the peace, and over their shoulders they saw another couple getting out of a car. The couple approached the beach but stopped short of stepping onto the sand. The woman produced a camera, aimed it at the ocean, and apparently took a picture, because a moment later they returned to their car, having accomplished whatever it was they'd come for. Eliot and Claire looked at each other and said, in unison, "People are weird." They laughed and Claire said, "I guess we are well-matched. We both like to make sweeping generalizations."

Eliot meant to remind her of this, but he forgot, then remembered when she was asleep, then forgot again. Soon it became clear that she had been on something of a plateau, because a sharp downturn began. She'd just begun to have less pain in her leg, to regain some mobility—at last she could hobble to the bathroom again, leaning heavily on her walker—when over the course of a few days her energy and focus vanished. She disappeared behind a veil, apparently irretrievable. Eliot said her name over and over and got no response. He held her upright and spooned sorbet into her mouth, and though she swallowed she didn't notice the dribble on her chin. Holly and Michelle came and played some favorite songs for her, holding a phone near Claire's ear: nothing.

"Is this it?" Holly cried. "Oh my God, this is it. I'm not ready."

When Eliot tried reducing Claire's sedatives, she remained absent but became agitated, calling "Help, help!" though unable to name anything she wanted. Sedation was critical, and so the veil thickened. She lay with her arms and legs close to her body, everything drawing inward.

Eliot was worried: very, very afraid of false hope. But did he mean hope for more time or hope for the end? She was clearly suffering, whether conscious or not. He was exhausted, which was helpful because it meant he couldn't ask anything of himself, including stability of mind. He was all over the place. He decided he'd discovered a central truth about life, which was that people spent too much time trying to consolidate their thoughts and feelings. Another generalization! People thought it was too important, far too important, to be consistent, always believing A, never thinking B. He was desperate to share this revelatory observation with Claire, even as he knew it was utterly banal.

One morning he woke disoriented, bright light flooding the guest room as if it were midday and he was waking not from a night of sleep but from a rare catnap. It was eleven thirty; he'd slept hours past his normal time. He almost always woke because he heard her on the baby monitor, not calling for him but making small noises, sometimes just the soft scratch of a sheet moving. But there'd been nothing, which could mean only one thing. He raced to her room, aware of some hubbub up ahead but still so certain she'd died during the night that he thought the kids must've been summoned (by whom?) and that they were saying goodbye to her (without him?).

Then the unmistakable sound of her voice. Indistinct but definitely hers.

He arrived at her doorway. The head of her bed was raised, and she was sitting up, a little glassy-eyed but very clearly and intentionally gripping one of Holly's hands with her right hand and one of Michelle's hands with her left. Holly and Michelle were seated on the bed, angled toward Claire with their backs to the door, so Eliot saw them before they saw him. He saw Holly's broad shoulders, her flamboyant hair carelessly pinned to the back of her head. He saw Michelle's neon-green running tank top and the way it pulled up in back to reveal an arc of skin above her black shorts.

Claire noticed him then. "El, where were you?"

It was all too much. Eliot was destroyed. "I can't stand it," he gasped, and he collapsed onto the floor and hugged his legs to his chest. Was it all going to start up again, cycles of relative wellness, brutal dips into the beyond state that in some way was worse than death? He was all the more destroyed for allowing himself to be destroyed. He was as bad at this as he was at anything he'd ever attempted. His face was between his knees, and he was assaulted by a toxic mix of underarm odor and feet smell and bad breath, fetid air trapped in the dark closet of his folded body. He was vile.

Holly was at his side, patting him, shushing him.

But he couldn't unfold. He couldn't look up and see her concerned face. She said softly that it was OK and he shook his head.

"Eliot," she murmured at last, "I need you to get up. This is upsetting Claire, so I really need you to get up now."

Half an hour later, showered and dressed, he sat on the deck drinking coffee. It was beastly hot out, but he was under the umbrella, bearing it. Sycamores shaded the lower part of the yard, heading down to the woods. He could hear Young Laura and Jay next door, playing with their children.

He would sell the house. Not right away, but he might not wait the full year everyone recommended. He and Claire had talked a few times about moving to New York in their dotage. He could do that on his own. He could get a small apartment and continue his culinary adventures in a tiny galley kitchen, for an audience of one. With all the drama of the last weeks, he'd missed July dinner club and had deliberately failed to respond to several emails trying to schedule an evening in August. New vistas: that was what he needed.

Michelle stepped onto the deck. "Feel better?"

"I suppose. Yeah." He shrugged. "Actually, I feel like an ass."

She came and sat with him. "That's love."

"Being an ass?"

"Claire once told me you know it's worth something if you're willing to be your worst self with the person. If, like, you can survive the shame."

"This was talking about us? Her and me?"

"No, no. Some guy I was dating. I was doing my usual hot and cold, and he called me on it. Which normally isn't what happens. This guy was like, 'You're really good at pushing people away.' And I had an ugly little interaction with him and figured that was that, moving right along. Claire asked me what it would feel like to call him up and tell him he had a point."

"Huh," Eliot said. "Then what happened?"

"I mean, I called him? Maybe?" Michelle shrugged. "I don't know, in the long run obviously nothing happened!"

The last words were delivered sharply, when a moment earlier she'd been warm and even-keeled. If nothing else this proved the guy was right. Eliot thought of one of Claire's parenting philosophies, that you tried to guide from behind. Seemed similar to whatever she'd been attempting to do with Michelle. For Michelle.

"Sorry," she said. "This is so awful."

Eliot thought she meant their conversation, that just this small exchange with him was unmanageable, undesirable. That their guarded relationship was as it should be. But no, she was offering an olive branch. She meant Claire's dying, the state of waiting for her death.

20

STACEY FROM HOSPICE SAID it wasn't unusual for there to appear to be a reversal. That a period of decline might end not at a new and lower plateau, but back where it had begun, though she preferred to think of it as Claire being available and unavailable, rather than up and down. She told Eliot many loved ones found that a more comfortable framework.

So Claire was available again. When she was awake she was quite alert. And she didn't want to stay in bed all day. Mostly Eliot wheeled her from room to room, but sometimes she used the walker, determined to stop the atrophy in her legs. Right after her fall Eliot had hired a guy to build a ramp, but once the osteoplasty was behind them they hardly used it, hardly left the house. "Circumscribed," that was the word. A circumscribed existence. Still, Eliot understood how hemmed in she felt—hell, he felt it—and when she asked him one day to drive her to East Rock so she could see the view, he helped her into the car and off they went. She was tired before and very tired after, but Eliot was glad he'd simply agreed rather than tried to talk her out of it. It was nice to be able to do a small, pleasant thing together.

That evening something made him think of the poem John had sent him in California, and once she was asleep he found it and read it again, slowly, this time zeroing in on some lines about the afterlife:

some bright nowhere
of broad fields and sunlight
that was my idea of heaven

Claire was, as she put it once, unagnostically agnostic. She was certain she didn't know if there was a God. He was pretty sure she believed there *wasn't* a heaven, or at least had believed that at the time when she rejected the idea that she'd miss anything after she was gone. He wondered if that had changed, but he thought not. What she'd said at that Fourth of July dinner the night of her fall: that was just another way to say she loved her family and friends.

One afternoon Holly and Michelle arrived with a carton of peaches, from a place in Georgia. They'd ordered them special— Claire's favorite fruit. They'd waited until the peaches were at perfect ripeness before bringing them over.

Claire was thrilled. She wanted peach cobbler—or no, peach pound cake. Or a meatball recipe Eliot had made once, served with sauteed peaches and basil. She hardly ate these days, might not end up having so much as a taste of any of these things, but Eliot said he'd run to the store for ingredients if Holly and Michelle didn't mind staying. He did a big shop, since he was there, coming home with three full bags. It was the first time he'd had such a large load since the construction of the ramp, and he realized it provided a better route to the kitchen than up the steps to the front porch and into the house that way. He managed one bag cradled against his chest and each of the other two dangling from a hand. At the gate he set one down and released the latch. The gate swung open, and there, coming down the ramp and just navigating the

180, was Claire pushing her walker, with Holly and Michelle just behind her.

"What are you doing?" Eliot cried. He dropped the bags and raced to intercept her. "What the hell, oh my God!"

"Your apples!" Michelle exclaimed, slipping past him to his spilled groceries.

"You could lose control of this thing so fast!" Eliot grasped the walker and the danger was over, but his heart raced.

"These guys were right here!" Claire said.

"Nothing could've happened," Holly said. She moved past Eliot and squatted to help Michelle. "We were totally focused on her."

"I wanted to visit the trees out front," Claire said. "I wanted to get hot in the sun and then go into the shade and cool off a bit."

"Then why not use the wheelchair?" Eliot said.

"Because I wanted to walk. That's why I have cement in my bones, remember?"

Later, the three women sat on the deck while Eliot started making the peach pound cake. In the chaos of retrieving the groceries the expedition had been scrubbed, but just in case he'd extracted a promise that Claire wouldn't try the walker on the ramp again. He said he'd take her out in the wheelchair later, or if Holly and Michelle wanted to do that he'd make sure they knew how to work the brakes.

One thing about baking, Eliot hated having to wait while the butter softened. Wally had recently emailed the group with a hack for this, and Eliot cut the cold butter into pieces, put them on a glass plate, and nuked them for a few seconds at a time until they'd warmed up enough that he could partly flatten them with his finger. A game changer.

The softened butter went into the stand mixer, along with sugar. He turned the machine on and put the equipment he'd used so far in the dishwasher. Was it really Claire who'd had the idea of pushing her walker down the ramp, not Holly or Michelle who'd suggested it? The more he thought about it, the more he felt it hadn't been her idea, or not her idea alone. Folie à deux—that was when two people conspired in something crazy. How about a folie à trois? The same trois who had spontaneously extended a trip to Amsterdam so they could visit a tulip farm. Who had flown to Oslo to see a band they loved, a trio of Australian sisters they'd first heard live during that summer in New York. No, Claire hadn't decided to risk a fall on the ramp, not without some encouragement, some cajoling, some badgering from her friends. *You can do it, Claire! Go, Claire!* He could just imagine it.

He turned off the mixer and cracked open the sliding glass door to the deck so he could hear what was going on.

"She grew up in Arkansas, of all the unlikely places. Both her parents were teachers." That was Holly.

"I literally thought it was Ar-Kansas when I was growing up," Michelle said. "From reading the name. I thought there was Kansas and there was Ar-Kansas. And then in some separate part of my brain I thought there was a state 'Ar-kin-saw' that people talked about."

"That is so cute," Claire said. "So you."

Holly said, "Lucia and Tori think she's weird."

"I thought they liked her."

"Tori thinks she's a robot. That's why she's a dentist, she empathizes with all the gadgets and machines."

So they were talking about Carmel. Holly quoting her doubting daughters.

"Eliot liked her," Claire said, and he was pleased until he remembered eavesdropping on them from the garage, back at the beginning. Claire talking approvingly about how he'd felt Josh and Alison weren't a good match. He had been like a crazy person, hiding in his own garage. And here he was again.

Once the cake was in the oven he put together the meatball mixture and cleaned the kitchen. Claire would want to nap before dinner, and he tidied her bed, folding back the sheet to make it more inviting. He straightened up the bathroom. He gathered things to launder and had just started the machine when his cake timer went off.

Until January, when he baked a spice cake for dinner club, Eliot had never made a cake in his life, and he was still nervous about checking for doneness, having experienced the results of both over- and under-baking during his short career as a pastry chef. Claire had told him to take cakes out of the oven and immediately close the door before checking them, to avoid losing oven temperature, so he did that, setting the pan on a pot holder. Very carefully he touched the surface of the cake. It remained slightly indented for several seconds before gradually resuming its shape, which meant not quite ready. But it seemed like the sides of the cake were pulling away from the pan, and in some recipes you were told to take the cake out *before* that happened. He didn't know what to do. Overbaking meant dryness, which looked OK but tasted bad;

while underbaking meant a gooey line of batter near the bottom of the cake, which looked bad but didn't interfere much with enjoying the rest of the cake.

He put the pan back in the oven for three minutes, watching the second hand on his watch carefully. When the moment arrived, he took the cake out and turned off the oven. There came a point when you had to just decide it was going to be OK.

He stepped onto the deck.

"Eliot!" Claire said, startled.

"What?"

She glanced at the others, something passing among them. What was going on? What had he interrupted? God, he was on edge. Abby had suggested he find someone to talk to, and while he didn't say so to her, he thought it was priceless that *this* was the moment when she thought he needed help. Who wouldn't be stressed going through this?

"Nothing," Claire said. "You startled me is all. But seeing as you're here, I think I'll lie down now. That OK?" she asked her friends. "You guys should see if he'll give you some of that cake."

"It smells insanely good," Holly said. "You're a wizard."

After dinner some nights Eliot connected his laptop to the TV, and he and Claire watched home movies. "Oh, this is a good one" she might say when a new video started. Or "Is this the one where Abby recites the Gettysburg address at school? I like this one."

She was curled up on the couch on one of these evenings, her bare foot touching Eliot's thigh, and he couldn't help it, tears leaked from his eyes. He didn't want her to notice so he didn't wipe them away, and soon salt water spilled onto his cheeks, dripped into the corners of his mouth. His nose began to run.

He was determined to hide this. He thought of leaning his face onto her shoulder so her top would absorb the wetness, but the top was thin and she might feel the moisture. She'd definitely notice if he pressed his face to the couch. There were already new medical bills piled up on his desk, and he imagined stealing away to deal with them, if only to allow himself a chance to wipe off his face and blow his nose. But he didn't want to leave her.

The onslaught of bills and out-of-network insurance claims and confusing EOBs: in the early years of her illness, Eliot had been in a constant state of high alert about all of that, feeling that he had to deal with everything as it came in. That had always been his way with administrative stuff: deal and be done with it. But he kept falling behind. There was just so much. Finally, talking to a colleague whose daughter had been in a terrible car accident necessitating years of surgeries and hospital stays and rehab, Eliot realized there was no being done with it. He was not a consultant with a single, finite task; he was a lifer. Catching up was a myth. His colleague had created dozens of spreadsheets before giving up on keeping track of expenditures and reimbursements. "You're going to pay more than you really owe," he told Eliot. "There's no way around that."

"Eliot?" Claire said.

The video they were watching had ended, and he hadn't noticed. He pulled his computer back onto his lap and found one of her favorites: Josh at ten or twelve picking out chords on his first full-size guitar. Eliot clicked Play, and a tear hit the keyboard. He was desperate to wipe his face. On the TV screen, a chair had been placed directly in front of a bookcase that had since been removed to make room for the media center containing the television Eliot and Claire were now watching. Josh entered the frame and looked at the camera, situated almost exactly where Eliot and Claire were now sitting. He said, "Can you guys go away and just let the camera record?"

"It's like he's talking to us from his childhood," Claire said. She waved at the screen. "Hi, Joshy."

Emboldened by her absorption in the video, Eliot sniffed hard and drew his sleeve across his eyes.

"You can pause it if you want," Claire said, "and go get a tissue."

21

HOLLY NEEDED HELP with an IKEA storage unit for her garage. She'd ordered it online, planning to assemble it herself because she'd never before tried to assemble IKEA furniture and had no idea of the labor ahead. Eliot only learned about the project because she asked if he would help her load the incredibly heavy boxes into a borrowed minivan in order to return them in person. Online IKEA couldn't arrange a pickup for several weeks.

Eliot knew the assembly would take hours, but he offered to do it for her anyway. When he and Claire took the kids to college, while Claire helped unpack or raced out for more towels or chatted with other parents, he sat on the floor screwing together unwieldy pieces of particleboard. Absorbed and quite content.

Plus: despite a few difficult moments, Holly'd been such a help.

The Patty Gruber Garage was separate from the house, big enough for three cars. The photo of Patty that Holly had hung on the wall depicted *Meltdown*'s one true innocent, the insurance executive's wife, as she arrived at the local courthouse for day one of the trial that would find her husband guilty of thirty-seven counts of wire fraud, among other crimes. In the previous episode her husband had been advised that his family's appearance, as they attended his trial, could be critical, and the photo depicted poor Patty in the prim outfit selected for her by the defense attorney's trial facilitator, a getup characterized by Claire and

Holly as something a Mormon flight attendant might have worn in 1962.

Holly and Stuart's architect had equipped the garage with clerestory windows that opened and allowed for cross-ventilation. Eliot had brought a kneeling pad, and he cued up a playlist of Josh's songs to keep him company. IKEA had packaged the parts in five separate boxes, but he got going at a good clip, his previous assembly experiences helping ease the way.

After an hour and a half, he took a break. Holly had urged him to bring his trunks, saying she and Michelle had been swimming almost every day and it was glorious. It was Eliot's first time in the pond since June, and the water was warmer now and lovely. He swam hard enough to elevate his heart rate and had nearly reached the far side when he turned back. It was beautiful, but he didn't want to be away from home too long.

That morning, when Holly and Michelle arrived at the house to spend the day with Claire, Holly said there was lunch stuff in her fridge, and Eliot made a sandwich and ate it quickly, then returned to the garage.

He started up the playlist again and one of his favorites of Josh's songs came on. There were some high notes that Josh sang so sweetly it made Eliot want to weep. Plus Josh's lyrics were charming. Was there another song in existence that rhymed "obtuse" and "ruse"?

By midafternoon he'd completed the assembly and fastened the storage unit to the wall. He half wished he'd saved the swim for now, a way to cool off and stretch all at once, and he spent a moment considering a second dip. But no, he wanted to get home. For dinner he had odds and ends in the fridge, plenty for himself and Claire. He hoped she'd feel like videos after dinner but knew that after a day with Holly and Michelle, this was unlikely. She'd probably be extra tired. That morning, before he left, she asked him to squeeze onto the hospital bed with her and just lie quietly for a moment, suggesting that she wanted fortification against the bustle of her friends' presence.

Holly's car wasn't in the driveway. Eliot had texted to say he was on his way, and she hadn't responded. Maybe she was running an errand. He gathered his tools and went straight to the garage to put them away. This meant entering the house via the kitchen, but the door was locked, and he had to go around to the front door. Also locked. Puzzled, he opened it with his key and entered what he knew immediately was an empty house.

"Hello?" he called.

The living room was empty. The kitchen was empty. The TV room was empty. Claire's room was empty, the hospital bed neatly made, the throw blanket she liked to drape over her legs folded over the back of a chair. He checked the rest of the house, but his initial impression had been correct, there was no one home. A couple days earlier Claire had said she wanted to go to the Yale campus before the students poured in, so maybe her friends had taken her into New Haven. He took a shower, rolling his shoulders under the hot water to try to loosen them. Holly could've had the courtesy to leave a note.

Unless there'd been an emergency and they'd taken her to the hospital, no time to think about him.

He pulled up the three-way text thread he had going with Holly and Michelle. He wrote: **I'm home. All good? Where are you?**

A moment later his phone rang. Claire calling.

"Where are you?" he said by way of answering. "Are you OK?"

"I'm fine," she said. "Everything's fine."

"Where are you?"

She didn't respond immediately, and he heard music playing softly, road noise. They were in the car.

"We're going away," she said. "I asked them to take me away."

Eliot was dumbfounded. "What are you talking about? Are you kidding me?"

"Please don't yell like that."

"Take you . . . where . . . I don't . . ." He couldn't complete a sentence.

"I'm sorry, El."

"But where are you? Where are you going? I don't understand."

"I know," she said. "That's what makes it so hard."

Incredibly, she wouldn't tell him where they were headed. They'd be back soon, she said. In a few days. He was not to worry, it wasn't a big deal, just a little getaway, she really didn't want him to worry. Once the call was over Eliot hurried to the shelf where he kept her medicine bottles: all gone. By insisting on moving back home, he'd driven her away.

He started a call to Abby but ended it before it could ring. He couldn't tell the kids about this. Whom could he tell? His male friends were the husbands of Claire's friends, a group she'd whittled to its slim essence over the years. Since the beginning of hospice, a couple of these guys had tried to take Eliot out for a drink, but he'd declined both times. His closest work friend had retired a year ahead of Eliot and now lived in Scotland. The truth was that Holly was his closest friend.

Though there was dinner club.

Got a minute? he texted John.

At a wedding. Everything ok?

Sorry to interrupt. All good.

Eliot stood in the kitchen and stuffed food into his mouth—long past the point of hunger, but what would occupy him when he stopped? Claire's request that morning, before he left the house for Holly's, that he squeeze onto the hospital bed with her: Was that goodbye?

No, impossible. She wasn't at the end yet. Just two days earlier, Stacey had been out to the house again and said they still thought it was weeks to months. So what was this? More death spa? She was far from the condition she'd been in back in April, laughing with her friends.

They went on a spa vacation once, Eliot and Claire. It was in the Caribbean, one February when both kids were in college. She was like a kid at Disneyland, wanting to do everything, the hot stone massage, the foot reflexology, the coconut body wrap. They had decided beforehand not to worry about the outlandish prices. They were going to do whatever they wanted. They had a shockingly expensive Champagne dinner cruise on a boat, just the two of them. There was a captain, a chef, a server—Eliot and Claire were outnumbered.

She was more interested in sex on that trip than she had been in years, waking him in the middle of the night, joining him in the shower after an afternoon on the beach. That interlude ended up being close to the end of precancer sex for Eliot and Claire. In the years following her initial diagnosis and treatment but before the discovery of her metastases, she developed an attitude of fond tolerance, devolving into fond and less fond submission. It became easier for him to pretend he'd grown indifferent than to see that she was enduring it rather than enjoying it.

Disgusted by his mindless snacking, Eliot left the kitchen and prowled around the house, not exactly looking for her but looking for traces of her, a drinking glass, a used tissue, something to take care of. He'd been gone for hours, but there wasn't a sign of her anywhere. Then suddenly he wondered: Was getting the chance to spirit Claire away the reason Holly had asked for his help with the IKEA thing? She hadn't actually asked for it, but she'd made it all but inevitable that he would offer. Plus: *You should take your suit and swim in the pond. It's glorious.* That would keep him occupied even longer. *Lots of stuff in the fridge if you get hungry.*

Had Holly bought the storage unit expressly to get him out of the house today?

He found his phone and pulled up Claire's number. Would she answer if he called? He couldn't because what if she didn't.

He turned on the TV, found a baseball game. He was enraged at Holly. He had heard Claire say she'd asked her friends to take her away, but in his mind it was all Holly's idea. Of course Claire was the love of Holly's life. And Holly was the love of Claire's. Michelle only reinforced this. She embodied the role of second best, proving the existence of rank.

So Eliot was third?

He tried to focus on the game. Nice double play, but he didn't care about either team. He turned it off.

He wondered if Abby and Josh knew. They'd reach out to him, wouldn't they? If they knew? Or would it feel too awkward? He was embarrassed by the idea of their conferring about it, deciding together. The next thing they shared would be his death, though unless he managed to be killed instantly in a grisly car crash, or to suffer a massive, fatal heart attack, they would first share his tiresome decline, then his alarming dotage, and only then his death.

Claire had made him get a life insurance policy soon after her diagnosis. It wasn't cheap, but it reassured her, since she'd always thought she would outlive him by at least a decade and be on hand to make sure the kids were well-cared-for and smart about their life choices. Meaning she expected to live forever. Once she knew that wasn't going to happen for her, she certainly couldn't trust Eliot to pull it off.

The problem was that the kids wouldn't get the money until he was gone. They might need it before then, to pay for his care. Eliot should've told Claire that instead of life insurance he would buy into a continuing care community, the kind of place where, no matter what, they had to take care of you until you died, so your kids wouldn't be stuck with the job. It wasn't too late. Instead of moving to a little apartment in New York, he could liquidate everything and pay whatever exorbitant amount it would take to become someone else's problem and keep the kids from being burdened.

He fell asleep on the couch and woke with the lights blazing and the TV on. He stumbled in the direction of the bedroom. He imagined falling onto the king-size bed—its crisp sheets and abundance of pillows, Claire with her bedside table and he with his, which she always made sure had what he needed: tissues, lip balm, Ambien cut into tiny pieces in case he woke in the middle of the night and couldn't get back to sleep. When he saw the hospital bed instead, he realized he'd been dreaming, and from behind him came her voice, saying "Fooled you!" He turned and she wasn't there, and he woke for real now with the lights blazing and the TV on.

22

IN THE MORNING ELIOT tried Claire: straight to voicemail. Holly: same. He tried Michelle, and her phone rang and rang, and he ended the call before her voicemail could start, to avoid hearing her chipper voice saying "Hi, you've reached Michelle Lee," which she pronounced "Mi-shell-uh Lee," the space between first and last name sharply articulated because she hated her nickname growing up, Michellie, based on how her name sounded when spoken quickly by a teacher calling roll.

During her visit right after Claire was diagnosed—breast cancer, just breast cancer; the five-year survival rate then at 80 percent—Michelle was like someone with PTSD: on edge, unable to focus, jumpy and apt to leave the room suddenly ("Gotta run pee," but said so breathlessly you knew she was in the middle of an anxiety attack). It bothered Eliot so much because it was how *he* felt; Claire explained that to him later. Michelle was so annoying that he did something very sadistic at one point: he showed her a website about Claire's type of cancer and asked her to read it, saying that given her medicine-adjacent career, it would be a big help to have her eyes on everything with him. At the time he believed his reasoning. It was so galling now, that illness-phobic Michelle had even partially taken his place.

In the kitchen he cracked eggs into a bowl. Three was his usual, but he added one for good measure. Plus—why not?—a pour of cream. Until dinner club he hadn't paid much attention to pots and pans, but he was now the proud owner of three different nonstick skillets, the better to scramble three different quantities of whisked egg. He was melting butter in the middle-size skillet when he got a text from John: **Everything OK?**

He replied with a thumbs-up, then reconsidered and texted: **Claire left.** But that was too confusing and dramatic, so he added: **Went away with her friends, didn't tell me in advance.**

His phone rang, John asking with grave concern what was going on, what had happened, was Eliot all right?

He ended up coming over, arriving as Eliot shoveled the last of the eggs into his mouth. He and his wife had returned from Vermont a few days earlier. Eliot described his summer: LA, Claire's fall on the Fourth, the medical procedures. John was a painstaking, curious listener. "Wait, you did or didn't talk to her while you were in California?" "So once she had her fall the friends were around more again?"

"You must feel so usurped," he said at some point, and there it was, in a nutshell.

John suggested a hike but Eliot was afraid to go anywhere with poor cell service, so they set off through the neighborhood. Eliot steered them to a street he'd always loved, deeply shaded by hawthorn trees. In the old days, when he and Claire walked on summer evenings they always came this way. The street ended at a T, opposite the back gate of an elementary school.

Eliot led John onto the school's playing field. Josh and Abby had gone to a different school, but Eliot had spent long weekend hours on this field with both of them but especially Abby, so she could practice her soccer moves.

"You have . . . three boys?" Eliot asked John. He was embarrassed that he was unsure.

John hesitated. "We had three. Now we have two."

Eliot stopped. "Oh, my God. I'm sorry. I know you've told us stuff about Jeremy's vet practice and Keith—it's 'Keith,' right?—with his twins, but I had this idea there were—"

"You probably saw a picture when you were over. There's a photo of the three of them near the bathroom."

Eliot nodded. He vaguely recalled a picture of three small boys.

There didn't seem to be anything to do but resume walking. "If you want to talk about it," he said at last.

John nodded but didn't speak. They arrived at the blacktop and walked across fading white paint marking four-square and hopscotch courts. The school itself was a three-story brick building, built in the 1960s.

Out front, Eliot indicated the route back to the house. Suddenly panicked, he whipped out his phone, but there were no messages, no calls.

"What are you going to do?" John said.

"What can I do?"

"Right."

But the question got Eliot thinking. Was there a way to figure out where they'd gone? Not far, surely. Claire would be uncomfortable on a long car ride.

Then he realized. It was staring him in the face: Maine. She would have wanted a last trip to Maine. Of course.

If only he'd put down the deposit, back in February. The idea of doing so had seemed foolish at the time, a gesture born of denial, but now he felt he'd made a terrible mistake. He should have left the option open, no matter how minuscule the chance that they'd be able to make the trip. As soon as John left, Eliot would call Bill Murphy, who owned the house he and Claire had rented for the last fifteen summers. Maybe Claire had called him to see if he had a vacancy?

In front of the house John said he should get home.

"Thanks for coming over," Eliot said. "I really appreciate it."

"No trouble." John hesitated. "You said if I wanted to talk about it. I don't. But that doesn't mean I can't answer questions. I'm happy to answer questions."

"OK," Eliot said.

"Do you have any?"

Just the obvious one, so Eliot asked it: "What happened?"

"He was born with a genetic condition, a metabolic disorder. He died a few weeks before his second birthday."

"That's terrible," Eliot said. "Awful. I'm so sorry."

John nodded, appreciating or acknowledging the sentiment, inadequate though it felt to Eliot.

"But you guys survived, you and Pam? I mean . . . your marriage did? I hear that—"

"Couples often don't," John said. "But we were very lucky."

Eliot called Bill Murphy but got no answer. He texted: **Any chance Claire's been in touch about renting?** He lay down, hoping to take a nap. It was noon, and despite his wretched night he was wide awake. He was a fool to have retired. What was he going to do for the next however many years? He had so much time ahead, so much energy. He wondered if Cindy had left the firm. God, what an evening that had been, at the bar in Middletown. It felt like a lifetime ago. He was still embarrassed, but the feeling had changed. He was less pained by what she'd said and more by the fact that he'd walked out rather than told her to go fuck herself.

His phone pulsed. **Sorry, reserved through September.**

It took him a moment to see that this was a response from Bill Murphy. But had Claire tried? That was the question he'd asked.

Did Claire ask?

Sorry, Eliot, I know you guys are going through a lot. When you couldn't make it this summer I went ahead and rented your weeks to another family. Really sorry.

Eliot bowed his head. He brought up the number and called.

"Eliot, I'm actually in the middle of something," Bill said by way of hello. "I could do the second week in October. Gotta run, but let me know if that might work."

"Don't hang up!" Eliot cried. "I'm not trying to book the house. I'm wondering if Claire tried. Did she get in touch with you?"

"Yeah, and I told her the same thing. Sorry, Eliot. Really."

"When was that? Last question, I promise. Was that yesterday morning?"

"Oh, no," Bill said. "It was at least a week ago. Maybe two? Sorry not to be more help."

Eliot was stunned. If Claire had called Bill a week or two ago, she and the others had been cooking up this trip for a while. Behind his back.

He found shorts and running shoes, the shorts snug enough that he thought maybe he wouldn't go after all, but he had to do something. For years he had been a daily runner. Competitively in high school, to let off steam in college. When the kids were little he ran three mornings a week, coming in sweaty as Claire was waking them for the day. He got lazy, though, and his knees complained.

He started slow, his legs heavy and awkward, his lungs burning before he'd even hit his stride. After four blocks he had to stop, heart racing, doubled over to catch his breath. He walked a block and ran again, his legs even heavier now. He was trudging more than actually running. He pressed on. After he'd covered four more blocks, he walked again. In this way, running four and walking one, he killed half an hour.

When he got home, Young Laura was out front watching her kids run through the sprinklers. "Got enough water for me?" he called out in a hearty voice he didn't feel. He put out his arms and Frankenstein-walked onto the lawn, saying "Monster time" and making the kids shriek with pleasure, especially the littlest, a girl who reminded him of Abby at the same age, keyed up in some indefinable way. The water was beyond refreshing. Laura held up a pitcher of lemonade, and he joined her on the steps and accepted a cup.

"How are you, Eliot?" she said. "I've been thinking of you guys so much this summer."

He drained his lemonade and stood up. "Hanging in."

Claire called again at the end of the afternoon. She sounded very tired and was so breathless she had trouble speaking, her words broken up by staccato coughs. She said she'd decided she ought to tell Eliot where she and the others were. They'd gone to Maine—just for a little while, a few days. It was a beautiful spot, right on the water. And she'd had wild blueberries for breakfast, such a treat. They were available at fruit stands up and down the main road.

Eliot was silent. He couldn't find any words for a response.

"I'll be home soon," she replied. "I love you."

He composed a text to Holly and Michelle, telling them that he was very disappointed in them, felt betrayed, wondered if they'd given any thought to what they'd do if Claire took a turn for the worse. It was nearly identical to a text he'd composed the day before. He hadn't sent that one, and he didn't send this one.

In April, when he learned that Claire wanted him to leave, he had focused on what her friends could give her that he couldn't. Now he wondered what there was in him or about him that she wanted her friends to help her avoid.

The therapist, back when the kids were little, asked Eliot and Claire each to make a list of five things they loved about the other and five things they'd like to change. Eliot's negatives about Claire were small things. Tell me when you're mad. Tell me why you're mad. Give me a minute at the end of the day. Ask before you schedule dinners with other couples. Don't schedule dinners with the Moultons. He included the last one because he didn't like the Moultons but also because he really didn't have five complaints.

Claire's about him were nebulous and expansive. I wish you didn't respond to stress with depression and paralysis. I wish you didn't have such rigid beliefs about what makes a good life. Hearing her list was tantamount to hearing that she wished he were a different person.

Eliot wasn't so far gone down this rabbit hole of misery and self-pity that he didn't recognize it as a rabbit hole of misery and self-pity. But still.

Right after her mastectomy there had been some pretty grisly wound care, and she was adamant about Eliot not seeing it, not helping her. He said it wasn't going to make him feel any different about her, and she said of course it wasn't, that wasn't the problem at all. He asked what it was then: She thought he couldn't handle it? No, it wasn't that either. She couldn't say, couldn't put it into words.

And in any case it ended up being moot. He had to help her, she couldn't manage on her own. But later, when he looked back on her instinctive refusal, he decided that her rejection of his involvement was something basic about women and bodies, inevitable even in someone as intelligent and well-adjusted as Claire. A body meant to attract had ipso facto been sorted into a category that barred other uses. This was a gender thing. All women felt their bodies were meant to attract; on some level they did. So the moment a woman's body was put to other purposes—and what was cancer but the hijacking of a body's purpose, an attempt to assign a single overarching purpose, the rapid and haywire dividing of cells—she experienced an automatic disconnect, a does-not-compute. *Husband, look not upon my wound.* Childbirth, the other site of blood and spectacle, got a pass, because it was the direct product of the body having attracted.

And now: *Husband, look not upon my death.*

He needed to get out of his head, short-circuit the rants and cries, the babyish complaints. Somehow it had gotten dark out. He drove to a bar, took a stool, and ordered a shot of Maker's Mark and a beer.

After two of each he was feeling wonderfully relaxed and unworried. After three of each he understood he'd done something foolish and was in danger, of a DUI or a wicked hangover or both. If he wound up in police custody, whom would he call? It was important to be married so you could phone your wife if that happened.

He drove as carefully as he ever had. It wasn't drunk driving if he wasn't drunk, and he wasn't drunk. Under the influence, yes, but not drunk. Funny how the word "drunk" meant something so specific, something having to do with fun! and celebration! Though there was also falling down drunk, and there were blackouts and all that.

At home he downed four glasses of water. He'd neglected to eat before going out and boiled an entire pound of pasta, which he consumed with enough butter to lubricate a car engine. Well, he didn't consume every bite. Three-quarters of the way through he realized he'd overestimated his appetite. He wasn't quite the glutton he thought he was. He dumped the remains in the garbage and left pot and bowl and plate and fork to wash in the morning.

The night before, once he was truly awake on the TV room couch, rattled by his dream, he staggered to the guest room and fell asleep in his usual bed. Now he made his way to Claire's room, once upon a time the room they shared, and got under the covers of the hospital bed. It was a small bed and not comfortable. A little soft, in fact. Soft landings. Happy endings. Claire hadn't known what that meant. Asked him once in all innocence what was a "happy ending" after a massage. "It would have to be a pretty bad massage," she said, genuinely confused, "to leave you unhappy." She didn't mind being laughed at. Certain goofy things she said, it was almost as if she were inviting him to laugh.

Back in his go-get-'em working days, he had a colleague who

at the end of a long evening of work would insist, before the group called it a night, on what he referred to as the mutually assured destruction game, everyone taking turns badmouthing any colleague who wasn't present. Why Eliot went along with it he couldn't remember; probably because before it was officialized as a game he said something indiscreet in passing and because of that one mistake was an automatic conscript. Maybe his indiscretion had launched the game. He couldn't remember, wondered if he was even remembering the game correctly except he knew he was because he came home on one of those late nights, maybe even before Josh was born, when Abby was a baby, and told Claire about that night's most hilarious round, when the ringleader—Steve something, but Steve what? What the fuck was his last name?—said that he'd led a recent hire into a maze of exaggerations and self-promoting lies so grandiose that the kid ended up giving notice the next day, having too late realized that Steve had known all along that he was full of shit. Eliot told Claire about it because it had left a bad taste in his mouth. But he hadn't fully caught up with his own experience and was chuckling as he relayed the story. "That is not called funny," she said when he was finished. "It's called persecution. There's a difference."

Eliot got out of the hospital bed and staggered to the bathroom. He urinated copiously into a toilet he'd once known on a daily basis but now approached only as an escort. The four glasses of water kept him standing over the toilet for a long time, and waves of drunkenness made him so unsteady that he accidentally splashed the rim, then sort of intentionally splashed the floor as well. The Eliot of tomorrow could clean it up. The Eliot of tonight staggered back to the hospital bed, ripped off the covers, dumped them on the floor, and made his way to the guest room. He was a guest in his own house.

23

THE LUNCH DISHES ELIOT HAD USED at Holly's house were still upside down on the drying mat by her kitchen sink. Of course they were: he'd been the last person in the place. Two days earlier, at the very moment Eliot was attaching her fucking monster storage unit to her fucking garage wall, Holly was probably driving Claire across the Piscataqua River Bridge from New Hampshire into Maine.

He wanted to find Holly's laptop. It wasn't in the kitchen: he could see that right away. The large living room contained a wall of built-in shelves, and there was a strange end table with a lot of shallow drawers, accessed from three of its four sides, so it took quite a while to determine the laptop wasn't there either. The dining room, no. Her bedroom, no. (The vibrator was still in its drawer. So was the navy blue book: though now the bookmark was near the end.) At last, having searched every likely and many unlikely places, he gave up. Odds were she had it with her. He was in the car, ready to drive home, when he thought of Michelle.

He reentered the house, entered the Carolina Hutchison Guest Room, and was astounded that for nearly two full months it had been his room. The time he'd lost with Claire: it pulverized him to think about it.

Michelle was very tidy, everything not just in its place but very neatly—exquisitely—folded. No laptop in evidence. Her T-shirts looked as if they'd been arranged in their drawer by someone working in a high-end clothing shop. Even her underwear was carefully folded, and rather than storing them in a stack, she had arranged them so one pair half-covered the next pair, which half-covered the next pair, and so on. Her bras were similarly placed and were surprisingly colorful: purple, lime green, pink. Carolina Hutchison, staring down at Eliot in her trench coat and sunglasses, seemed unfazed by his snooping. She was about to start spying on her father, so perhaps that made sense.

He went into the bathroom. Lots of cosmetics, arranged on the counter from tallest to smallest. Michelle was so OCD.

There were magazines on a small table next to the toilet. What did Michelle read while emptying her bowels? The top one was a generic travel magazine. He slid it to the side to see if she had a secret soft-porn habit like her friend, and there was her iPad. Michelle's iPad, right in front of him. He touched the home button and brought it to life. He was briefly delayed by a password request, but damn if Michelle wasn't exactly as sentimental as Holly, using Claire's birthday for her code.

Eliot took the iPad back into the bedroom and sat on the bed. Michelle's recent browser history contained a lot of links to websites featuring group travel packages for singles and dermatologist-recommended sunscreens. He found a twenty-minute period when she looked at seventeen different pop psychology articles about getting through rocky times with a friend.

The idea that Holly and Michelle were getting on each other's nerves created a small but delightful lift to his spirits. Claire and Holly talked all the time about why Michelle had never married: She was a perfectionist. She was rigid, unwilling to compromise.

On one occasion Holly quipped: "It's not that she's unwilling to compromise. It's that she's unwilling to give in." Which made Claire laugh, but later, when Holly was gone, Claire told Eliot that Holly was the one who couldn't give in—or it was a trait she shared with Michelle. That made sense to Eliot. Holly, when you disagreed with her on a matter of opinion, at first attempted to adjust her opinion to match yours, but if she couldn't find common ground that way, she dug in deeper, repeated herself, seemed to need to win you over. She couldn't bear any distance. This could be a matter as minor as whether a restaurant had a nice Sunday brunch. Or as major as whether climate change was the biggest challenge facing the kids' generation. Holly had refused to concede this in a conversation with Josh on the Fourth of July but also refused to leave him alone about it.

Eliot continued deeper into Michelle's browser history. He went back a week, more. Finally he found a long string of Maine vacation rentals, spread across five different rental companies. On one website Michelle was still logged in, and Eliot read over a dozen message threads with homeowners telling her that yes, their calendars were accurate for August, and no, their houses weren't available. The date of this browser activity was July 26.

July 26, July 26. On the 27th old friends of Eliot and Claire's had dropped in for a quick visit on their way from New York to New Hampshire. Eliot remembered the date because they'd told him about it way in advance, hopeful it might turn out to be a good day to say hello (meaning goodbye) to Claire. The four of them spent a half hour on the deck, everyone with a plate of Eliot's—

The 27th was the day after the Georgia peaches. Eliot remembered being under the shade umbrella with Claire and the couple, slicing pieces from the cut center of the peach pound cake and wondering how it would taste on the second day.

So the 26th was the day of the peaches. The day he went shopping and came home to find Claire with her walker coming down the ramp. And later, when he stepped onto the deck at the end of the afternoon, she seemed rattled by his sudden arrival and exchanged looks with her friends.

He found Michelle's message app. Her thread with Holly was endless and trivial.

> **Be there in 10**

> **Kk**

> **You have any nail polish remover?**

> **Almost out but it's all yours baybee**

> **Finally remembered her name. Alexis Phelps.**

He scrolled and scrolled. Past a series of photos of different types of yogurt, sent by Michelle to Holly. Past a link to an article about tinnitus, sent by Holly to Michelle.

> **Going to sleep now, too tired to come say goodnghi**

>Salmon looks good.
>y/n?

Lucia coming
September! So excited.

>Yay!

A selfie of the two of them with Claire.

Soooo hot today

>Remind me to
>tell you about T

At last he hit a long back-and-forth and scrolled up to start his reading with the initiating text. Sent July 26 at 8:09 p.m.

>Told you

Told me what?

>I found one

One . . .

>Maine rental! I sent 33
>inquiries and there's a
>place that seems possible.

Srsly?

>YES

You're incredible. It's
fucking high season.
Is it hideous?

>Can you please
>come in here?

This is superhuman,
M. Did you book?
We should book
ISTANBUL

ISTANBUL

Fuck

instantly

>COME IN HERE. I think
>YOU should book.

>But as a new inquiry. I was
>slightly pushy with her.

And that was it. A gold mine. And yet . . .
   He already knew they were in Maine. He was no closer to

knowing precisely where. Massively frustrated, he quit the browser and stowed the iPad. He'd invaded Michelle's privacy for nothing.

The grocery store was empty on a Monday morning. Eliot loaded his cart with the usual: milk, bread, eggs, fruit, vegetables. He bought the largest rib eye they had, then asked for a second one, thinking he could either freeze it or annihilate his arteries in one fell swoop. He was almost to the checkout when he decided to confront the empty hours with a big cooking project. He remembered Piotr talking about a spiced lamb dish and found the recipe on his phone. He went back to the meat counter for half a dozen lamb shanks. He found bottles of fennel seeds, cumin seeds, and coriander seeds. Carrots and a couple of turnips. Parsley, dill, basil, mint.

At home he printed out the recipe and propped it on his recipe stand. He sprinkled salt and pepper on the lamb shanks and put them in a pot along with a chopped onion and some other seasonings. He filled the pot with water and set it to simmer.

When Eliot was growing up, lamb was an exotic and slightly suspect food, served very occasionally by his mother during her Julia Child phase. His father found it "gamey"—no doubt parroting *his* mother—and greeted his wife's time-consuming (and, in Eliot's view, delicious) efforts with a not altogether kind air of amusement. "Mom's doing it fancy tonight," he might say. Or "Your mother should be French—shouldn't she, boys?"

Lately Eliot felt very sorry for his mother—no doubt identifying with her powerlessness. He was retrospectively frustrated on her behalf; she never complained, never stood up for herself against his father. She was anxious, which he hadn't really understood until Claire pointed it out. He'd known his mother's temperament, of course, but less as it pertained to her and reflected her inner life than as it pertained to him and curtailed his options. She'd been dead ten years, but he still sometimes heard her voice fussing after him: watch out, be careful, slow down. The voice of her middle-aged self—the mother of his school days, his twenties—pouring small worries into his head in a high-pitched voice generally preceded by a sharp intake of breath.

For many years, in his forties and fifties, Eliot assumed he still had the chance to know his mother more deeply than the minimum guaranteed by the basic structure of having been a good boy who became a responsible adult son. Did he want to know her more deeply? No more than he wanted to avoid it, and so the years marched on. It was only after she died that his ambivalence gave way to yearning. He had the hunger of a man who'd sat outside a busy restaurant for hours, not in the mood to eat, until the restaurant closed and he realized he was starving.

Claire was impatient with him about this. She thought he didn't really wish the relationship had been closer, he just wished he'd gone through the motions of trying to make it closer so he could feel better about himself as a son. He argued that he wished he'd been closer to his mother for *her* sake, not his, and Claire said maybe his mother had been perfectly happy with how things were between them. Maybe she never tried for more intimacy because the idea was unappealing. Had Eliot thought of that?

Eliot hadn't. It helped, a little.

His mother had been poignant to Claire—in her self-editing, her constant self-erasure from any decision-making or debate. Claire thought Eliot's mother put men in a different class, found them not above but outside of reproach, in the way that a thunderstorm was outside of reproach, or a wave of geese flying overhead and darkening everything. Claire said Eliot had been brave, marrying a woman who saw him as belonging to her species. But did she see him that way after all? She'd wanted her friends, she'd wanted women to take care of her.

To start the sauce, Eliot browned a chopped onion and added garlic and saffron, tomato paste and honey. He found an orange and used a small paring knife to cut off strips of peel for flavoring. Next he'd add lamb broth, but it wasn't ready, the shanks were still simmering, so he took his laptop to the deck and composed an email to Michelle and Holly. It was similar to the unsent texts from the day before and the day before that, but he was more expansive now, befitting the different format. "I understand your desire to make Claire happy, but the very choice to steal away in my absence suggests that you understood I would have concerns." On he went, detailing the dangers of taking Claire so far from the superb hospice service she had carefully selected to make sure she would stay comfortable during her last days. "Never did I imagine, when Claire was diagnosed just over nine years ago, that the final battle would be against her closest friends rather than . . ." That was terrible. One thing Claire said from the start was that it wasn't a "battle against cancer"; she hated that. War metaphors were inappropriate. Cancer was cell division. Rather than a battle, it was a series of attempts to halt a biological process. To halt biological processes. Or just to slow them down. "At the end of all of this, when we have lost her, it'll be Abby and Josh and I who will have to reckon with . . ."

Fuck it. He pressed the backspace key and made the words disappear, all the way back to the formal and unfriendly salutation: "Holly and Michelle:" He erased it. He erased his subject line: "Claire." Now nothing remained but the two email addresses:
hollymccarthy1963@zeemail.com
michellesusanlee@gmail.com

Gmail was dual verification, we-don't-recognize-your-browser, all that crap, but Holly was still using ancient and clunky Zeemail, where a failed login attempt might not trigger anything more than a chance to try another password.

Thinking of her front door code and Michelle's iPad code, he tried Claire's birthday: no. Michelle's birthday: no. Sam's birthday, embedded in Eliot's text thread with Stuart, from when Eliot needed to get into the Beverly Hills house: no. Lucia's birthday: same and same. Holly and Stuart's youngest was Tori, and there Eliot's luck ran out, because Stuart had only two door codes. He tried Facebook, but Tori was evidently too young or too hip to have a Facebook page that might supply him with her birthday. Stuart wasn't on Facebook either, and while Eliot was pretty sure Stuart's birthday was in April—same month as Eliot's—he wasn't going to try thirty combinations to see if Holly had used the birthday of someone she more or less hated.

Besides: people didn't use birthdays anymore. Or all numerals for that matter. These days it was password apps that created impossible combinations of uppercase and lowercase letters and numerals and "special" characters. Who had decided they should be called that? Why the obsession with specialness? It was the scourge of the twenty-first century. Claire wanted a special death.

He returned to the kitchen and found that the lamb was tender and the broth ready. He set the shanks on a plate and strained the broth, measuring out what he would need for the recipe and saving the rest to freeze. While the meat cooled he returned to the sauce pot and added white wine, orange juice, the orange peel, the lamb broth. He brought this to a boil just so he could inhale the steam: as lovely as he'd hoped. He turned off the burner because it was way too early for him to eat. He was aiming for a beautiful and elaborate meal for himself at seven, the kind of thing known as self-care in some circles and pigging out in others.

He went back outside and checked the weather in midcoast Maine: clear and seventies. Sometimes, usually as they were preparing to leave Bill's after an amazing three weeks, Claire said they should retire to Maine, not Manhattan. They could escape every February and go somewhere warm. For the other eleven months, they'd have what they'd only ever had all too briefly: the quiet, the simplicity, the salt air, the granite, the ocean.

A child's cry sounded from next door. For a while Eliot had been aware of Young Laura and Jay on the other side of the fence, playing with their children. Now one of the kids was wailing. The tones of the voices changed. The adults cajoled. The child screamed. Young Laura spoke in a soothing monotone; Eliot couldn't make out the words, just the maternal rhythms, the calm. Jay had a deep voice, and Eliot heard him delivering what sounded like a modern ultimatum: heavy on the empathy but with an undesirable consequence mentioned as a distinct possibility. The child shouted her displeasure. Eliot was pretty sure it was the little girl. He recognized in her misery an echo of her delighted shrieks in the sprinklers the day before.

"Five," he heard Jay say. "Four. Three. Two. One."

The child emitted a final scream and was evidently carried into the house, because a moment later the only sounds were Young Laura speaking brightly to the remaining children in the voice of a parent who's been bested by the most powerful weapon in any child's arsenal.

Wait.

Eliot reopened his laptop and found the Zeemail login page again. He took a deep breath and into the password field typed M-E-L-T-D-O-W-N. He was in.

24

IT WAS GETTING DARK when Eliot found the road that would take him to 431 Porter Way. He had driven well over the speed limit and was exhausted by the adrenaline coursing through his veins. He was also famished, his lamb dinner abandoned. GPS said he was eight minutes from his destination.

He was driving just inland from the ocean, which for the last several miles had become visible for short stretches, only to disappear behind stands of evergreen trees. Farmhouses appeared sporadically on both sides of the road. True to Claire's report, he'd passed a number of farm stands advertising wild blueberries, closed now at the end of the day.

No fool Eliot, he had not informed the ladies of his plan, but when he was just two minutes out he pulled over to reconsider. It would have been one thing to tell them before he left home; they would have tried to stop him and he would have come anyway and everyone would have felt bad. Would it be better or worse for him to send a quick text now? He imagined the hubbub as they read his message, as compared to whatever hubbub would be caused by his sudden appearance. Claire learning he was nearby versus Claire hearing his voice and seeing him in the flesh. He wouldn't text.

The ocean became visible again. There were a couple of boats on the water, out for a sunset sail. In the distance, a small island. He passed a two-story house with new cedar shingles, not yet weathered to gray. The water disappeared behind more trees, and he came upon a cluster of mailboxes at a sign that said PORTER WAY. He made the turn and drove another half mile, and the trees gave way to a group of small houses on a bluff overlooking a sheltered cove.

431 Porter Way was the last of them, a yellow cottage at the end of a gravel driveway that bisected a lush field, green going to blue in the late light. Eliot slowed as his tires crunched over the gravel, wanting at this final moment to soften his arrival when for the last four hours he'd made the three women into a coven that deserved no consideration.

Holly's car was in front of the cottage. Eliot parked next to it and got out. He breathed in deeply: wanting, deeply yearning for a dramatic moment of return. Return to Maine. Had he feared he'd never come back? Abby and Isaac had mentioned that they might start spending a week in Maine every summer. This was at the end of the June visit. Claire and the children were in the TV room reading one last book together, the kids' farewell moment with their grandmother, though of course they didn't know it. "What do you think, Dad?" Abby said, a note of pity creeping into her tone. "We could always get an extra bedroom so you could come too." A sweet offer that made him want to die.

"Stop and breathe," Claire said each year when they first stepped out of the car. She meant it, and she wouldn't let him give it a pro forma moment, either. It had to be real, deliberate. He had to move away from the car, no bags in his hands yet, and take in the crisp air.

Today there was no scent to ground Eliot, no cricket song or woodpecker. He climbed the steps to the porch, which looked even smaller in person than it had online. The place was more ramshackle than the photos Eliot had found after clicking a link in Holly's correspondence with the homeowner. He recalled Holly asking Michelle if the place was hideous. It wasn't grand enough to be hideous, but it was certainly a dump, and Holly had paid top dollar.

Eliot knocked. No answer, and he waited a bit and knocked again. No answer, and he looked through the front window and saw a small living room with a braided rug, a dining area with a wooden table, a kitchen. All empty as far as he could see. He knocked a third time but didn't wait, instead circled the house and saw, on the edge of the bluff, three Adirondack chairs occupied by three women.

He started toward them. Mosquitoes dove at him, and he pinwheeled his arms to drive them away. They must be covered in Deet, the women. Or they were getting eaten alive.

His steps were muffled by the grass, so he was nearly upon them before they saw him, all three looking up in unison.

Holly scrambled to her feet. "Eliot, my God!"

"Eliot!" Claire's skin looked waxy in the fading light. "Oh, honey." She bowed her head and began to weep.

He circled the chairs and crouched in front of her, taking her hands in his. He waited for her to look at him and said, "It's OK, my love. It's OK. I came after you." Holly and Michelle were exclaiming over his arrival, but he wasn't listening. "I couldn't just let you go like that. But why didn't you say something? How could you have . . ." He broke off. He wasn't going to ask how she could've done this to him. "Why didn't you tell me what you wanted? I would've brought you. I would do anything for you."

She shook her head, a protest clearly forming behind her distressed eyes.

"What?"

"You wouldn't let me leave the house. I couldn't go down the ramp."

"No no, that was just—"

Claire looked at her friends. "You guys. Help me."

"You kind of . . ." Holly said. "You kind of treat her like she's already dead."

Eliot felt as if he'd been struck. "What?"

"Even months ago, that first dinner . . . you didn't want her to go out for *lemon cake*." She looked at Claire again, then Michelle. "It's like she can't actually live, she's just supposed to wait to die."

Incensed, he straightened up. He was glad for the seven inches of height he had on her, the breadth of his shoulders. He said, "*That's* absurd. But this"—he swept his arm to encompass the cottage and the three chairs—"is outrageous. Bordering on criminal." He turned back to Claire. "Do the kids know about this?"

"Eliot," she pleaded.

"What? What do you want me to say?"

He had not thought beyond the moment of arrival. That he now felt foolish was proof of the injury he'd suffered. He turned to the water. The bluff gave way to a steep fall with rocks at the bottom. Holly and Michelle had stolen from him, not Claire but his right to her. Had they considered the possibility that her cognitive abilities were in decline? Had they considered the possibility that any moment now, she could move into the next phase, or that she could be there already? Days to weeks. Claire could have mere days to weeks left, and her friends thought it was acceptable to load her into a car and drive hours to a place where her family couldn't find her? All so they could restart their little death spa? He was suddenly certain Holly had spearheaded the whole thing, way back at the beginning. Claire, talking about the moment when a rope was thrown, when one hand had let go and the other hadn't yet reached out. She'd been trying to hide the truth. Yes, she'd been intoxicated by Susan Simmons's death, but it had been Holly's idea. Holly's idea, but it never would have happened without Michelle, because Michelle made them a group. She was the means by which Susan Simmons's house full of female energy could be duplicated.

And yet, Holly and Michelle would be nothing once Claire was gone. Less than nothing: an old connection that was vaguely embarrassing because it had gone on much longer than it should have. Eliot was certain of this. How to get through rocky times with a friend? They weren't going to.

Someone touched his shoulder. Holly, standing just behind him. She smelled of mosquito repellent and wine. There were platters of fruit and cheese behind her. Three wineglasses, nearly empty. They were having a sunset wine party.

"Eliot," she said in a parody of gentleness. "Claire just really wanted—"

"Right," Eliot broke in, his anger finding its footing again, his sense that he'd been grossly mistreated. "This has nothing to do with your wants! Nothing to do with how upset you were about being booted after your little death spa. Well, let me tell you something. You two?" He turned to include Michelle. "A year from now you won't be talking. You're only all together because of Claire. I don't know if you two even like each other."

"Eliot!" Distraught, Claire struggled to get to her feet, and Michelle moved to help her. Eliot charged at Michelle, shouting "Get out of the way!" as he yanked her away from Claire. "Go!" he yelled at Michelle. "Go away!" he told Holly. "Now!"

Dead silence for a split second and Holly said, "We're not leaving her with you when you're like this."

"How about this!" Eliot shouted, taking hold of one of the empty Adirondack chairs. "How about when I'm like this!"

"Eliot!" Claire cried again, but it was too late: he raised the chair over his head, stepped toward the water, and launched it over the bluff. It landed on the rocks with an enormous crash and broke apart.

"Eliot!"

"No!"

"Oh, my God!"

He was hot with rage. Claire's mouth hung open as if midscream, her eyes wild with terror. Holly and Michelle hurried to help her out of the chair.

"Stop!" he cried.

They didn't stop. They moved away from him, toward the cottage, almost as a single being. At one point Claire glanced back, but when her gaze found his she looked away.

Overwhelmed by shame and regret, Eliot looked down at the wreckage. The chair was in pieces on the rocks. One of the arms lay close to the water, just inches from the approaching tide. Nearer the bluff, the seat back had detached from the seat.

In the distance, a screen door slammed. He couldn't walk past the cottage and get into his car. He couldn't stay where he was. The last light was holding in the sky, but not for much longer. He heard a car, but it was the neighbors, arriving home. He was lucky: if they'd been around they might have called the police. He stepped closer to the edge of the bluff. The rocks were ten or twelve feet below. No access here, but there was a wooden staircase about thirty yards up.

He moved along the bluff, hoping it was dark enough now that he wouldn't be seen. The staircase was fastened to the rocks. At the bottom, the beach was a field of boulders and large stones, jagged, crisscrossed with seaweed. The second rock he stepped on tilted suddenly under his weight and he nearly fell. It was a slow, tricky walk to the destroyed chair. The arm that had come off had broken jaggedly, leaving a splintered stub bolted to the seatback. Eliot took the seatback to the foot of the bluff and returned for the seat. To reach the severed arm he had to move from the rocks to a field of kelp overlaying squishy pebbled sand. There was a crack down the center of the arm, originating at the rounded end and extending almost all the way to the jagged broken edge. Eliot tried to split the arm along the crack but got nowhere. He set it on an angular boulder, one side hanging over the edge, and tried to finish the split that way, with leverage. Nothing. Evidently he was no longer angry enough to break things.

He dropped the arm with the other pieces. The moon was halfway up the wall of the sky, and he sat next to the pile of chair and looked at the water. His shirt was stiff with dried sweat. His day had started twelve hours earlier, prowling through Holly's house. He unlaced his shoes and took them off, took off his socks. It was close to dark now. He rubbed his face. By habit he touched his pocket and realized his phone was in the car. Had he locked the car? It didn't matter.

He stuffed his socks into his shoes and struggled to stand. The walk back to the steps was slow and painful, rock edges digging into his bare feet. At the top he saw that the cottage lights were on. He had no choice.

Claire herself answered his knock. She looked as if she'd been in a strong wind, not rumpled but flattened.

He said, "I'm really sorry."

She pulled open the screen door and stepped back so he could enter. An intake of breath as she noticed his bare feet.

Holly came in from the kitchen, and Claire held up her hand. "It's OK." She reached for Eliot and led him out of the room, holding onto him for balance. A small bedroom opened off a hallway, and she took him inside and closed the door. Twin bed with a fuzzy bedspread and a big dip in the middle. Her overnight bag lay open on the floor.

"Let's sit a minute," she said, easing herself onto the bed but keeping hold of his hand so he had no choice but to sit next to her. He pulled his hand free and leaned forward, elbows on his thighs, head in his hands. Her palm came to rest on his back and she gave it a pat, then let her hand rest there, above his belt. The degree to which he didn't deserve her kindness.

"I know you're angry," she said, and he began to sob. His first instinct was to stand, get away from her, but she wouldn't let him, she pulled downward on his belt. He bent lower, arms around his calves, head sideways on his knees.

"It's OK," she said, but it would never be OK. There was nothing after this moment that would be better than this moment. When he stopped crying it wouldn't be better. When he sat up it wouldn't be better. When he stood, when he slunk back to the car.

"Do you want to take a shower?"

He shrugged. Maybe it would feel good. Maybe it would just prolong the agony of being here.

She got to her feet slowly, fingertips on his shoulder, and moved to the door. She opened it and pointed across the hall.

His feet were filthy, sand stuck in the crevices alongside his toenails. In the bathroom he looked around for an unused towel and was about to step back out when she appeared in the doorway and handed him one, so threadbare it was barely an inch thick though folded several times. She raised her eyebrows and gave him a familiar, skeptical smile, then backed away and closed the door.

It was a shower over tub with a vinyl curtain missing a couple of rings. The only soap was pink and in the shape of a shell. It didn't make much lather, and the water didn't get hot enough, but it was good anyway. He washed his hair with something fruity. As he rinsed off he felt closer to normal, though he understood that he would never again move through the world without shame.

He turned off the water and stepped out, glad the mirror over the sink was fogged. There was barely enough towel to dry off.

"Eliot?" The door opened a crack. Claire's hand appeared, holding a striped bedspread or possibly tablecloth. "Wrap up in this."

She was in her room waiting, one hand against the wall for balance. She had him drop his dirty clothes on the floor and sit on the bed wrapped in the stripes. She used her foot to slide his clothes into the hallway and stepped out, closing him inside. He heard voices. Movement. He lay down and buried his face in the pillow, searching for her scent, but it wasn't there: just detergent, an attempt at lemon. He had to keep his knees bent so his feet wouldn't hit the footboard. More voices. Doors. A car started. He became aware of an aching emptiness in his belly and hoped someone was going to get food. He could eat and go. He could be home by one, two at the latest. Or whatever, find a motel once he was back on the Interstate. Would she ever come home now? Home home? If only he'd left well enough alone, she'd've been back with him in a few days, wasn't that what he'd been told? It was just a getaway. A little getaway to Maine. He should've waited. There was still time, it was still weeks to months, but now he'd ruined it. Lost all chance because he'd been afraid of a sudden slide downward while she was gone. Or backward. Inward. Away. He couldn't remember how the hospice woman said he should think. Unavailable, that was it. Where would they take her now, Holly's house? Weeks to months, then days to weeks. He imagined a y axis with ever smaller sections marked off, hours to days, minutes to hours, seconds to minutes. It was a version of Zeno's paradox. If you kept reducing the increments, death could never arrive.

The door opened. Claire stood in the doorway. "They're gone," she said.

25

HE WOKE IN DARKNESS, his head on a skimpy pillow. There was an unfamiliar, musty smell. He felt for something that might orient him, a lamp, a clock. He sat up, felt a rug under his feet. He was in Maine. At floor level he saw a line of lighter dark where there seemed to be a door. He found a switch on the wall. He was in a small room with a double bed. Claire was down the hall. Her friends had left.

The evening rushed back and broke him all over again.

In the kitchen, a plug-in night-light helped him find the oven, where an ancient clock said 2:20. Earlier, he and Claire had tried to have a snack together, but she hadn't been up to it. Had been exhausted, had felt terrible. He helped her to the little room and she said, "I just wanted to come back one more time."

"I understand." He turned down the bed for her, fluffed the pillow. Helped her out of her clothes and pulled the blanket over her shoulders.

"I did ask them," she said. "Hospice. About traveling. They said whatever I felt I could do."

He folded her discarded clothes, set them on a chair.

"I wanted to see the ocean. And smell the air."

Eliot didn't like the way "coming to Maine" was edging out "coming to Maine without Eliot," but what was he going to say?

"Eliot," she said. "It was wrong. I don't know what I was thinking." She covered her face with her hands. Was she on the edge of tears? Did he want her to cry a little? Maybe so. Maybe he was a sadist.

He pushed that away. "Do you suppose . . ." He wanted to ask if she thought it had been her brain, her brain lesions affecting her mind, her decision-making, but (A) that was silly; and (B) the idea put him in mind of the participation trophies handed out at children's sports. Everybody won.

She said, "I need to go to sleep."

Back in the kitchen he had eaten a bowl of cereal with wild blueberries while steps away his clothes swished in a small washing machine. He went into the room Holly and Michelle had shared and climbed into the bed.

And now it was nearly two thirty. He'd slept a few hours. His skin vibrated with exhaustion. He was desperately thirsty and drank from the kitchen faucet, using his hands cupped together so he wouldn't have to waste time looking for a glass.

The wash cycle was finished. His clenched shorts and underwear and polo shirt hugged the washer wall in three separate clumps. He put them in the dryer, and the unbalanced load knocked like tennis shoes. He went to Claire's door and listened. Nothing.

Wrapped in the stripes, he went outside and found his phone in the car. There were a lot of messages. He didn't read them, instead left the phone on the dashboard and circled the cottage, grass prickling the soles of his feet. Moonlight silhouetted the two remaining Adirondacks. He reached the top of the bluff and the tide was high, no rocky beach visible, no broken chair. The ocean moved gently. Unlike Bill Murphy's house, this cottage overlooked calm water. Bill's place was on open coastline, perched high above pounding surf. Claire loved sitting nearby when the tide was in, the reliable drama of the waves.

A breeze came off the water, and Eliot turned back. In the cottage again, he sat in the living room. He was wiped out but not sleepy. The cottage wasn't bad. He couldn't remember the rental period and thought perhaps he'd see about extending it. If she wanted so much to be in Maine. Blueberry season would probably continue for another couple weeks. Maybe they could transfer her care to a hospice here.

It was strange how you could be thinking about where you were and where you might go and when, and even why and how, while a crowd of the unbearable shuffled their feet outside your tent and waited for you to open the flap. The unbearable was guilt over what he'd done, it was how he'd failed the most basic tests. How she'd die anyway.

He no longer thought very often of life before her cancer. Neither married life nor his life as a boy, a young man. This seemed a grave error. Negligence. It was as if everything from before had been backfilled by the bad thing that had happened, had been distorted by it and finally erased. Each important event, each ordinary Saturday morning, each squabble or kiss—all behind a screen now. Had this been true since the beginning, since the first time he and Claire sat in Steiner's office and began to learn about grades and stages and the array of poisons available for help? There must've been a moment when they lost what had come before, but had it been the same moment for each of them? Most likely not. And wasn't it a fool's errand to try to identify it. To try to imagine it into being, as if once established it could serve as a marker that would matter in some way.

A milestone.

He was pacing. He wandered back to the bedroom where he'd slept: such a small bed for Holly and Michelle to share. From the doorway he saw a scrap of something bright against the baseboard. A yellow sock, or half-sock—the type that didn't show inside shoes. Michelle's, most likely. He set it on the dresser. They would be home by now, at Holly's house. What were the kids going to say when this all came out? If it hadn't already. The pull to retrieve his phone had gotten stronger.

A twinge of pain stabbed at his gut. He'd been feeling it for some time, disappearing, returning. Suddenly it was worse. He lay on the bed. This happened sometimes, often when he was hungry, though it happened with overeating too. He just had to wait it out. One night on a business trip to Germany, under the twin assaults of jet lag and gut misery, he tossed and turned until 4:00 a.m. He lay on his right side and waited and waited and waited until finally, surprised, even peeved that nothing had changed, he rolled onto his left side, and the pain briefly disappeared before coming back just as relentless. Hours went by like that. There was no good position. There was nothing to do. It hurt like hell and it wasn't going away. It was like waiting for Claire to die.

In the kitchen, he rooted in the refrigerator for something bland. There was a mild cheese. He cut slices and ate them with a piece of sandwich bread. Only a little; too much would backfire. He checked his clothes—still damp. He returned to the living room and sat. When Claire called out he was sort of asleep but not really but yes he was asleep because they were talking about

Old Laura next door and how Claire needed to go over there even though she was exhausted. He was trying to dissuade her. They were right about him, they were all right.

He hurried to her room. She was on her side, coughing. When she saw him she pushed up a little for a better look, then dropped back onto the bed. "My head aches." Her voice faint and raspy. "It's killing me. I need something."

He brought the pain medicine and helped her sit up enough to swallow it. She was clammy but not hot. He offered juice, tea, but she just wanted to lie there. The bed seemed too flimsy for him to perch on its edge, so he sat cross-legged on the floor.

"I'm dying," she said.

"I know."

"No, it might be soon. It might be soon." She spoke with her head on the pillow, dreamily. Eliot was terrified.

"What are you feeling?"

"Tired."

After that she stopped speaking. She seemed to fall asleep, but a little later she opened her eyes and said, "This is only a little part."

"What?"

"Of us. Just because it's the end, that doesn't make it bigger."

He wanted to say he'd been thinking the same thing, or rather the opposite but along the same lines; the point was that they were in sync, circling the same ideas. But she was nearly dozing and he didn't want to disturb her. He put a hand on her shoulder, but she seemed to flinch and he pulled it away.

She slept. After a little while he lay down next to the bed. From her overnight bag he took one of her sweatshirts and folded it into a pillow. Near dawn he woke. She was out, breathing quietly. He found his clothes in the dryer and put them on.

There was an old coffeemaker, an actual Mister Coffee, and a plastic package of filters, tacky with age. He carried his steaming cup outside. He could make out the shape of his phone on the dashboard, but he continued past it, headed for the bluff again. A mist had come in, making him cold as he sat in one of the chairs and drank half the cup in a few scalding mouthfuls. He could just make out a small boat motoring parallel to the shore. Probably a lobsterman. He twisted to look at the cottage. From this perspective it was snug, cozy. The other houses on the bluff were snug too. Quiet.

When his cup was empty he started back to the cottage. As he watched, a large rock emerged from under the back porch and moved at a stately pace toward the house next door. A few steps closer and he saw it was a porcupine. Its quills were magnificent. His first time seeing a porcupine, as a teenager, he believed they would fire a quill at you if disturbed, and he backed away. This was a myth. It was a pet that might get into trouble. A dog. Getting too close to the porcupine and racing away howling in pain.

Nevertheless, out of respect, Eliot stopped. The porcupine trundled onward. It crossed the neighbor's driveway and disappeared around the back of the house. Eliot took a few steps backward to see if he could track its progress, but it was gone.

He stopped at the car for his phone. Seven texts from Abby, three from Josh, two on the Holly-and-Michelle thread, three from solo Holly. Entering the house, he lowered the volume so nothing incoming would disturb Claire, and he read the texts. He read them a second time. It wasn't so bad. It wasn't as bad as he'd feared.

He found flour and salt. Baking powder—nearly empty and probably not fresh, but usable. Butter and cream: thank God for Holly and her lavish habits. Plenty of blueberries in a green cardboard box in the fridge, its edges soft with damp. But there were no eggs. This was so surprising that he searched the fridge a second time. Eggs were nearly all Claire ate. Maybe that's why there were none, she'd eaten them all.

He gave up and returned to the couch. He sent out short texts. It was getting lighter out. Brighter. Abby sent lots of questions, spread over three messages. A fourth arrived with a long block of text that he only skimmed.

A sound from Claire.

The room was dark, stuffy. She was on her side, a hand pressed to her temple.

"Oh, your poor head," he said, crouching next to her.

"I'm really dizzy." Barely more than a whisper.

"I'm sorry, baby."

She rolled onto her back and covered her eyes with her hands. "Tell them we'll decide by tomorrow."

He didn't know who she meant and waited for more. Who or what she meant. Had he heard right? Her voice was faint, difficult to understand.

"OK?" she said.

"OK." He hesitated. "Tell who?"

"The kids. And if they keep asking maybe it's a no. They have to learn to be patient."

He eased himself onto the floor. Her hands still covered her eyes, and he thought they were muffling her voice, making her harder to hear. "What's a no?"

"Eliot. I can't keep being asked." She rolled to face him, her hands coming away from her face. Purple shadows under her eyes.

"I'm sorry."

She coughed.

"Water?"

She nodded and burrowed deeper into the bed. He went for fresh water and came back.

"Let's sit up?"

"I can't."

He set the water on the windowsill. He wondered if he should ask her to repeat herself, about telling the kids. But what was he supposed to tell them? They'd decide what by tomorrow?

"I need the bathroom!" She pushed the covers away and attempted to sit up. He rushed to support her. Upright, she tried to stand and crumpled. He caught her as she went, one arm under her legs, the other around her back. "The *bathroom*," she insisted, but she was coughing as she spoke and the words were mush. He lifted her and carried her to the toilet. He had to hold her upper body so she didn't fall. Urine trickled into the toilet, not the rush he'd expected. He managed to free one hand to tear off toilet paper.

Back to bed. He arranged her under the covers. He tried again with the water, and this time she managed to swallow some.

She slept again. Eliot ate what he could find. He cooked a vegan hamburger in a scaly, cast-iron pan. Finished off a package of gourmet crackers.

He stepped onto the porch. It had turned into a bright, perfect day. Salt water, conifers. The other houses appeared empty, every car from the previous evening already out for an adventure, even as small an adventure as a run for supplies.

A text pulsed in. John, with a single question mark. Eliot returned the phone to his pocket.

Back inside, he cleaned the cast-iron pan with salt. He found vegetable oil, carefully applied it to the cooking surface of the pan. He turned on the oven so he could reseason it.

What were the kids supposed to be patient about?

There were half a dozen jigsaw puzzles in battered boxes. He found a lighthouse and dumped the pieces on the table. What time was it? It might be 11:00 but it might be 2:00. Later than 2:00. He looked at his phone. 10:15. The minutes were creeping by. He was suddenly exhausted but didn't dare lie down. If he fell asleep he might not hear her.

He had one edge of the puzzle finished and the other three well underway when she called again. This time she was much more alert. She asked for water and sat up under her own steam to drink it. Asked for something to eat, and as he turned to go said no, she wanted to go out there with him. He helped her into a sweatshirt and soft pants. She moved OK with his hand under her elbow, panting a little and coughing but her color was better.

"Oh, a puzzle!" she said. "You are so cute."

Eliot began scraping puzzle pieces into the box.

"No, no, stop! I'll sit in there."

She had let go of him to hold a chair back, and she held out a hand for help getting to the couch.

He cleared the coffee table and pushed it close to her knees.

"There was beautiful fruit," she said. "And cheese."

He brought in a plate. She pinched up handfuls of blueberries and brought them to her mouth quickly, losing nearly as many to her lap as she managed to consume.

"Come here," she said, gesturing impatiently. He was just standing there watching. He sat next to her. She put a palm on his thigh while with her free hand she continued with the berries.

He said, "What you said earlier?"

She stopped eating and looked up, her lips stained blue.

"About how we'd tell them tomorrow?"

Total blank. She had no idea what he was talking about.

"The kids?" he persisted. "You said we'd tell them tomorrow and they had to be patient?"

"No, I didn't."

"You did. They had to learn to be patient or it might just be no."

"Eliot." She was fighting a smile. "Are you sure you weren't dreaming?"

"I was with you in your room. Right after you woke up the second time."

"Maybe I was dreaming. Maybe I was still asleep."

"You were awake."

She shrugged and reached for more blueberries.

"Sorry," he said. "I just—if there's something I need to tell them I want to make sure I do. So if you remember."

Claire's let a pinch of berries fall back on the plate. "Eliot."

"What?"

"Why can't you let it go?"

Embarrassed, Eliot rose and took a few steps. He kept his back to her, his face burning.

"Don't do that either."

He turned around.

"Do you understand?"

"Not particularly." He stayed still for a moment, then picked up her plate and headed for the kitchen.

"Maybe I wasn't done!" she called.

"Just getting a refill!"

This was awful. He'd left the flour out, the baking powder. If only there'd been eggs he could have made blueberry scones and none of this would have happened. He scooped more blueberries onto her plate, added a sliced plum, cut a little more cheese. There was a jar of cornichons and he added a few because every now and then she liked a sharp flavor, a puckering taste.

He set the plate in front of her and fetched a dining chair so he could face her with the coffee table between them. She looked exhausted.

"Please explain," he said, sounding stiff to his own ears, sounding like a jackass.

"I can't," she said softly. "I don't have it in me, Eliot. I'm tired."

He sighed and regretted it immediately. If only he could retrieve the sound, the body language. Everyone should have a little vacuum cleaner that they carried around to suck up their errors. He said, "Maybe you were confused."

"Why say that?"

"It makes sense. Crossed wires. Like the day you fell—you talked about Juno as if Josh and I had known him."

She pushed her plate away and repeated: "But why say it? What's the point of saying it? What good does it do?"

Everything was so precarious. Times like this, but tranquil moments too, companionable hours, peaceful days. "Talking on eggshells"—who had said that? The therapist. When the kids were little. Sure, OK, Eliot tried to be careful—but then if he spoke bluntly he sounded to himself like his father in the grip of one of his angry moods.

The grinding work weeks, how tired and grumpy you were on the weekends.

"Forget it," he said. "Never mind."

"I wanted to forget it. You couldn't let it go."

"Claire, let's not do this, baby."

"Holly said this would happen."

"What?"

"A fight."

"We're not fighting."

"You decide?"

"Claire. I just want to be with you. While we can, while I still can."

"That's not true," she said. "You want to be with me and you want to be right."

Eliot stood up quickly, and she . . . did she flinch? Had he made her flinch? The chair yesterday, the crash when it hit the rocks.

"Sit down."

He lowered himself back onto the dining chair.

"No, here." She patted the spot next to her. "Come here."

"Have I scared you?"

"Come sit."

He circled the coffee table and sat on the couch, but he left space between them. He stared straight ahead, heard her labored breathing. A cough.

"I'm so sorry," he said, still unable to face her. "This is terrible."

"Maybe so, but it's not going to kill you."

He turned. She was studying him dispassionately. He hadn't frightened her, he'd disappointed her. Even so, the words that came out of his mouth were wrong: "You said you were too tired."

There was the weary look. Disappointment intensified. It was true, he had to be right.

"I see," he said. "I get it. Is this why I had to leave?"

She pulled the neckline of her loose sweatshirt back onto her shoulder. It was so big on her he could barely make out the contours of her body. He thought suddenly of her first weeks as a person with cancer. Disgust: that was her reaction. One of them, one of the early reactions. Cells and their avid, revolting behavior. Fear was another. But they were so tiny, the cells, fear was wrong; she wasn't afraid of them, only of what they did. They were disgusting. On a slide they were like maggots.

It was intolerable to consider the bedlam inside her body.

"No," she said. "This isn't why."

"Why then?"

"I wanted—"

"What was *wrong* with me?" he cried. "Not what was right with them—what was wrong with me?"

"That's so reductive, Eliot. I *felt* like it."

"And did it make you happy?"

"Happy?" she said with disgust.

"Sorry. I'm sorry."

She was silent for a long moment. She said, "In fact it didn't. I was wrong. I imagined it would be . . ." She trailed off.

"Stuart thought there was a category error maybe. Like you wanted your last months or weeks or whatever to feel how *you* felt while Susan was dying, not how *she* felt."

"You discussed it with Stuart?"

Eliot shrugged.

"Eliot."

"Sorry."

"Never mind," she said. "Forget it." She gave him a long look. "For what it's worth, I think on some level you were right, that I wanted it to be pretty. Or something. Girly. There was... there was a component of denial." She paused and coughed into her elbow. "Maybe Stuart's right and I wanted to feel like I did with Susan, not like she did. I mean, who knows? Who knows how she felt?"

Eliot nodded. Even if Susan had told Claire and the others that she was glad they were there, who knew what it was really like for her? As she got sicker, as she approached death, as she literally lay dying.

"The thing is though, Eliot?" Claire said. "Despite all of that? I think the truth is that you couldn't have stood it. You couldn't have tolerated it. Can't. You've been great, you've been wonderful. You got a raw deal, me getting sick sucked and you handled it really well. But I think on some level I didn't want to watch you fall apart. I didn't want to have to put you back together."

Stricken, Eliot could hardly speak. "When did I fall apart?" Other than last night.

"That morning a few weeks ago? When you overslept?"

It was true, he had fallen apart then. The morning he stumbled out of bed and found her sitting up with Holly and Michelle, after days of being unconscious.

But that was after he'd come back home. After she'd fallen, after the medical interventions. "You made me leave before that. Way before that. You didn't know I'd—"

"Eliot. I knew."

"Holly and Michelle get upset. *They* cry."

"With me," she said. "They cry with me."

He let his head fall back against the couch. When the brain lesions were found, via an MRI following weeks of headaches and dizziness, he sobbed in his car, but he was alone. He remembered very clearly inventing an errand after the call from Steiner because he didn't want her to see how upset he was. More upset than when they found the lung mets. Her beautiful and extraordinary brain. He drove to a large supermarket parking lot and sat behind the wheel and sobbed. Still wearing his seat belt. At one point he looked up and a teenaged boy was looking at him. He gave the boy a quick wave and started the car and drove home. Had he left Claire alone that day?

No. He'd gotten Holly to come over.

Plus: the day in June, when Abby and her family left. Claire said she felt like she was abandoning Abby and he told her Abby would be OK. And later that afternoon Claire wept with her friends while he listened from the hallway.

She was right about him. She was right.

"I think," she said, "that we should pack up and go home."

"No, wait, I want—"

"I want to go home, Eliot."

He stripped the beds and started a load of towels. He packed the remaining perishables into a grocery bag and sponged down the kitchen counters. He returned Claire's things to her overnight bag and zipped it closed.

There was a question he needed to ask her, but he was too afraid.

She said, "Let's go look at the water one last time."

She was too weak to walk, so she put her arms around his neck and he carried her like a groom carrying a bride over the threshold. She was very light. At the top of the bluff they looked down at the beach. The tide was at the halfway point, heading out. The chair arm had been washed away, but the two larger pieces lay on the exposed rocks.

"Still there," he said.

"Not your finest moment."

"That's your take?"

"What should I say? Proof of your essential toxic masculinity?"

You're like this benign blob walking around. At least benign was better than toxic. Josh had said "benign," that was something.

"You lost it," she said with a shrug. "People do things that are . . ."

"Suboptimal?" he said.

"Exactly."

He set her in the chair she'd occupied the evening before. She was thirsty, and he hurried back to the cottage for her water bottle. He brought the remaining blueberries back with him and set them at her side.

"Aren't you going to sit?"

He sat. Reached into the box for a few berries and leaned back in the chair. He said, "I was going to make scones. This morning, before you woke up. But there were no eggs."

"Nice thought."

"We can pick some more up. Blueberries. First place we see. I'll make them at home."

"Scones don't need eggs, you know."

"Yes, they do."

"OK."

He ate a few more and it was time to go. He closed up the house and joined her in the car, but he didn't start the engine.

"Aren't we going?"

He had to ask. No matter what she would say, he had to find out now. "I need to know who will be with you," he said. "For the rest. I'm sorry, I just need to know."

"You will."

Eliot felt himself unclench: the muscles around his mouth and behind his ears, his biceps and glutes.

"And the kids when they can," she continued, but the words were like water now, easy, nothing behind them but more of the same. "Holly and Michelle will come over. It'll be how it should've been all along." She sighed deeply. "I'm sorry, Eliot."

He couldn't respond right away. "It's OK," he said at last. "Totally OK."

"You're being very forgiving."

"There's nothing to forgive."

There was quite a bit of traffic, reminding Eliot that it was still high summer in Maine. He bought a quart of blueberries at one stand and another at the next. Claire dozed as he got on the Interstate and headed south. Didn't even stir when he stopped to fill the car with gas.

Getting back into his seat, he took a moment to stare at her sleeping face. Their first night together, decades earlier—a very deliberate sex date, the opposite of the way he'd normally gone to bed with women; he and Claire sober, serious, gradual in their progression toward the moment when he entered her for the first time—that night, when they were finished and happy in each other's arms, and Eliot was starting to drift off, she said she'd never fall asleep, she was the lightest sleeper, a prima donna of sleep, she'd still be wide awake come morning. He said he was sure she'd conk out eventually, and she said, "If you ever see me sleeping, you'll know I trust you. This," she added, indicating their naked and intertwined bodies, "takes trust too, but it's nothing compared to sleep."

Eliot buckled his seat belt. Back in the cottage, the things she had said: speaking as she had about him would have taken trust too. Saying he had to be right, saying she didn't want to have to put him back together again. Telling him those things had been a gesture of trust on her part, trust that she could speak the truth and he wouldn't feel like the recipient of a final verdict, permanently judged. Which meant his task was to not feel permanently judged. He sat very still, thinking this would be tricky but not necessarily impossible. Like reaching for something fragile that you could break if you came at it clumsily.

She woke up when they were about an hour from home. It was overcast, the kind of low ceiling that had given her headaches before menopause. Her head hurt now. And her back. He pulled off at a rest area and gave her some Vicodin. Left her in the car while he ran in to pee.

"How *did* you find us?" she asked as he pulled out of the parking area and got back on the Interstate.

He looked at her. She was genuinely curious, entirely unsuspecting of his trespasses. "I found Michelle's iPad. And I hacked my way into Holly's email."

"Eliot!"

"Don't tell."

"Why would I do that? Good God."

"I wasn't just being mean, by the way. Last night, about the two of them. Michelle was googling articles about what to do if your friendship hits a rocky patch."

"That was about her friend Tina!" Claire exclaimed. "She has this friend Tina who honestly sounds like such a pain."

"OK."

"You're wrong about them. A hundred percent wrong. They need each other. They love each other."

Eliot shrugged.

"They do. And they love you. Holly texted me that a bit ago. She took some farm stand tomatoes over to the house, said she bought too many—typical Holly humble-gifting. Anyway she said it looked like you'd been in the middle of cooking something? Lamb shanks?"

"Oh, shit, did I leave them out?"

"Just the recipe, I think. She sent me a picture of it." Claire pulled out her phone and squinted at it, reading: "'Tell Eliot this lamb recipe looks amazing. Just like the chef making it. Give him my' and then there's a heart emoji."

"How do you like that," Eliot said.

26

IT WAS EARLY EVENING when Eliot and Claire arrived home. He got her settled and went into the kitchen, a little worried he'd left the lamb out in his rush to get to Maine, but he hadn't—just the recipe in the recipe stand, a memento of his ambition. The sauce was in the fridge and he dumped it, along with the cooked lamb. He knew Claire would have no appetite for such a heavy dish. Months later—in the winter, long after she was gone—he would try it again and be delighted by the result, spicy and succulent. The evening would be an experiment, an attempt at having people over: John and his wife, Pam, and Holly. A very cold February night with lots of red wine and a surprising and hilarious conversational detour into one of *Meltdown*'s most minor characters, Carolina's gorgeous and admittedly not-very-bright boyfriend Max Mattingly, on whom it turned out Pam and Holly had each harbored an intense secret crush. Up to that point Eliot would have done nothing but live without Claire. He wouldn't have moved or planned to move or signed up for a hiking trip in Nepal or made a profile for a dating app. He wouldn't have visited Abby and the grandchildren, he wouldn't have visited Josh. He wouldn't have quit dinner club. He wouldn't have started running regularly, though of all the things he wouldn't have done, he would have come closest to doing that one.

He would have to feed himself though. For a time it would be little other than cereal and sandwiches, an inadvertent diet that would take ten pounds off almost without his noticing. Occasionally he would yearn for soup and spend long afternoons making stocks from chicken carcasses and veal bones. At Christmas, the milestone first Christmas without her, he would bake cookies with the grandchildren and spend the heartbroken weekend after their departure finding red and green decorating sugar all over the house. And when summer arrived, the first summer without her, he would recall the blueberry scones he made almost daily in the week after they got home from Maine, and though he'd always used the same scone recipe he would launch a project to compare methods, to discover the effect of buttermilk instead of cream, more sugar versus less, sifting the flour for an extra fine crumb. Searching for recipes, he would discover that you *could* make scones without eggs, and he would recall Claire in the Adirondack chair on the bluff, hearing him insist that scones required eggs and replying without hesitation: OK. Remembering this would mark one of the many occasions when he would engage in the small calculus of elevating her grace over every other trait. For a while he would be at risk of reducing her to a collection of excellent qualities. But that would turn out to be a temporary phenomenon in the long story of his life after his first wife died. Eventually he would remember how pissy she could be when he forgot to ask how playgroup was when the kids were little. Her impatience with how often he worked deep into the night. "You're such a *man*," she said once, with the same disgust Josh used when he pronounced the words "career" and "company."

After the long drive home Claire wanted a bath, and Eliot was sitting near her, perched on the closed lid of the toilet, when a calendar alert informed him that his car registration renewal was due in one month, on September 12. Which meant the current date was August 12, which meant it had been exactly five months since the beginning of hospice. She could still make it, he thought, though he wasn't sure if he meant die within the predicted six months or outlive them.

It was dark when she finished her bath and she was obviously exhausted, but she wanted the head of the bed raised, the light on. She wanted her iPad so she could text the kids with an easier keypad than the one on her phone. When she asked him to flatten the bed a little later, he found she'd started a text to Abby but hadn't finished it. **Sweetheart, I had the loelist ti in Maine the kis**

She stayed in bed all the next day. Holly and Michelle came the day after that, and Eliot wheeled Claire to the deck so the three of them could sit outside together. The day after that it was bed again. Her breathing was labored. Abby came for twenty-four hours and spent most of her time at Claire's side, though she also had an urgent conversation with Ifeoma, from hospice. Days to weeks, Ifeoma told her, and Abby remarked to Eliot that she'd always known Claire would die within the initial six-month hospice period. Eliot asked why, and Abby said because Claire had spent her life not rocking boats. She'd spent her life steadying them.

Stacey came to assess and said yes, hospice would be coming more frequently now. She told Eliot this was the period when most loved ones felt they were beginning to understand what it meant for someone to be actively dying. Eliot considered hiring a nurse to sit with Claire overnight but ultimately decided against it. When he'd had several hard nights in a row, Holly or Michelle came to spell him. Claire often seemed to be asleep with her eyes open. Her lips were dry and cracked, her saliva production so reduced that the edges of her mouth stayed together, webbed, and only the center opened for sips of water. She frequently woke at two or three in the morning and spoke as if she were dreaming. There was a baby she was worried about. "Don't you hear him crying?" she pleaded one night. "I can nurse, I can still nurse."

Her best time was early afternoon. She asked to be taken to the kitchen one day and had Eliot open various cabinets because there was a bowl he'd brought her from Finland that she wanted to see again. He didn't have the heart to tell her it had broken years earlier, so he opened door after door and pretended frustration that he couldn't locate it.

Another day she wanted to find her mother's bumblebee earrings. A pair of topaz stones for the lobes of each body, wings of gold. She wanted to give one earring to Holly and the other to Michelle. Eliot said he thought her jewelry was going to Abby, and Claire said yes, of course, most of it, but the bumblebee earrings had always reminded her of that summer in the un-air-conditioned fifth-floor walkup in New York, when one Sunday she and Holly and Michelle had gone to a flea market and happened upon a nineteenth-century framed engraving of a bumblebee. They loved it but were astounded by the price tag—$100—and the picture became a measuring stick for them. "That dinner cost more than the bumblebee." "She bought herself a six-bumblebee coat."

Eliot found the earrings. Claire presented them to her friends while he ran an errand, to give them privacy. After Claire was gone, Holly would have the earrings made into a pair of necklaces, and for years and years she and Michelle would wear them almost every time they got together, often sending Eliot a selfie of the two of them with their faces close, forefingers pointing at the bees.

Applesauce was all Claire could eat. She had a few spoonfuls once or twice a day. When she was thirsty, Eliot had to hold her head forward so he could position her drinking straw in her mouth for sips of water. Afterward he eased her back slowly, carefully sliding his hand out of the way before the full weight of her head hit the pillow. This because his watch had scraped her scalp once and bothered her.

Even now there were reversals. One early evening Eliot believed she was dozing and lay down in the guest room, thinking he should try harder to sleep when she slept so he could be alert in the middle of the night. He was drifting off when her voice came over the baby monitor. Sharp and clear: "Eliot? Can you come in here?"

He found her with the head of the bed slightly raised, the remote in her hand. She hadn't operated it herself in at least a week.

"Can you open the window?"

He pulled open the curtain and raised the sash. "Better?"

"Yes. Sorry."

"Don't be sorry."

"I am." She gave him a pained smile. "Your whole life is tending to me."

He drew a chair close. "Shh. I'm happy to."

"You're my tender," she said. "My tender tender," she added dreamily.

He leaned forward to kiss her shoulder and let his head rest near her for a moment. He smelled perspiration and detergent and something bitter that he thought of as the cancer, though it was probably a by-product of one of her medicines as it broke down in her body.

She said, "I'm not mad that you talked about me to Stuart."

That he'd told her about it had completely slipped his mind. The cottage came back to him, lying on the floor in her tiny room with her sweatshirt under his head, sitting in the misty dawn above the ocean.

"Thank you," he said. "I needed . . ."

"To talk," she said. "Of course you did." Her voice had grown gravelly, but her meaning was clear, her mind was clear. "I'm glad you went out there. I want you to do things," she added, meaning after she was gone.

"I don't want to." This was the deepest truth he knew.

She reached for his hand and closed her eyes. The head of the bed was still elevated, and with his free hand he found the remote and pressed the button to lower it. She opened one eye as the bed adjusted, then closed it again.

"Eliot," she said when he was nearly at the door.

He turned back.

"I'm not scared."

"I'm glad."

"I'm just going to slip away. And then I'll be . . . nowhere."

"A bright nowhere," he said, remembering the poem. "Of broad fields and sunlight."

"That's lovely," she said, closing her eyes again. "Maybe I'll see you there."

He returned to the guest room, but he was wide awake, he couldn't nap now. He washed his face, wanting to leave the idea of sleep behind. Had she called for him so she could forgive his having talked about her to Stuart? And if so: Was that something she'd been meaning to do or something she'd thought of out of nowhere? "People talk about each other," she pronounced once, apropos of some minor hubbub in her circle of friends about someone saying something about someone else, the censoring its own secondary gossip. "It's what we humans do."

There was a load of laundry to start, pairs and pairs of her pajamas because it was pleasing for her to change into clean ones. He stuffed the items into the machine, poured detergent into the dispenser. He'd been talking about Claire for nearly forty years, but it came to him—as he started the washer, as he stepped back into the kitchen—that going forward when he talked about Claire he would be talking about someone who was fixed in time, who had stopped being. The idea pierced him with its strangeness. He would never again just talk about her—Claire, his wife: in the other room, at home for the evening, back in Connecticut; discussing her with someone who knew her, describing her to someone who didn't but might meet her someday, or even to someone who would never meet her though it wasn't an actual impossibility. A literal impossibility. Once she was gone, the valence of how he talked about her would change completely.

A day of rain draped a cloak over the house. The reversal reversed. She pushed away the applesauce. Eliot tried Jell-O and she didn't want that either. A sip of water here and there.

Her last time out of bed was the day after Josh arrived. Enlivened by his presence, she asked to be taken outside. Josh pushed her onto the deck, moving furniture until he could situate her under the shade umbrella. Eliot watched from the kitchen. Josh squatted in front of Claire and they spoke briefly, his hands reaching for hers, hers reaching for his face.

It was the end of August, very humid. The air-conditioning gave her chills, and Eliot had to layer three blankets over her to make her comfortable. Then fever and sweats, and he ran cool washcloths over her arms and legs. He was at her side for hours every day. He had imagined that this last part would be difficult, that the agony of the impending loss, the agony of her discomfort, would make it hard for him to be with her. He had expected to feel alienated, to have to fight an urge to flee. It was not like that at all.

Her hands came together, but inside out, the back of one hand against the back of the other. She stopped speaking. Abby came back.

Then it was hours to days. She was very far away. Unavailable. Everyone took turns administering morphine because they wanted to share the work.

ACKNOWLEDGMENTS

I've had the extreme good fortune to have not one but two amazing Sarahs in my corner. First and enormous thanks to my agent, Sarah Bowlin, for her extraordinary warmth, her thoughtful and generous attention to . . . absolutely everything, and her brilliant and sensitive literary guidance. Geri Thoma brought us together, a final and unsurprisingly perfect bit of agenting after twenty plus years of splendid literary care. Thanks also to Rich Daniel and to the team at Aevitas: Erin Files, Vanessa Kerr, Allison Warren, Kayla Grogan, and Ruby Rechler.

To my other Sarah, my editor Sarah Stein, second in chronology only: gratitude for general loveliness, for exquisite attunement to the novel's texture and aims, and for providing both excellent editing and excellent editing. I'm grateful to everyone at Harper: Jonathan Burnham, Doug Jones, Katie O'Callaghan, Leah Wasielewski, Lindsay Prevette, Joanne O'Neill, Jocelyn Larnick, Lydia Weaver, Bonni Leon-Berman, Shelly Perron, and the wonderfully helpful Jackie Quaranto.

Many thanks to the following, for advising me on a variety of matters: Jane Aaron, Robin Black, Suzie Bolotin, Sylvia Brownrigg, Steve Byrnes, Natalie Doyle, Benjamin Dreyer, Richard Goldberg, Eleanor Jackson, Jamie Mandelbaum, Susie Merrell, Carol Papper, Sam Parker, Meg Wolitzer, and Patti Yanklowitz.

I'm grateful to Christian Wiman for permission to quote from his poem "Night's Thousand Shadows" from the collection *Hard Night*. In addition to the apt and beautiful lines quoted in the text, the poem provided the perfect answer to the question of what the novel should be called.

Finally, to my husband Rafael Yglesias, my first and best reader, my literary soulmate, my dedicatee: endless gratitude, though that doesn't begin to describe it.

ABOUT THE AUTHOR

ANN PACKER is the author of five previous works of fiction, including the bestselling novels *The Children's Crusade* and *The Dive from Clausen's Pier*, which received the Kate Chopin Literary Award, among many other prizes and honors. Her short fiction has appeared in *The New Yorker* and in the *O. Henry Prize Stories* anthologies, and her novels have been published around the world. A Bay Area native, she currently spends most of her time in New York and Maine.